Claiming The Reaper

REAPED BOOK TWO

Copyright

Dedication

To our readers, new and old, we thank you for taking this journey with us one final time.

Prologue

Selene

I've always hated the zoo. I would watch all the animals pacing along the cage, eyeing the people watching them, and in my mind, they were waiting for a weak point to escape. They looked depressed, and some of the more aggressive ones always looked ready to strike.

That's me right now.

I'm a red-assed Orangutan, pacing the length of this room, just waiting to toss shit at the next person to come near me. Then I will beat my fists on my chest, showing them who's boss, just before I sink my teeth into their jugular.

I'm *that* red-assed Orangutan.

I don't know how long I've been here, but it's had to have been days, and my patience is running out. If my guys don't get here soon, I'll get myself out of here, hunt *them* down and toss some shit their way, too. It can't take this long to find me, what the fuck are they doing? Playing hide the pickles without me?

They better fucking not be, there aren't enough holes. They need me.

The door creaks open, and I watch as heavy boots clunk down the stairs, one slow step at a time. Must be fat-assed Mack Delaney.

I wish I'd taken a shit.

The chains around my wrists clank as I cross my arms over my chest, waiting for his huffing, sweating self to reach the bottom. Yeah, they learned their lesson the hard way when I got out of their ropes, *twice.* Now I'm chained, and I'm trying to figure out how I'm going to take these home with me when I get out, Darius would squeal with delight.

"Hello, Reaper." Mack's toothless mouth grins when he finds me waiting for him.

"Hello, Gingivitis." I grin back, and his face falls.

"You have a smart mouth, you dumb whore." He retorts, and I look at him with confusion.

"Which one is it?" I toss my hands up, "am I smart, or am I dumb?"

"You're a whore." He spits.

"I know," I nod, "and you're toothless. Are you asking for an hour of my time? I'll *bite*—since you can't—I'm a little intrigued. I'd let you have me sit on your face, just to find out what it would be like to have my clit gummed."

"Jesus," he mutters, and shows me a pair of scissors. "I need a lock of your hair."

"You're barking up the wrong Orangutan if you think you're getting anywhere near me with those."

"The wrong *what*?"

"I'm a caged beast, Gummy Bear!" I clap my hands, making the chains clink together. "I will rip you to shreds if you get any closer."

"Don't make me call a few guys down to help restrain you," his smirk is sinister, "they may have their way with you after."

"Oh, cute." I snort, "you think a man threatening to rape me will make me compliant?" I snicker, "call them down, it's been a while," I grab my pussy through my pants, "I could deal with a dick or two."

He curses and turns on his heel, heading back up the stairs. "Let's see how you feel when you've missed a few meals."

"It'll feel like my crack-whore mother forgot to buy groceries, Gummy Worm." I yell at his retreating back, "been there, done that."

A few hours later, and I would kill for a glass of water. I've been cushioned, babied, *spoiled.* I drop my head back against the cement wall of the basement and growl in frustration. I've softened up, and I can't let it continue. As soon as I'm out of here, it's back to training. I got some Diablos to take down.

The door opens, and another pair of boots come down the stairs, he's holding a tray, and I see a tall sweating glass of cold water sitting on it. Okay, after this meal, I'll begin training.

"Boss says we need some hair first." The thug in front of me says.

"Since it's been a while, I can offer my coochie or my head." I throw him a grin. "And if you pick between my legs, you'll have to pay the toll."

"Just a bit from your head, whore." He rolls his eyes, and I snort.

"You're boring." I wave for him to come closer, "why does he need the hair?"

"To send to your pretty boys." He says as he snips a lock off.

"They are pretty, huh?"

He puts the tray down in front of me and I attack the water like a dried-out raisin. They put bread and butter on the tray, but I've eaten way worse, so I dig in. It's about fifteen minutes later when I feel my mouth dry out and things around me begin to grow foggy. The door opens again, and I hear the boots on the stairs, but I can barely lift my head.

"We're moving you, blondie." Someone says as they tip me over a shoulder.

"I'm going to set my Orangutan on you." I mumble.

“The fuck did she just say?” I hear someone snicker, and then everything goes black.

Chapter One

Zander

We're back in New York after Blaze followed Selene's trail. We don't have much, but someone has been leaving us nuggets of information along the way, wanting us to follow. We left Nevada and the Dientes Afilados assured us that if we needed them, they'd be there.

Santos has been quiet, understandably. He's found his long-lost father and a new brother in the few days we were there, telling me we're all just tangled in fate's big-ass, sticky web. How else could you explain the coincidences? Darius has been silent but strong, watching Santos for any signs of a temper flare. None of us are completely finished with Nevada, not with Santos *and* Selene both finding family there.

With Selene missing again, the air around us is crackling with a dark energy. Not the same as the first time, we were depressed and missing her, but this time, knowing she's been taken, we're on the cusp of something fucking explosive. Santos has been too quiet, too still. Darius has been thrumming, his body practically vibrating, Blaze looks sinister and excited, and I'm coiled tight, waiting to unleash.

The crumbs have led us back to our turf, and that can only mean one thing, Los Diablos. As we slowly drive through the streets, we see more of their presence, like they thought it would be a good idea to move into our town while we were gone. Big fucking mistake.

Blaze growls when he sees a drug deal go down, and I'm next when the block has more prostitutes than ever. We cleaned this place up, made it respectable, and ran drugs on the down-low, not being blatant about it. But this is just sloppy.

"Someone is dying today," I snap.

I'm greeted with crickets, usually I'd get a hoot from Santos, a chuckle from Darius, but instead it's an eerie silence. We've never been in this space before. Not where we're all in the same frame of mind, we're usually pretty even keeled. Santos and Darius are psycho, Blaze is dangerous, and I'm handsome. I mean *level-headed*. But we are balanced, right now we're tipped to one side, and that scares even me.

We pull up to Blaze's house—now our compound—and as we wait for the gates to open, I see something attached in the center.

"What is that?" But before my sentence is even out, Blaze is already striding up to the object, and ripping it off the metal bar.

"We need to check the cameras." Darius murmurs, and I give him a nod.

Blaze gets back in the car and tosses a plastic Ziplock bag into my lap. I hold it up, but it looks like a piece of paper inside.

"What is it?" Santos croaks, his voice shocking me, it's the first he's spoken since leaving the MC's compound in Nevada.

"Not sure," I shake my head as we pull up to the front of the house, "let's get inside and take a look."

Once we file into the house, everything feels solemn, and the silence just keeps adding to the emptiness we're all feeling. We sit at the table, Blaze kicking out his long-ass legs, Darius straddling his chair, and Santos drumming his tattooed fingers along the tabletop. I open the plastic baggy, pull out the paper, and unfold it. Out falls a long flaxen lock of hair.

"Is that…?" Santos leans forward and snatches the hair from off the table, immediately bringing it to his nose. He's up and out of his chair, the wooden legs scraping along the floor. "It's Selene's."

"What does the note say?" Blaze interjects.

I throw the paper to the center of the table, my jaw clenching, and my stomach twisting with a fiery rage. I can't even speak right now and reading it to them would be impossible. Darius snatches it up much to Blaze's irritation and begins to read.

"There once was a Little Reaper, her hair so blonde and fair, she loved causing mayhem without a single care. But now she's a prisoner with her hands shackled tight, spreading her legs without much of a fight. Leave town before morning's light, or she'll be dead by the end of tomorrow night."

"Poetic," Blaze snarls, "doesn't sound like Los Diablos."

"Not unless they're working with someone." I grunt.

The kitchen falls quiet, and then I watch as Santos' face begins to light up, the spark coming back to his eye. "Does this mean war?"

"I guess so," I shrug.

"You hear that, San?" Darius stands and holds out his fist, "looks like we're getting the machine guns and Kevlar."

Santos smashes his fist to Darius' and hoots, *finally*. "Who the fuck are these guys? Telling us to leave our town."

"A bunch of fucking idiots," even Blaze is grinning, the scary fucker.

"We need to find out where she is first," I scratch my chin.

"On it." Blaze stands and heads to the back room where we have our surveillance.

"Should we call in a favor with Dientes Afilados?" I ask Santos.

His nose crinkles and then he chuckles, "your pronunciation is like a white boy ordering Taco Bell."

"I am a white boy." I huff.

"You're lucky you're cute," Santos ruffles my hair. "Let's see what Blaze comes back with, then we'll decide if I think it's worth it to call my asshole father."

Asshole father indeed. Santos may be a fucking handful and he may be the most chaotic person I know, but I can honestly say, thank fuck he wasn't raised by Papi Loco. The name really says it all.

"Let's go try on our vests and see how many weapons we can strap to our bodies." Darius says, leading an excited Santos out of the room.

We really are a bunch of psychos if the prospect of blood and war excites us.

Blaze

I stretch out in the chair, waiting for the computer to boot up, and clenching my fist. She better not have let anything happen to herself; I will kill her if she did. She doesn't get to make me question what the fuck my heart is doing and then disappear again. I'm sick to death of tracking her down, and I'm not going to want to do this for the rest of my fucking life.

But I will if I have to.

There, I admit it. I would do just about anything for the annoying woman with the blonde hair, and filthy mouth. She fixed something inside of me I didn't even realize was broken. I roll my fucking eyes at my own-damn-self and wait for the computer screen to boot up.

I have a camera at the front door, at the front of the gates, and the backyard. Another quality I acquired from my abusive foster father—paranoia. Well, it's coming in clutch now. The screens boot up, and I zoom in on the one at the gate. My cameras aren't the blatant ones you see on most homes, I have stealth cameras hiding in areas as small as a screw hole. Again, paranoia.

I shuffle through hours of footage, and finally stop when I see a large red pickup truck park outside of the gates. Two guys approach, their faces covered and the plastic baggy in their possession. They look around, probably trying to spot a camera, and then proceed to tape it to the gate. They were here four hours ago.

I can't tell who the fuck they are or who the fuck they work for because they were smart enough to hide that, but not completely intelligent. I zoom in on the truck and right smack there in the center is the license plate. *Bingo.*

I write it down and head back out to the kitchen, finding Zander sitting alone nursing a beer. He looks up at me, his eyes sad but hopeful, fuck's sake, we're all goners.

"Did you get anything?"

"Yeah," I put the paper down in front of him. "I need you to find out what you can on that."

My expertise is hunting and watching, Zander's is tech, and the other two like shooting things. Zander jumps up quickly, rushing into his room, no doubt to do geeky tech shit while jerking off. This woman has us all kinds of fucked up.

I grab my own beer out of the fridge and sit at the table, taking down half of it in one swig. I hear Santos' excited voice from somewhere in the house followed by Darius' laughter. I was a little worried when he became sullen after leaving the compound. Finding his biological father like that must've been a hard blow, and then to learn he's a cunt, even worse.

"Got something," Zander skids back into the kitchen, his socks making him glide across the floor. "Reginald James."

"Who the fuck is that?" I snort and finish my beer.

"Don't have a fucking clue, but I got an address to where the license plate is registered to."

"Sounds good." I stand and nod. "Round up the idiots, and let's pay *Reginald* a visit."

"Santos! Darius!" Zander bellows as he rushes back out of the kitchen, "we got something!"

The sound of thundering hooves hits the floorboards and my whole second story sounds like it's going to split down the center. Bunch of fucking pansies.

"Did you find her?" Santos yells.

"No, but we found who dropped her hair off though." Zander calls back.

"Let's kill them!" Darius adds in.

Fucking pussy-whipped assholes.

I grab my keys and rush for the front door, my heart beating with the prospect of a lead. I make it to the front stoop when I hear Zander call out to me.

"Bro!" He snickers, "you may want to get some shoes on."

I look down at my sock-clad feet and let out an exaggerated exhale, "yeah."

Pussy-whipped asshole.

Santos

My mood has perked up slightly at Zander and Blaze finding a lead on Selene. I'll bring my little demon home one way or another, but I hope I get to shred an army of people to do it. I'm numb but unhinged at the same time, trying to block out my feelings while letting it slip into my mind enough to drive my murderous thoughts.

Finding the man who helped create me, is pulling me in two different directions. Relief at finally finding him, but also anger. He abandoned me, raised his other fucking son as if I didn't matter, and left me to fend for myself.

I am giving myself whiplash as I replay that moment in my head, the one where I met eyes with Papi Loco and reality smacked me in the face with full force. Loqi seemed just as surprised as I'd been, but I doubt the prick is having an internal war with his demons like I am.

I sense Darius' concern before it has even happened, always so attuned to my emotions, knowing when I'm quiet, something is wrong.

My boys always have my back, but Darius has my fucking heart and soul in his hands.

Now that Blaze has his shoes on, we all pile into the car to chase down whoever this Reginald fucker is, Selene's face flashing through my mind and causing me to temporarily forget about Papi. She's all I care about right now.

Blaze drives while Zander sits in the passenger seat, leaving Darius and I in the back, pretending they can't hear Darius as he speaks to me. "You good?"

I'm not fucking good, not by a long shot, but I shrug and try to keep calm.

"Yeah. I just want our girl home where we can chain her up in the basement. No one's going to get the opportunity to snatch her again."

He grunts in agreement, not hesitating to thread his fingers through mine to give my hand a firm squeeze. "We'll get her back. If we're lucky, she's already ripped half their limbs off and is casually leaning against the door, whistling while waiting for us to arrive. She's fine."

I smile at that, knowing he's probably right. No one gets to restrain Selene and live to tell the tale. Well, other than us in the bedroom, if we ask real nice. *Great, now my dick's getting hard.*

Darius raises an eyebrow, glancing at my groin with amusement. "At least you're in a better mood. I don't like it when you're quiet. It's scary."

"Keep looking at it like that, and we'll both be scaring Zan and Daddy Blaze," I joke, annoyance flashing in Blaze's eyes in the rear-view mirror.

"Don't even think about it, you crazy piece of shit," he growls, his eyes narrowing as Darius surprisingly runs his fingers through my hair and yanks hard, his face close to mine.

"Sounds like fun, San." He's fucking with Blaze, but I sense he's trying to keep me occupied while my mind is in a better place. I hate sinking into that dark pit I've been spending so much time in lately, knowing my silence and fury will eventually turn to violence and lashing out. Darius is always the one to take the brunt of it.

I chuckle, wrapping my fingers around his throat and forcing him back, his fingers slipping from my hair. "As much as I agree with you, a bullet in my ass isn't on my plans for the day."

"You calling my dick small or deadly?" he says with a fake gasp, making me snort.

"There's nothing small about your dick and you know it. I was referring to a real bullet. Daddy Blaze looks mad, and I don't want to push him until we have our girl back to protect me."

Zander smothers a laugh, while Blaze flicks his eyes from the mirror to the road with a grunt. "Try me, you little shits. See what happens." Grumpy bastard.

Darius relaxes back into his seat, but his eyes remain on me, his hand resting lazily on my thigh. It soothes me to know he's always so close, and the banter we've been having keeps my mind from wandering.

His fingers flex against my thigh, my dick stirring from the simple touch. I've been hornier than usual lately, probably because we had Selene in our grasp again, but the more Darius looks after me, the more I want to bend him over and nail his ass. He knows it, too, because he gives me a cheeky smirk before turning his attention out the window.

Darius

It's risky to push Blaze, but it makes Santos smile, so I continued to tease him. I'm staring out the window, but I can sense Santos' eyes burning into the side of my head. Sex and violence is Santos' language, so until the violence comes, I'll distract him with sex. Well, I'm not about to fuck him in the backseat, not with Blaze's hand twitching on the steering wheel, his gun close by.

I suck in a breath as Santos grabs my hand resting on his thigh, dragging it further north until his solid bulge is under my palm, my gaze snapping over to his. He smirks, raising an eyebrow in a playful challenge.

Living life on the edge is one thing, but living life on the edge of Blaze's gun? No thanks.

When I don't move, Santos rolls his eyes and grips my wrist firmly, lifting his hips a fraction to force his dick against my hand, more than happy to risk Blaze murdering us. Zander grins from the front seat, finding amusement in our impending doom, keeping his mouth shut to avoid the drama for as long as possible. He doesn't give a fuck if he sees us doing anything, he's cool like that, but Blaze would blow a fucking fuse. Probably because he isn't getting laid until Selene's back home with us.

I squeeze Santos through his pants firmly, forcing a quiet growl to leave him. I'll play along if he wants, but we aren't going to get off while Blaze is here, that much I know. He's only torturing the pair of us.

Blaze slams on the brakes, spinning to glare at us with all the anger he can muster—which is a lot—ignoring a car as its horn blares behind us. "If you two don't leave each other alone, I'll make Zander sit between you. Clear?"

I grin, giving Zander a wink. "Hear that, Zan? You're invited to the party too. I'll even let you top instead of bottom," I tease, his eyes filling with amusement.

"I'm flattered, honestly. But if you think I'd be anything other than the top, you're delusional."

"Don't fucking encourage them!" Blaze barks, turning his annoyance onto his best friend. "If you start acting like those two, I can't be held responsible for my actions! I need at least one of you to not be thinking with your dicks all the time!"

All three of us laugh, but Santos pushes me off his dick and takes my hand in his, the gesture so normal it's almost strange. Santos can give me whiplash sometimes with his moods. Sometimes he's stupidly horny, other times he's angry, but the playful, softer side of him is one of my favorites. It's good to see him relax.

"So, what are we doing with this Reginald cunt when we get our hands on him? If you won't let us fuck, at least let us have a play by play of the murdering we will do. That way, I still get to come in my pants," Santos drawls as Blaze starts driving again. Zander turns in his seat, glancing at the grip Santos currently has on my hand, understanding taking over his face. Santos needs to focus on something to keep his temper in check.

"Maybe we can torture information out of him?"

"What if the vehicle was stolen and this has nothing to do with him?" Santos frowns, making Zander raise an eyebrow.

"Do you give a shit?"

"Not particularly. I'm killing him for having such a shitty name to begin with. Did his parents hate him? Who the fuck looks at a cute screaming little baby and decides he looks like a Reginald? Angry parents with an unwanted pregnancy, that's who," he scoffs.

"Like Santos is any better? You were named after the sacred image of saints," Blaze deadpans. "What the fuck is sacred or saint-like about you?"

"My big-ass dick is pretty sacred. Makes Selene scream out to God, anyways," he throws back without hesitation, glancing at me to back him up. "You think it's pretty good too, right, babe?"

Vulnerability flashes in his eyes behind the mask he tries hard to keep in place, earning a wink from me. "You know it, *amante*."

Blaze mutters about killing us, but Santos grins at me like a kid in a candy shop, his demons soothed for another few minutes. I don't give a shit if it makes me sound dick whipped. I'll call him my lover every damn day if he keeps looking at me like I fix everything for him.

Chapter Two

Selene

My mouth is like sandpaper, and my throat feels swollen shut, completely dried out. I have to force my eyes open because they're crusted shut, and when I look around, I see I'm in another basement. This one is dank and musty, and the smell is making my stomach twist.

Fuck, I'm starving.

My head feels heavy as I lay it back against the cement wall behind me, the cool surface seeping through my skull. Maybe I shouldn't have threatened Gum Disease with my Orangutan, maybe he thought I was going off the rails, or possessed.

Once my head clears, I sit up and lift my hands, I'm still chained. This basement is smaller, and it's filled with damp boxes. I'm fucking breathing mold.

Where the fuck are my guys? I would've found *them* by now. They can't think I disappeared on my own again, right? They're smarter than that, right? I drop my head with a groan, I actually don't know the fucking answer to that because all we've done together is fuck and kill people. But I mean, they've survived this long, and Blaze did track me down to Nevada.

I begin to relax just as the door opens and two sets of boots hit the wooden stairs.

"Is she awake?" One asks, and I close my eyes.

"Doesn't look like it."

"Do you think Mack gave her too much?"

"I don't care." The second one has a bit of an accent, maybe Latin. "I need to get home to my abuela, she likes to pray the rosary together."

"Man," the first laughs, "you're gonna have to skip the Jesus humping today, this is our mission until Mack and the guys get back."

"What if her guys show up? Reggie, I'm not willing to die for this shit." The first whines, "let's just kill the chick and leave."

I let out a groan and hear them shuffle back, bunch of pussies.

"Water." I croak, putting on a show.

A water bottle is rolled across the floor, bouncing off my feet. I pick it up and open it in record time, guzzling down the cool liquid like a Nun on a Priest's cock. I choke on the liquid as my swollen throat has problems getting it down and I sputter, the water going everywhere.

Both guys look young, but they're dressed like thugs, and one has a black bandana around his head while the other has a white one.

"She looks possessed." Jesus Boy exclaims.

Huh. Maybe I could really work that. I'm chained and I can't lure them with my pussy, so possession it is. I need to get out of here and it looks like I'll have to do it myself, then I'm killing my guys.

"Fuck," I stare up at him wide-eyed, still choking on the fucking water, "you called him."

"What?" The fucking pussy thug grabs the crucifix around his neck, "are you insane?"

"She's fucking with you," the first one laughs. He'll be a harder nut to crack, but I only need to crack one.

"I have something inside of me," I make my voice creepy as fuck, "deep inside, and he's mean."

"What?" The kid holds out the crucifix, "what's inside of you?"

I close my eyes, making sure the whites show as my eyelids flutter, making the religious fuck gasp. "He's big, and hairy all over," I open my eyes up and look at him, "he has a bright, red ass and walks on all fours."

"What the fuck?" The first guy bends over laughing, "a red ass?"

"Don't laugh, my abuela says demons can come in any appearance, it would explain how she can kill like she does."

Finally, the guy wearing the black bandana eases up and looks at me, wondering if I do indeed have a red-assed, furry demon inside of me who helps me kill people. Are these two on drugs?

"Nah," he laughs again and pushes the guy wearing the white bandana, who's still staring at me in fear. "Don't be a pussy."

"I think we should uncuff her and set her free, maybe she won't kill us."

"Don't even take the keys out of your pocket," Bingo, "Mack will kill us even if she doesn't."

"I'll get out of here." The second guy is shaking his head, those brown eyes wide in fear. "Jesus will protect me."

I cross my arms over my chest, the chains clanking as I continue to listen to them bicker, and then when it turns a bit more physical, I roll my eyes. So fucking predictable.

I watch as they argue over my sanity, shoving each other back and forth, and when the little God-fearing cunt shoves his buddy a little too close to me, I wrap my shackle chain around his neck. He struggles but I hold tight, all the while smiling at the kid who's praying about his father up in Heaven, or something like that.

When the guy passes out in my arms, I release him, and his unconscious body hits the ground. "Keys." I hold out my hand, and they're thrown at me, landing at my feet.

I unlock the cuffs around my wrists, snickering when the guy starts panicking, looking around for a place to run.

“I could’ve sworn you said to kill me.” I say as the metal hits the cement floor.

With the second key on the ring, I unlock the padlock holding the chains to the industrial loop drilled into the wall, and then swing them up over my shoulder.

I turn and look at the trembling guy again as he clutches his cross around his neck, “boo, bitch.” I say, and he startles just before taking off in a run up the stairs.

“Hey!” I hear a few voices upstairs shout, “where the fuck you going?”

More people to terrorize. *Goody.*

I sling the shackles over my shoulder, and begin to whistle *Twinkle, Twinkle, Little Star* while I stomp up the stairs. “Bloody, bloody little shits, gonna scream while I saw off dicks. Breaking necks makes me high, but circumcision is fun I can’t deny. Bloody, bloody little shits, gonna scream while I saw off dicks.”

I think I missed my fucking calling as a recording artist. The door is open at the top of the stairs, thanks to the little Christian boy who ran out of here with shit in his pants, *praise the lord.*

“Reggie,” a gruff voice calls from another room, “what happened to Pepe?”

I follow the sound and find two other guys sitting on a couch, watching TV, and smoking a joint.

“I told him I was a demon, and the little fucker pissed himself. You think his piss would be considered holy water? You know, because he’s a Bible fucker?”

“What the fuck?” The guy who’s watching TV, jumps to his feet, while the one smoking a joint, struggles to get up.

I swing out the heavy metal shackles, catching the guy standing hard in the face. He drops like a sack of potatoes just as his buddy finally gets his ass off the couch. He looks at me through squinted eyes, swaying back and forth on his feet.

“How’d you get out?”

“I’m like Houdini,” I give him a wink. “Wanna play a game?”

“No,” he pulls a familiar looking knife out of his back pocket, and I gasp.

"You have my baby?" My belt has been feeling so empty without it, and the last I saw it was sticking out of Henry's chauffeur's eye.

"It is nice," he advances on me. "It's mine now."

"No can do," I shake my head with a tsk, "that knife chose me, like Harry Potter."

"Put those things down," he points the knife at the shackles over my shoulder as he advances.

"Sounds good," I say when he's less than a foot in front of me, I drop them to the floor, and still grip them in my hand.

He lunges for me at the same moment I swing the large metal chains, catching him on the ankles. He cries out and drops to his knees.

"Those ankles are sensitive as fuck, huh?" I snicker as I grab my knife and flip it in my hand, "toes too," I say just as he gets his feet back under him, I drop the shackles down onto his socked toes.

Once again, he's screaming on his knees, and I begin to hum along. His friend groans from his spot on the floor, and rolls over onto his hands and knees, slowly working his way up to his feet.

This is so much fun.

My giddy feeling is cut short when the guy does stand and swings a gun around to my face. His whole left side is swollen and bleeding, and he's looking really mad.

"Back downstairs." He growls.

So, they've been ordered not to kill me, even fucking better.

"Let's play a game," I grin at him. "Your friend wouldn't play with me." I point to the guy still moaning on the floor, crying about broken toes.

"Let's play doctor," he sneers, "I fill you up with some holes."

"Yes!" I nod, "doctor is fun, I'll be the brain surgeon."

"Get the fuck downstairs." He grinds out, and I shake my head with a snicker.

"Fine," I roll my eyes, "I'll go first." I grip my knife and swing my wrist quickly, throwing it with expert precision.

The sharp blade sinks into his eye, making him drop the gun, and his mouth gaping open. But not a single sound comes out as he crumples to the floor.

"I think I won that round," I say to the sobbing baby on the floor. "Are you my next patient?"

"No," he blubbers out as he begins to crawl backward, "I'm not even a part of Los Diablos, I just came here to buy some weed."

"Is that right?" I crouch down, "how'd you get my pretty knife? Hmm?"

"Carlos gave it to me." He points to my first patient.

"I see." I nod and stand.

He deflates with relief, his head hanging, and his brown shaggy hair slipping over his forehead. None of them are innocent, they all partake in kidnapping girls to sell. I'm not about to let a single one of them live, and I'm eager to send a message back to Delaney.

I'm going to need a lot of blood, though.

"Is this Delaney's house?" I ask my second patient.

"No, this is Reggie's house." The guy passed out in the basement.

I walk over to the dead guy on the floor and yank my knife out of his eye, the sound like music to my ears. I wipe the blade off onto his shirt and stand just in time to see the other fucker trying to make a run for it with broken toes.

"And here I was thinking I'd go easy on you, not all patients end in death." I call out to him as he disappears around the corner. I walk past my shackles, reminding myself to come back for them, and watch as his shaggy hair disappears into another room.

"I'm tired and don't have the energy to play hide and seek, come out so we can do your much needed open-heart surgery." I giggle, the sound manic. I may be tired and weak, but the prospect of gutting someone always perks me up.

I walk into a kitchen, there's open takeout containers everywhere, flies, and beer cans scattered. It smells like fucking death and in the center of the room is my patient number two holding a large butcher knife.

"Oh, you want to play butcher instead?" I cock my head to the side, "do you even know how to fillet a human?"

"Don't come any closer," he hobbles back a few steps.

"The best place to get meat is off the ass," I slap my own, "like a rump roast." My mouth salivates at the prospect of roast anything.

"Stop talking," he's trembling, like one of those little Taco Bell dogs, and his eyes are just as buggy.

"How very *Silence of the Lambs* of you," I snicker, "but looking at you right now, you'd make a poor Hannibal Lector, not me though. Did you want to try your own brain?"

"No," his voice is high-pitched, filled with fear, and I can't deny I'm inhaling it like a fresh breeze.

"Fine, open-heart surgery it is." I throw my knife and it slams in to the hilt, moving through his shirt and skin like butter.

The knife he's holding crashes to the tiled floor, and he wraps his hand around the hilt of mine, shock registering on his face. His hand tightens, and he pulls the knife from his chest, a strangled wheeze coming from his throat. He drops to his knees as his shirt blooms quickly with blood.

"Dang it!" I stomp my foot, "that's two patients in one day. Doctors have such a tough job."

He falls forward, his face making a sickening sound as it connects with the floor, and my knife still gripped in his hand. I stride forward and yank it back, cleaning his blood off onto his shirt. I walk back to the room where I left my shackles just as I hear slow measured steps coming up from the basement.

Reggie. I clap with excitement.

I stand by the semi-open door and wait, my stomach bubbling with excitement over our cat and mouse game. *I love games.* His hand appears first, shoving open the door, and then his foot hits the floor as he pokes his head out. I grab onto his hair quickly, wrapping my arm around his windpipe and pressing my knife to his throat.

"Reggie!" I squeal, "caught ya! You don't make a good mouse."

"Let go of me," he struggles a bit until I press in deeper with the knife.

"Why am I here? What was Delaney's plan for bringing me here?"

"Fuck you," he snarls, not at all afraid of dying like the others. He must think he still has a chance out of this, and I kind of want him to think he does, too. I love when the cat chases the mouse.

I shove him away from me and slip my knife back into my belt as he stumbles into the room with my first patient, his blood still pooling out of his eye socket. I hear him curse as I come in behind him, making him jump back, and narrow his eyes.

"Are they all dead?" *I like him.*

"Nope," I shake my head, "your little Christian friend ran out." I point to the front door. His eyes skate to the door, his mind trying to work out how he himself can run as well, and the excitement builds. "Shall I close my eyes and count to ten?"

His throat works hard on a swallow, and I watch his Adam's apple move slowly under the thin skin. I'm hoping he takes me up on my offer. I loved Hide and Seek as a child, and the last time I played it was around nine years old with Jan. Just the thought of her has my chest aching, but I can't let the thought of her mess up my fun right now. She's safe, and I'm in the middle of the most fun I've had in ages.

I close my eyes, making sure one stays cracked open, exactly how I did it as a kid. Then I begin to count, my mouth curling upwards as Reggie squirms. I get to three and the fucker bolts, making me squeal in delight. I scoop my shackles off the floor and give chase, both of our feet cracking against the hardwood.

"Ready or not! Here I come!"

"You said you'd count to ten!" He yells over his shoulder, his hand reaching for the door handle.

"I lied!" I exclaim as I throw the cuff end of my shackle, hitting him on the back of the head.

He stumbles, his left shoulder hitting the wall beside the door, and his hand coming up between us. He's panting, his skin is pale, and the defeat in his eyes is palpable. He knows he's about to die.

"They won't leave you alone after this, you will be a target forever." He tells me as he breathes heavily against the wall.

"Not forever," I smirk, "only until I kill them all."

His eyes darken, the irises threatening violence, and my excitement ramps. Then he comes at me, a growl slipping from between his lips, and his hands wrap around my throat, but only because I let him. His fingers tighten, his teeth are bared, and when I choke out a laugh, his eyebrows crash in the center.

I slip my knife out from my belt, and stab him in the stomach, reveling in the feeling of his warm blood coating my hand. Shock registers in his features and then his hands loosen as he falls back against the wall.

"Unfortunately," I grip the handle of my knife and yank it back out, "your death needs to be the messiest. I have a mural to paint."

He begins to cough, blood splattering out of his mouth and landing on my face, "you won't get away with it."

"Sure I will," I slap his cheek leaving behind a bloody handprint, "I'm the motherfucking Reaper Incarnate."

I slash my blade across his throat, giggling when his blood spurts out, and his body slinks down to the floor. I slip my blade back into my belt, and crouch down in front of him, scooping his blood into my hand.

I begin to paint out what's become my very own branding, a bloody scythe. The dripping blood is an added bonus. I get to the end and stare at it, knowing it needs one final touch. So, I scoop up more of Reggie's cooling blood and get to work. Just as I'm finishing, I hear gunshots outside in the driveway, and groan as I rush through the final word.

Welcome to Hell, you've been reaped.

I wipe off my hands in Reggie's shirt and take a deep breath as I swing open the front door.

Blaze

We start pulling out all the dead bodies from the car that pulled up to Reginald's house, and just like we thought, Los Diablos. I wanted more than one to interrogate but Santos got fucking trigger happy. At least the kid in the trunk of my car will do. He's in there now, sobbing and praying to Jesus to save him. Dumb piece of shit.

Once we have the bodies piled together, Zander starts taking a video, and Darius whips out his dick to piss on the mound.

"Are you fucking serious?" I snarl at him, and he tosses me a wink.

"I can't hold it, I'll get a UTI."

"Is that when your dick starts to make cheese?" Santos asks, and I watch Zander gag.

"That's syphilis, you dumb asshole," he says between retches.

"I can't wait until the day I can kill you three and live the rest of my days in peace." I snarl as I stride for the front door.

"He could never," Darius snickers, "the fucker would be bored out of his mind."

He's not wrong.

I reach the door and before I can grab the handle, it swings open revealing the one thing my heart beats for. She's standing there, covered in blood, chains draped over her shoulder, and a shit-eating smirk on her face.

The organ in my chest races, and before I can even form thought, I have her wrapped up in my arms, bloody chains, and all.

"Miss me, Daddy?" She purrs, and my dick solidifies instantly.

"Yeah, baby," I smother my face into her hair, "I really fucking did."

"What took you guys so long?" She mumbles into my chest, her body finally relaxing.

"It's only been twenty-nine hours." I tell her, "We came as fast as we could."

"That's it?" She pulls back and looks at me, "it felt so much longer."

"Is that my baby girl?" Santos calls, and I pull away just in time for him to barrel into her, lifting her up into his arms. "Did you kill everyone in here?" He asks as he looks around her into the house.

"Yeah," she giggles as she snuggles into his neck, "except for one, he ran out on me." Her pout is exaggerated as she sticks her bottom lip out, and maybe a little adorable.

"We caught a kid running out earlier," I say as I fold my arms over my chest and lean against the door frame, "he's in the trunk praying."

"That's him!" Her eyes light up.

"We're going to play with him later," Santos coos into her ear, and she giggles.

"I love games, I've been playing them all day."

I look around her into the house and see carnage everywhere, "looks like it."

"Give her to me," Darius shoves me aside and grabs Selene out of Santos' grip. "Baby, do you have chains?" I can hear the excitement in his voice.

"Not just chains!" She squeals, "shackles!"

The groan that comes from Darius' mouth is guttural and primal, and I can't help but admit this woman is perfect for each of us. Zander is next. He steps up into the house, slow and steady, and watches as she excitedly shows Darius how the shackles fit over her wrist, then gives him keys on a ring. He's patient for his turn to claim her.

Finally, her ocean blue eyes lock onto him, and she wiggles out of Darius' hold, running to Zander. He wraps her up into a tight grip, his face also burying into her hair.

"I love you," he says, and the rest of us pause, the air suddenly thick.

We haven't said that yet, not to her anyway.

She pulls back from him and looks up into his face, "really?"

"Yeah," he nods, "I needed you to know that because you keep disappearing on me."

"Does that mean you'll be making love to me now?" Her face falls.

"Hell no," Zander grins. "Let's get you home so I can fuck you sore."

I look at both Darius and Santos, seeing their expressions and trying hard not to laugh in their faces. Both looked pissed that Zander chose to be the first one to say it, but I'm buying my time. I won't mind being last because I'll be the most memorable.

They start walking to the car, Selene swinging her shackles as the boys follow behind. I take one more peek inside the house and see she's painted a large scythe with blood, with a sweet message underneath.

That's my girl.

Zander

Selene's wedged between Darius and Santos in the backseat as we head toward home, her sinful smile causing my heart to tug in my chest. I've been unsure whether to confess my love for her but watching her being reunited with the guys had sealed the deal. She's the only woman for me, and there's no point in putting it off.

I'll never forgive myself if something happens to her and she doesn't know how much she means to me.

"Bad Santos!" she scolds, her laughter peeling through the car as I glance back to see Santos hauling her into his lap, not hesitating to bury his face between her tits to motorboat them. Darius is watching them with a big grin, happy to have them both back to normal.

We all know Santos' mood has been affecting Darius too, so seeing him relaxed makes me relax. If he doesn't pick up any concern, then we have nothing to worry about, Santos is alright.

"You like me bad, my bloody queen," Santos mumbles from her chest, leaning back while keeping his hands firmly on her waist to stop any escape plan she may concoct. Blaze is fuming in the driver's seat, probably upset to be left out of the titty party Santos is currently having with our girl.

"So true. You know what else I like? Orgasms. You have any of those stashed away for me when we get home? Apparently being kidnapped and murdering a bunch of people makes me stupidly horny," Selene says with a moan, making me snort.

"You're just figuring that out now? You're soaking wet panties didn't give it away as you played with those bastards?"

She goes to speak but Santos grabs her throat and yanks her against his chest, devouring her in a kiss that causes a groan to fill the car. I can't tell you which one of us makes the noise, but I don't give a shit. She's lucky I didn't haul her into the front seat and make her ride me.

She peers over her shoulder at me with a devilish grin, grinding down on Santos' lap and making him groan. "Pretty sure my flaps are chaffed from them. I did a lot of running around playing games today."

"Wait until we get home, your flaps will be chaffed by the time I'm done with your cunt," Santos growls, his eyes darting to Darius seriously. "At least my dick will be nice and wet to slide right into Darius." Jesus Christ.

Selene moans her approval at the idea, but her eyes never leave me. "You'll kiss it better, won't you, Zan?"

"That depends," I snort. "If your cunt's dripping with cum, Darius can kiss it better instead."

"Can you guys talk about something else? Ever?" Blaze demands, his angry eyes moving to the rear-view mirror to glare at them in the back. "We get it, you're horny little rabbits."

"Don't act like you can't wait to bury your monster cock inside me too," Selene coos, finally taking her eyes off me. "I've been looking forward to going to pound town with you."

Blaze's hands tighten on the wheel, but his eyes soften a fraction, not being able to tell her no. "You'll be the death of me."

"Excellent. Because I have a feeling you'll be the death of my pussy. I'm so wet right now, Daddy," she smirks, licking her lips, a surprised shriek leaving her as Darius suddenly grabs her and tugs her into his lap, kissing the shit out of her like a man starved. Santos pouts, watching as Selene doesn't even put up a fight.

"How come you don't fight him on it? I had to wrangle you like a wild animal to get you in my lap."

"You like the chase," she giggles as she pulls back from Darius slightly, her eyes sparkling with amusement. "It's foreplay."

Blaze looks mad at the banter, but his lip kicks up into a tiny smirk as he keeps his eyes on the road, seeming glad to have us all back together. My best friend is a grumpy bastard when he wants to be, but we are family. Our happiness makes him happy.

"If you come sit back on my lap, I'll make you come," Santos exclaims, causing Selene to jerk her attention away from Darius who was kissing her neck.

"Promise?"

"I'd never joke about orgasms. Come here," he orders, making Blaze curse as Selene moves across the backseat to do as she's told. First time for everything.

"You are not fucking while I'm driving!" Blaze barks, but Santos chuckles darkly, shoving his hand down the front of Selene's pants, a gasp of surprise leaving her as his fingers press inside her.

"I wasn't going to fuck her. Not unless she begs me."

"I'm begging," Selene pants as she grinds down on his hand, making me laugh. Santos growls, leaning forward to bite her bottom lip sharply.

"You get what you're given until we get home. Got it?"

"Daddy! Santos is being mean!" she huffs, and Blaze can't stop the grin that forms on his face.

"What was that? You want us to give you more orgasm torture and not let you come?"

She clamps her lips shut, giving Santos a dirty look, daring him to hold out on her. He moves his fingers in and out of her, her scent filling the car and causing my dick to harden behind my zipper. Darius leans back to watch the show, chewing on his lip as Santos works to get our girl closer to release.

Sure, I wish I was the one to get her off but seeing her come apart on Santos' lap is almost as good. Whatever he's doing to her is working, because her head drops back, and her eyes flutter closed. Her muscles tighten and her hands dig into Santos' shoulders, a hiss leaving him at the twinge of pain she gifts him.

"Oh my God!" she screams suddenly, her eyes flying open as Santos fists her hair firmly.

"Look at me!" he snaps, some of his control vanishing. I knew it wouldn't take long.

He doesn't slow down, and she doesn't stop screaming for God, my face scrunching as I suddenly hear something like an echo. I listen closely, not understanding what it is until Selene finally becomes quiet, and Santos lets her forehead fall to his, whispering sweet promises that probably involve blood and violence.

"*Please, God! Save us from these devils!*"

Blaze glances at me with a frown as he drives into our driveway and kills the engine. "What the fuck was that?" He snaps as he gets out of the car.

"*Please, God!*"

Darius sniggers as he opens the door to climb out. "Seems our Bible buddy thinks he's having a prayer session with our girl. Do you think God heard you, baby?"

Santos cackles as he helps Selene adjust her pants before they climb out too, even Blaze is finding amusement in the situation. I scramble out just in time to see Blaze open the trunk, revealing the babbling idiot we've locked in there.

His eyes blink against the light, but they find Selene and his eyes widen. "God heard us? He saved you from the Devil? Your demons are gone?"

She grins, leaning down to peer at him closely. "I am the fucking Devil. My demons are my friends."

"Why were you praying then?!" he exclaims, seeming ready to piss his pants as she giggles like the maniac she is.

"Praying? I was coming. Hard, might I add. My baby sure knows how to send me to Heaven."

Santos bats his lashes at her like the lovesick fool he is, ignoring the guy as he starts praying again. "Speaking of Heaven. Let's leave Blaze and Zander to lock this fucker up while we go and fuck our souls into each other's bodies."

"What if we don't have souls?" she questions as Darius and Santos start guiding her toward the house, pretending like they can't hear Blaze and I cussing them out for ditching us.

"There will be orgasms there, who gives a shit," he whoops like an idiot, eyeing the shackles she's dragging alongside them. He better make it fast, because the moment Blaze and I are done tying this dude up, we'll be in there to join the party, and I want her on my dick one way or another.

Santos

Selene is taking too long to walk, so I grab the back of her thighs and hold her against my chest, making out with her like crazy as Darius fists my shirt and drags us through the house with Selene's shackles in hand, guiding me since I can't fucking see. We need to slow down to make sure Selene gets off multiple times, but the selfish part of me doesn't give a shit right now. I just want to be buried inside her and fill her with my cum.

Darius kicks the bedroom door shut behind us and drops the shackles, prying her from my arms, not hesitating to yank her shirt over her head.

"Wait! I need a fucking shower," she states, making him shrug.

"Alrighty then."

I grin, knowing what he's going to do before she does. He strips her bare and throws her over his shoulder, ignoring her protesting and cursing, carrying her to the bathroom and turning the shower on. I get naked, not wanting to wait for her to be done, my eyes lingering on Darius as he places her on her feet and yanks his clothes off, too.

"You're not joining me," she snaps, crossing her arms as Darius guides her under the hot spray. I roll my eyes, ignoring her as Darius and I climb in with her. She goes to tell us to get out, but I shove her back against the wall, plastering my body to hers and kissing the words right out of her mouth. She slaps at my arm, trying to remain angry at our intrusion but not wanting me to stop.

She bites my lip hard, drawing blood before sucking it into her mouth as her nails dig into my back. I feel like a teenager again, almost coming down my fucking leg as her body rubs against mine.

Rough hands run across my back as Darius sandwiches me between them, his lips moving across my shoulder lightly to remind me he's there, too. I don't stop what I'm doing, but I reach around until my hand rests on his hip, giving it a squeeze.

Being between them is something I thought about regularly, both of them completing me in ways I didn't know was possible. I realize I'm crazy and irrational, but they love me for it, and they help center me when it's needed.

I lift Selene against the wall, sliding inside her where I belong, her low groan telling me it's what she needed too. I fuck her hard, my butt bumping back against Darius' solid length as he lets me take what I need from her, my mind drifts to the disgust in Papi's eyes when he found out I let Darius touch me. The way he made what we have seem like trash. The fact that he never thought to tell his other son about me, not expecting his two lives to collide like they have.

Anger burns inside me the more I think about it, until I realize I've zoned out as someone is trying to yank me back from Selene.

Selene? Fuck.

"Santos, snap the fuck out of it!" Darius shouts, managing to get between us and put Selene on her feet, her eyes wide as she peers at me over his shoulder. What the fuck happened?

As if sensing my thoughts, Darius grabs the back of my neck in a tight grip, his voice low. "You good, man?" My breathing's rapid, and confusion fills me as I try to look at her, but he stays in front of me so my attention can't waver. "You're back with us now?"

I shake my head, trying to control myself as I try to piece together what happened. I can't hurt Selene, it's impossible, and even if I do, no one can stop me. Making her bleed and bruise is something she craves, soaking in the violence we create from pleasure. So why is Darius stopping me?

Once my breathing calms, Darius releases my neck and takes a small step back, turning the water off as he goes. "It's like you were possessed, babe. You weren't hearing or seeing anything. What were you thinking about? You almost fucked Selene through the damn wall." That's nothing new, I always fuck her hard.

My eyes seek her out, seeing her reddened skin, finger shaped bruises on her thighs and a streak of blood in her light hair. "The fuck?" I mumble, noticing a blood streak on the shower wall. Selene can handle anything, we fuck with no restraint all the time, but this is different. I don't like not knowing what's happening.

Did I smash her head into the wall? That's a little rough, even for me. If she's bleeding, I want to know what I did. I hate being in the dark with my own actions.

I must look completely crazed because Selene's eyes track my face with concern. I climb out of the shower, putting my fist through the wall on my way out.

"Santos! Get back here!" Darius growls, but I keep going, needing to break something. Papi isn't allowed to live in my head rent-free and mess with me. I don't give a fuck about him, that's what I tell myself, but a small part of me is fucked up from finally finding him.

"You want to put some clothes on?" Zander teases as I almost run him down in the hallway, his eyes narrowing when I slam him back with my hands, needing him out of my way. I need the gym, the punching bag being a better alternative to the walls.

Footsteps follow me, stopping to linger in the gym's doorway as I stalk over to the heavy bag and start throwing my fists at it, my dick swinging and slapping my thighs. They've seen me naked plenty, so I don't give a fuck. I need to release the rage before I use it on one of the guys.

I feel Blaze's thunderous gaze before he even speaks. "What the fuck is wrong now?"

I don't look up, but I sense Selene enter the room, her scent surrounding me, breaking through some of the anger. It's stupid to let a man I hardly remember have so much control over my emotions, but knowing he ran off to raise his other son? Choosing him over me? Yeah, it isn't good for my mood.

"Leave him alone. He just needs a minute," Selene demands, my eyes darting across the room to hers. She approaches me, not being afraid of my fists like any other woman would be, resting her hand on my hip as I continue to throw punch after punch, making sure to stay back enough to avoid getting clipped with my elbow.

She doesn't stop me, doesn't tell me how to feel, she simply lets me know she's there, waiting for when I'm done purging my demons.

"San, you're alright," Darius says confidently, trying to make me believe it. I'm not though, I never black-out in a fit of rage like that. I'm pissed I can't remember my actions, but even more pissed for the reason behind them.

"I'm not fucking fine," I growl, swinging my arm as hard as possible, my knuckles cracking on impact as the bag swings.

"Come back to the bedroom, you'll burn your mood out on Selene and me," he answers, making me scowl.

"No."

"What the fuck happened?!" Blaze barks, sick of being kept in the dark. I turn my attention away from the bag, trying to relax as Selene's arm goes around my waist.

"I don't fucking know, that's the problem!"

Darius cringes, "we were messing around in the shower. He was banging Selene and zoned out. She's fine, but we were trying to snap him out of it."

"Did I smash your head into the wall or something?" I ask Selene, making her chuckle.

"No. You can't hurt me, silly."

"There's blood in your hair. I'm not worried about hurting you, you're as psychotic as I am," I chuckle dryly. "I'd just be really mad if I made you bleed and didn't remember it."

"It's your blood. You had your face in my hair and were biting the hell out of your lip," she murmurs as she lifts up on tip-toe, licking my lip, making me frown. I lift my hand to touch it, feeling the sting from a nasty cut. I groan as she leans forward again and gently sucks it into her mouth, tasting my blood without taking her eyes off mine.

She gives me a cheeky smile as she steps back, fisting my dick and giving it a few long strokes. "Now, can you come back to my room so we can finish what we started? You were fucking me so hard I almost saw stars. I'd like to finish. What made you mad, anyways?"

"Papi," I grunt. "I remembered how he spoke about Darius and me, then started thinking of Loqi and lost my shit a little."

Selene watches me with confusion, but Darius snorts. "I don't give a shit what he thinks."

"Excuse me? Why would you listen to that dumbass piece of shit?" Selene demands, her eyes rounding in surprise as I sigh.

"He's my Papi. The one who left me as a kid."

Darius

Selene kicks us out of Santos' room, wanting to talk to him in private. I've never known him to have blackouts like that, and I hate not being in there with him. Blaze and Zander are quiet as I wander into the kitchen, dressed and needing a beer.

I plonk down on the couch, sighing before taking a long drink to center myself.

"He blacked-out?" Zander mumbles, sitting down to watch me.

"He was banging her, then went harder, zoning out in the process. Selene's fine, as you could see, but she was worried about him when he didn't respond to either of us. His dad's really fucking him up, I could kill him," I scowl, glancing at Blaze who looks ready to march back into the bedroom and haul Selene out. "Leave him alone, Blaze. He needs a moment."

"What if he's fucking lost complete control? For real? It's never good when Santos loses it. You know that since you're usually his fucking punching bag," he grits out.

"Selene isn't some flimsy bitch we dragged in from a party. She can protect herself and doesn't need us to hover. She's worried about him, not scared of him. Jesus," I spit. "Let her have a heart to heart with him. He obviously has a lot on his chest he needs to vent, and he can catch her up on everything she missed. Papi was a real dick about me being with Santos, but we also didn't expect to run into him either. His mind's spinning, and Selene will shake it out of him. How's the bible basher?" I ask, changing the subject. Blaze gives me a filthy look, telling me he knows I did it on purpose, but he answers my question.

"He's tied up and ready to be interrogated later. I was hoping to nail our girl first."

"They won't be long," I shrug, hearing a moan from the other end of the hallway, making me chuckle. "Well, they won't be too long. She's obviously fucking him better."

"Is that a good idea after what just happened?" Zander asks, and I shrug again.

"Let them fuck their demons out of each other, then you two can nail her as a welcome home gift."

"What about you?" Zander says with a raised eyebrow, but I'm not worried about missing out. I have all the time in the world to fuck her.

"I won't die without her pussy for another day, I promise. You two feel free to tag-team her while I stay with San. I don't want him alone right now. There's a fifty-fifty percent chance of him running off to massacre his old man and half the MC, so I'll keep an eye on him."

"You're good to him."

"Of course, I am. He's mine," I answer, meaning every word. I'd be missing a part of myself without that crazy bastard. If he ran off on a suicide mission, then we'll all go to war to bring his ass back home.

Chapter Three

Blaze

There's something snapping into place as the three of us sit here in silence. I've always known about the connection Santos and Darius feel, and yet, hearing the confirmation and having Selene solidify it, is making me see things I didn't before. I used to be so afraid of a woman coming between us, weaseling in, and tearing us apart. As much as she's weaseled her way into all of our hearts, she's also healed us in places we didn't even realize were broken.

"I think we should go question the altar boy," I grunt as I stand, "you want to join us?" I ask Darius who looks deep in thought.

"Nah," he shakes his head, "I'm good here."

"Let's get this done," Zander yawns, exhaustion finally hitting him.

We head to the basement door and Zan grabs my shoulder, "do you remember Santos telling us anything about his family or how he grew up?"

"Very little," I shrug, "his mother struggled to raise him and worked a lot. He practically raised himself on the streets."

"I remember when we first met him and Darius, do you remember?"

"How could I forget?" I roll my eyes, "they both almost received a bullet between their eyes."

Santos and Darius were at a Los Diablos house party that Zander and I crashed. They were there looking for a few missing girls, and Zan and I were there to get info for Henry. A fight broke out and just in true Santos form, he went around shooting the place up with Darius at his back. When they found us in an office pulling files, I had my gun pressed to Santos' forehead, and it was downhill from there. We found the girls they were looking for and they decided to join our cause.

We never questioned how easily we blended, never thought too long on the chemistry we had as friends, and not until a few moments ago did I truly believe in fate. We were all meant to walk this life together, causing mayhem.

We head down into the basement, our nostalgic moment over, and find the little altar boy trembling in his binds.

"I can't believe he's a Diablo," Zander kicks his foot and chuckles when the kid whimpers. "Do they not have standards?"

"Let's ask him." I say as I grab a chair, straddling it to face the kid, "take the gag out of his mouth."

Zander yanks the dirty cloth out, tossing it on the floor as the kid begins to choke. "I'm… a… new… recruit." He forces out between coughs.

"What made you want to join a gang, kid?" Zander asks as he crouches in front of him, "shouldn't you be studying to be a priest or something?"

"Just because I'm devout Catholic doesn't mean I don't need the money." He spits out, "and I'm not a kid, I'm twenty-three years old."

"Under-developed then," Zander lines his words with pity, and I can't hold in the snicker.

"Why Los Diablos?" I ask.

"They approached me at church, they saw my grandma was frail and old, and asked me if I wanted to make extra cash."

"Diablos are recruiting at churches now?" Zander gives me a shocked look.

"Praise be to God." I mumble.

"Amen." The guy says from the floor.

"What's your name?" Zander asks.

"Joey, but everyone calls me Pepe. Look, I'm all my grandma has, and if I don't get home soon, she'll worry."

"Should have thought of that before joining a dangerous gang, *Pepe.*" I tsk.

"Sometimes choices are limited for guys like me." He mumbles.

"Guys like us." Zander corrects him. "We all have issues, but it doesn't mean we have to sacrifice ourselves to survive."

"What is it you guys do? You're with that woman, right? I could feel the evil coming off her." He looks sincere, but I don't like anyone talking shit about my girl.

So, I slap him across the face, hard. The impact busts open his bottom lip and blood begins to run down his chin.

"I think you should reword that."

"She killed everyone in the house!" He exclaims.

"Did you miss the part where she was kidnapped? Or how about *shackled* to a fucking wall?" Zander grits out, his fists shaking. He wants to hit him, too.

"They told me she killed people, innocent lives. She's the Reaper Incarnate." He leans in as if telling us a secret.

"We know who she is." I roll my eyes. "Tell us," I hold out my hand, "what is it you know about the Reaper Incarnate?"

"She kills businessmen around the city because she hates men."

"He's not too far off," Zander chuckles.

"She kills men who take advantage of women and children, all of whom have bought and sold people for a long time." I inform him.

"Like slaves?"

"Exactly like slaves." I nod. "Los Diablos and Mack Delaney are right now head of that trade here in New York, and you just signed yourself over to them. How would Jesus feel about that?" I widen my eyes.

"What would Jesus do?" Zander says, working hard to hide his smirk.

"Jesus would try to enlighten them about their ways and then pray for their souls." Pepe says.

"Well, there you have it," Zander claps his hands. "All the answers will be found in Jesus."

"All praises be to Jesus Christ." Pepe's chin hits his chest.

"We're going to help Jesus," I clap my hands. "Let's make the Diablos see the errors in their ways."

"Amen!" Pepe exclaims.

"I have an idea," Zander looks at me with a twinkle in his eye, "we can't let them know we're cleansing them of evil."

"No," I agree, "they would fight it."

"Exactly," Zander continues. "Let's instead infiltrate them and bless them from within." He holds out his arms.

"Yes!" Pepe nods emphatically, "like a soldier for Christ!"

Zander begins to untie him and gives him a stern look, "we need you to be our soldier, Pepe. Can you handle it?"

"They can never know who you're really working for." I add. "Which is Jesus." I tag on.

"I can keep the secret, in the name of the Lord." Pepe nods solemnly and then crosses himself, "I am a faithful soldier."

"Perfect," I stand. "And if you fuck up, Pepe," his eyes shoot up to mine, "I will crucify you, much like Jesus himself."

He swallows thickly and nods as Zander covers a chuckle into his hand. "I won't let you down."

"Try to infiltrate where they're going to be on the next pick up. They will have women and children." Zander tells him. "Then you come and tell us so we can save them."

"I will." He nods quickly. "You can count on me."

We walk him upstairs and to the front door, just as Selene screams out for Jesus, making Pepe sign himself.

"Peace be with you," Zander snickers as he opens the front door.

"And also with you." Pepe nods and hurries out.

"Do you think this will work?" Zander laughs as he shuts the door.

"Yeah," I grin, "it'll work fucking beautifully."

Selene

I leave Santos snoring in bed, and head out to look for the rest of my boys. I honestly don't know how I let the similarities between Santos and Loqi sail over my head. They were way too similar for me not to notice, but I was so consumed with Jan that it didn't fully sink in. Papi Loco is in for a world of pain when we meet again, and we will because I have shit to settle with my sister.

I find Darius asleep on the couch, his chest moving slowly, and his fingers twitching. I kiss his forehead and cover him with a blanket. From the moment Zander professed his love for me, I've been thinking nonstop about my feelings for them in return.

Santos and I were cut from the same cloth and sewn together with the same parental issues, no wonder we fit the way we do. Then there's Darius whose heart is five times too big and sees the good in us, no matter how unhinged we become. I brush my fingers through his hair, and head into the kitchen to find Blaze making bacon. My big Grizzly bear, who has a hardened crust, is just a soft gooey teddy bear underneath.

"I thought you might be hungry." He mumbles as he begins to put the strips on a plate.

"I am," I hurry to sit at the table, yanking Santos' shirt down below my ass. I'm not wearing panties and my sore little flower will not be happy if she's smushed into the chair.

He puts a full plate of bacon in front of me and a steaming cup of hot chocolate. I haven't had hot chocolate since I was a kid. I stare down into the mug, and he clears his throat.

"I figured coffee would keep you up and you probably need your rest." He looks bashfully grumpy, and it makes my heart squeeze in my chest.

"Thank you, Daddy."

His dark brown eyes flare with heat, and my pussy clenches with anticipation, I haven't had him inside of me since Henry's basement. He may have joined us in Nevada, but I know that's not his thing, Blaze won't always want to share me like Santos and Darius do.

With his eyes still on me, I begin biting into the crispy meat, the salty flavor making me moan, and I suck my fingers clean after each piece. Once my plate is nearly empty, and my hot chocolate done, Blaze leans on the table.

"Can I ask you a few questions about how you were taken?"

"I was wondering when you would," I grin at him, "where the others are all action, you like to analyze everything."

He sits on the chair in front of me and grabs my foot up into his lap, his deft fingers kneading into my aching flesh.

"I was stupid," I begin, not liking to admit it, "I recognized Henry's old driver and hopped in his fucking car."

"That was stupid, but," he shrugs, "an honest mistake."

"He knocks me out and tosses me in the fucking trunk," my fist hits the tabletop, my rage coming back full force. "I kill him and find these punks standing around with Delaney."

"We know him as Mack," he tells me, "He and Henry worked closely."

"Well, he's going to be working closely with my fists as I knock his gums down his throat." I snarl, "anyways, I ended up back here in New York in a basement, and it really felt like days."

He nods, the scar on his face pulling with his grimace, "I thought maybe you had run again."

"I thought you guys might have given up on me." I smile and grab his hand in mine, "this is new, for the both of us."

"Yeah," he brings my hand to his mouth, brushing his lips back and forth over the skin. Goosebumps rise along my arms, and he grins, knowing his effect on me.

I'm suddenly overtaken with a yawn, my mouth gaping open, and my body stiffening. When I finally open my eyes again, he's grinning at me, and I can't help but notice how handsome he is.

"Let's get you to bed," he stands and hauls me up. I jump up into his arms and wrap my legs around his waist.

"Are you coming too?"

His big hands land on my bare ass and he groans into my neck, his cock straining between us.

"No," he licks my neck. "You need rest, but I'll be there to wake you up."

"I need another shower," I moan.

His fingers swipe into my pussy and he growls, "am I touching Santos' cum?"

"And mine," I snicker.

He sinks two of his large fingers inside of me, pumping in and out as he takes me back to what's become my bedroom, the one Zander tried to lock me in so long ago. I giggle when I remember jumping out of the window and discovering his tracking app.

"Any reason why you're laughing while I finger fuck you?" Blaze snarls.

I grab his face between my hands and kiss him, my tongue dragging over the hard ridge of his scar. "I was remembering the first time I was here."

He pulls his fingers out of me, gripping my ass once again, and leaving it wet with mine and Santos' release. "I was so pissed off with having you here." He kicks open my room door.

"Only because you wanted me so bad." I tease him, and he graces me with another one of his rare smiles.

"Maybe, brat." He drops me on the bed, "now go shower and then sleep."

"Yes, Daddy." I say to his retreating back, and then laugh when he grumbles down the hall.

I can't wait to fuck the grump right out of his ballsack.

Zander

I finish my shower and find myself heading to Selene's room, missing her filthy mouth and warm, tight body. I step in her bedroom and my ears are once again assaulted by the sound of her singing. Is she making up her own words to Twinkle, Twinkle Little Star? I snort as she sings about cutting off dicks, and fall onto her bed, resting my arms behind my head.

There's a new atmosphere in this house, we're all more relaxed, and it feels lighter. I wish it could stay this way forever, all of us here, fucking our girl whenever we want, and not give a fuck about what's going on on the outside. But that's just not what we signed up for. The four of us banded together years ago in an agreement to take down the industry that took something from each of us. We're reaching the end of our goals, but it's still a ways away.

The water shuts off and I hear the blow dryer start, snickering when I think about her washing Santos off of her, only to have me on her next. This will be the story of her life; she'll forever walk funny with a sore pussy. The door opens and she steps out of it, completely naked and my cock tents inside my boxers.

"Every time I see your cock, I'm reminded of the fact that you took your daddy's dick and said, '*hold my beer.*'"

"Is this gonna be a forever thing?" I groan into my hands, "you talking about my dead father's dick?"

"It's not every day a girl can say she fucked a dude and his daddy." She prowls toward me. "Now take those off and fuck my ass."

"Jesus," I moan and quickly shed my boxers.

"No more praying," she holds up her hand, "I've had enough of Jesus today."

She grabs lube out of her side table, and crawls over my body. I lie transfixed as she squirts some into her hand, coating my cock and then her ass.

"You really want me to fuck your ass?" I breathe, my dick jumping with the prospect.

"No, Baby Walton," she rolls her eyes, "I was hoping Daddy Walton would come back and do it for you."

I snarl and lift her up, finding her tight asshole. I line myself up and slam her down onto me. The squeeze is so fucking tight and when she screams out, I jerk inside of her, making her cry out again.

"That hurt, asshole." She slaps my chest.

"That's what you get for constantly bringing up my father." I grit through my teeth.

She begins to grind into me, a sly smirk on her face, and I sense something coming before she even has to say it, "did you think rough sex was gonna teach me a lesson? Wrong thought you, Yoda."

I chuckle as I grab her hips, pumping up inside of her, knowing I won't last long. I've missed her, I'm afraid to lose her, and I fucking told her I loved her. She must see something in my eyes because she falls forward, her mouth brushing against mine.

"You love me, Baby Walton?"

"Yes," no hesitation.

Her ass clenches around my cock, making me see stars.

"I love you, too." Her words are spoken so softly but they slip down past my ribcage and wrap around my heart.

I thrust up into her a few more times, and we both come at the same time, her head tossing back as she cries out. She falls down beside me and wraps her arm around my waist.

"You're the second person I've said that to, ever."

"The first?" I begin to feel the burn of jealousy low in my stomach.

"Jan." She says softly, and I pull her in closer.

"We'll figure this all out and get you back with your sister, you both need each other." I kiss her head, "now sleep."

"Can you tell me a story?"

I chuckle at her request, my fingers skimming lazily along her back, "what story?"

"The one about John Dempster's death, I want every detail."

I groan and cover my face with my hand, "I am really not the one to tell you that, maybe Blaze, fuck even Santos. They were the ones who enjoyed it the most."

"But you're here now and I want to hear it."

So, I tell her because that's what my woman wants. I go over every disgusting detail, even gagging at the gorier parts. But it's all worth it to see her face light up with glee, even though her eyes are drooping with tiredness.

Just as I gag my way through John's lungs being lifted from his body, I hear her soft snores, and breathe out a sigh of relief. I gather her closer to my body and close my eyes, finally feeling at peace enough to sleep.

Santos

I awaken to find an arm tightly wrapped around my waist, prickly stubble pressing against my shoulder blade as I go to move. I can sense Selene isn't in the room with me like she was when I fell asleep after banging her brains out, but I don't mind. I'm just happy to wake up to someone.

Being alone in my own head is dangerous lately because my emotions seem to be controlling me a lot more than usual, but something simmers it all down when Darius or Selene are close.

"D?" I mumble, rolling over to face Darius, his eyes cracking open as a soft smile takes over his face. The bastard is making me too soft, but I wouldn't change a thing.

"You better this morning?" he asks, snuggling closer to me and playfully biting my pec. We have shit to do today, so as much as my dick likes the idea of choking him while he swallows my cum, I know it can't happen. After my night with Selene, I'm not sure I have anything left in my damn ballsack, anyway.

"Yeah. I don't think there's any anger left, Selene fucked it right out of my body," I grin, grabbing his wrist as his fingers brush against my dick. "Not this morning, you sex fiend."

"Why not? It's still early," he groans, but he rolls away from me, knowing I'm right. I usually am.

"The others will already be awake, so we might as well get this show on the road. I need a hot shower and a strong coffee," I grumble, rolling out of bed and wandering toward the door, making Darius chuckle.

"You want pants?"

"Not particularly," I reply on my way out, beelining to the kitchen to make a coffee. Zander's sitting at the counter, looking ready to bust in his pants as he handfeeds Selene toast and bacon, her tongue poking out to lick the grease off his fingers in a way that shouldn't look so damn erotic, but it does.

"I've got something better you can suck on," I wink, leaning back against the counter to wait for the coffee to brew.

She raises an eyebrow, sounding offended. "What's better than bacon? I'll tell you right now, nothing is."

"How about bacon wrapped around my dick? I'll even let you lick the grease from my sack," I offer, Zander giving me a dirty look for ruining his moment with her. Tough shit. If I can lure her away with a bacon covered dick and a greasy ballsack, he isn't doing a good enough job.

"Good morning. Why don't you put pants on? You're ruining my view," Zander grumbles, eyeing my dick like it's the Devil.

"Keep looking at it like that, and you'll have to deal with it," I throw back, my dick hardening slightly as it joins the conversation. Zander's eyes widen before he darts his gaze away, making me grin in victory. He's so easy to rile up.

Darius wanders in, smirking at me but keeping silent, knowing I'm pissing people off, but having one hell of a good time doing it. I should dunk my balls in Blaze's coffee. Might be a tad hot though, and I'm pretty attached to my balls.

As if on cue, Blaze wanders in freshly showered, his scowl hitting me immediately as he catches an eyeful of my junk. "The fuck is wrong with you?"

"You want the book or the dot points version?" I ask seriously, the other three sniggering while Blaze continues to look at me like I pissed in his cereal. I might do that, too.

"I wrote the fucking book about what's wrong with you. I just wanted to know what I was adding to it this morning," he barks. "Now, go cover up your dick before you lose it."

"Wait, you want my dick? Why didn't you say so? Come here, Daddy Blaze. Let me give you some loving!" I exclaim gleefully as I move toward him, risking my manhood as I dart around to climb on his back like a monkey, my dick and balls pressing into his back.

"Santos!" Blaze bellows, trying to shake me off, but I'm like a leech once I have a good grip. I laugh loudly over his cursing, holding on for dear life as he twists his big body to try and throw me off.

"Yee-fucking-haw!"

"You little fucking shit! You're dead!" Blaze shouts, failing to get me to let go, resorting to slapping at me. His hand cracks again my butt, and I let out a fake as fuck groan.

"Harder, Daddy."

"Get him the fuck off me!" Blaze demands, glaring at Darius who's smothering his laughter, walking over to help with the situation.

"San, let him go."

"Not until he promises to finish what he started. All this yelling and spanking is making me horny," I smirk, almost losing my grip as Blaze twists again while I'm distracted.

"You filthy cunt! Get your boner off me!" Blaze is basically screaming the house down like a woman terrified of a mouse, but I know my life depends on me doing as I'm told.

"Okay! Stop moving and I'll get down!" I chuckle, waiting for him to stop before grinding my dick against his back before jumping down. He turns on me, his fists clenched and ready for murder, but

Selene darts in front of me, giving me her back before lifting her shirt and blinding him with her tits.

He halts his attack, staring at them like a beacon in a storm, suddenly snapping out of it to glare at her. "That's a dirty trick."

She fixes her shirt, much to everyone's annoyance, giving me a wink. "No one hurts my baby boy."

"Your *baby boy* is the biggest dick!" Blaze snaps, making her grin.

"We're talking about big dicks now? Have you seen what monster you have in your pants, Daddy?"

"I can't fucking deal with you," he grumbles, but his lips lift into a smile, giving him away. He's been finding more humor in things lately, something else we can give Selene credit for. Then again, seeing the big grumpy cunt smile is just as scary as his anger sometimes.

She stands on tip-toes and kisses his cheek, heading over to the coffee machine to grab my coffee and handing it to me. "Here you go. Drink that to keep your damn mouth shut for five minutes."

"You really know how to turn me on, baby girl," I chuckle, taking it and sipping the liquid gold without complaint.

They discuss Pepe and Mack, wondering where to go next with our plans, and I stay silent like a good boy until my coffee cup is empty. Then I make the most annoying noise I can think of, drawing their attention before shaking my hips to cause my dick to slap against my hips, cackling as Blaze's murderous eyes meet mine.

I dart up the hallway as he goes to stand, shutting myself in the bathroom for my shower before I push my luck any further, hearing Selene and Darius laughing loudly as Blaze snaps at them for finding it funny.

Darius

After our interesting morning with Santos being back to his usual self, we tidy up after breakfast. I'm surprised when there's a knock at the door and I find Pepe on the doorstep, Blaze stepping in beside me to glare at him. "The fuck do you want?"

Pepe swallows, his Adam's apple bobbing as he glances between us with concern.

"Um, you wanted me to let you know about any shipments?"

"So, you thought you'd just stop by for a coffee to talk about it?" Blaze growls, making the man step back and mutter a prayer to Jesus before he nods.

"I didn't want to waste time."

"You're wasting time now. Fucking talk!" Blaze barks, grabbing the front of his shirt and dragging him inside, shutting the door behind him. I lean back against the wall and cross my arms, eyeing the shaking idiot with amusement. We don't make a habit of letting people into the house, but Blaze obviously wants to play games, which is fine by me. Before the guy can open his mouth, Santos wanders out from his shower, halting when he realizes we have company.

"What's Pipi doing here?"

"It's Pepe," the dumbass states, making Santos grin wide. At least he could take his stupid mood out on this guy instead of Blaze.

"That's what I said! Come here and talk to San, I don't bite! You have gossip for me? I looooove gossip!" He exclaims with excitement, scaring Pepe as he marches over to him and drops an arm around his shoulders, pulling his gun out of the back of his pants and pressing it against Pepe's temple. "Now, speak. Before you and Jesus have an early meet and greet."

Pepe isn't far off pissing his pants, but Santos is having a blast, so I let him have his fun. Selene's grinning from her place beside Zander, loving every second of it, but not wanting to disrupt him by joining in. *Yet.*

"I'll talk! It's why I'm here! There's a shipment being delivered today!" he blurts out, his eyes widen as Santos presses the gun harder against his skin.

"And?"

"It's got a handful of women and about ten teenagers. The youngest is twelve, and they're supposed to be getting some more soon. It's happening at one of our warehouses," he chokes out, his eyes not leaving Santos until I step closer with a low chuckle, dropping an arm around Santos' shoulders to tug him back a step.

"C'mon, babe. Give him a second to think. It's a bit hard to do if you blow his brains out."

"Might give the wall an artistic vibe," Santos grumbles but does as he's told, moving the gun away from Pepe's face to lean against me. "Maybe we can make him bleed just a little? I need more lube."

"If you think you're using this cunt's blood in my ass, you have another thing coming, dick face," I scowl, Pepe's eyes becoming as wide as saucers.

"You're gay?"

I frown, turning to eye him with annoyance. "I'm not gay, I just like his dick in my ass sometimes. Why? You wanna come play trains with us?"

"No! Jesus, please help heal the minds of these men! The Devil has taken them, but it's not too late! Take them in your loving arms and forgive them for all they've done, teach them the right path to Heaven!" he exclaims to the ceiling, making me snort. Jesus couldn't save us if he tried. We've been soldiers for the Devil for too damn long, and we like it.

Santos flashes Selene a dark grin. "What would Jesus do if he knew I came in your cunt then Darius licked it clean?"

"With the volume you call to him, I'm pretty sure Jesus knows," Zander deadpans, eyeing Pepe as the idiot babbles prayers under his breath, praying to let us into Heaven. The guy's lucky we find it so amusing, or Selene would have slit his throat by now.

Santos has a glint in his eye, telling me he's not done being a dick yet. "Hold him still."

Pepe goes to move, but I grab his arms tight and press against his back, having no idea what Santos wants, but letting him do it anyway. The moment Santos drops his pants, I almost choke on my own damn tongue. I've seen way too much of that dick this morning, and not enough of it going inside me.

"What are you doing?!" Pepe practically screams, fear filling the air at not knowing what's happening. Hell, I have no idea either, but I am here for it.

Selene moans, eyeing Santos as he gets naked, but Blaze drops an arm around her waist, trying to look casual as he makes sure she doesn't jump on Santos, and fuck him in front of our guest. That might be a little rude.

Santos is smiling so damn hard his face is going to crack soon, and I love every second of it.

"Jesus is lying to you, Pipi. My dick is so good it's in the Bible. He gifted me with this love weapon, and he wants me to use it. Come on, touch it. Let it fuck the straight right out of you."

"No! Keep that Devil dick away from me!" Pepe begs, trying to get out of my grip but having no chance. "Jesus says being gay is a sin!"

"It's sinfully delicious! Why do you think people scream to God when it's in them?" Santos asks as he steps closer, letting his dick rub against the poor man's leg. "Feel that? That's the gay soaking into you. Give it a minute, you'll be shitting rainbows by the time I'm done."

Zander's chuckling as he watches the show, and Selene looks ready to murder Pepe for letting Santos' dick anywhere near him, matching the pissed off glare Blaze is throwing our way. He should be grateful Santos has found someone new to taunt with his dick.

Pepe is hysterical, and Santos finally laughs as he steps back, pulling his pants back on. "You're funny, Pipi. I like you. Now, give the big, grumpy fucker over there the address for your secret warehouse so we can go and save those women and kids. They need to find Jesus and be saved from the Devil, remember?"

The moment I let him go, Pepe darts across the room to Blaze as if he'll save him from our gayness, firing out the address before taking off like his ass in on fire, leaving Blaze to glare at us. "Was that necessary?"

"Yes," Santos and I both chuckle, ending up in a fit of laughter the others soon join in with.

Zander

It doesn't take us long to find the warehouse, and once Blaze and I check it out, we know it's going to be easy. There's only a handful of men guarding the place, and from what we can tell, there aren't many inside.

"Come on, let's go play '*put the knife in the idiot*' so we can get out of here. I'll drive the van," Selene offers, making Blaze and I both snort. There's no way in Hell she's driving. She's not a bad driver, but she'll forget what we are supposed to be doing and probably stop at the diner on the way out for some lunch.

"I'm driving," Blaze answers bluntly, ignoring the glare she throws at him.

"I wanna go play that game," Santos smirks, "but I'll use bullets."

She pats his arm affectionately and smiles, "Yes. You're really good at that game. Tell you what. If you kill more people than me, I'll let you shackle me to the bed and have your wicked way with me when we get home."

His eyes widen as he rubs his hands together. "What if you win?"

"I'll shackle you to the bed while you watch D fuck me," she teases, a growl leaving him as he grabs her waist, jerking her firmly against him.

"You make it sound like a bad thing. I'm more than happy to watch you two fuck each other. For the record, I'm going to win, and I'm bringing my knife."

"Promise?" she moans, Blaze cutting the conversation off with a groan.

"Shut the fuck up, both of you. Are we being stealthy or…?"

"No chance in Hell," Santos says. "Look out, fuckers! Pew, pew!" Santos shouts at the top of his lungs as he starts running into the open like the idiot he is, making Selene and Darius chase after him, yiping and screaming random crap as they go.

Blaze glances at me with a sigh, the sound of gunfire filling the air around us. "You know, they really get on my nerves some days."

"Haven't noticed," I chuckle, following him as he runs after the others, dodging bullets as they shoot in our direction.

Blaze takes out the guys by the door who Selene seems to be chatting with, her angry eyes meeting us over her shoulder. "I was playing games with them!"

"We're here to kill them, not play with them!" Blaze barks, making me laugh as Selene shrugs.

"Same fucking shit."

We clear the outside fast, heading inside to find Santos massacring two guys across the room, laughing, and boasting loudly to Selene that he's winning. She lets out a huff as she joins him, stabbing her knife into one of the men's necks and tearing it open, the blood splashing over her arms and face.

"Zan!" Blaze snaps, drawing my attention to the guy who's sneaking up on me. I shoot him between the eyes, surprise on his face as he drops to the ground, making me snort.

"As if you didn't see that coming, idiot."

Blaze and I work our way through the room, taking out anyone who tries to sneak up on the others, but we don't expect Santos to drop to the ground on top of one of the bodies, humping them with a loud groan. "How do you like that, dick head?! Thought you could shoot at my baby girl and get away with it?!"

Blaze groans, seeing way too much of Santos' weird behavior for one day. I can't stop grinning as Selene smiles at him, loving his show of affection. He's crazy, but he loves her with all his heart, we can see it.

Darius laughs as he shoots at someone else, the body dropping to the ground. "Hey, San. This guy looked at our girl too!"

Santos is on his feet and across the room in seconds, dropping to his knees and unzipping his pants, showing us his dick for the hundredth time today. Anyone would think he's proud of it. He rubs his balls on the man's forehead, slapping him with his dick. "Taste the rainbow, asshole! Here's your teabag, minus the cup!" he cackles, finding way too much enjoyment out of rubbing his junk on someone else's face.

"Santos! Get my dick off him!" Selene snaps, clenching her fists around her knife as she dodges some guy who tries to grab her out from nowhere. I roll my eyes and shoot him, wishing they were staying focused, but knowing that ship has sailed.

"Your dick? You already have one!" he answers, halting her as confusion fills her eyes.

"Where?"

Like the idiot he is, Santos heads over to her and pushes her to her knees, ignoring her growling as he suddenly slaps his dick against her forehead. Shock fills her face for a moment as she stares at him, anger taking over as he speaks again. "There! Now you're a dick head!"

"You're fucking dead, *estupido*!" she screams, jumping to her feet to chase him, his cackling sounding over the bullets still firing around the room.

I gun down anyone who goes near them, giving them a flat look as they continue to play tag. "Knock it off!"

"Bite me!" Selene snaps, swiping her knife at Santos who just jumps out of the way in time, his laughter bouncing around the room.

"That's right, baby girl. Come get me!" he notices a bullet whizzing by his head and glares at the man who fired it. "Oh, yeah. Gun fight. My bad."

I smack my palm against my forehead as he continues to run away from Selene while shooting at the threat, and he's two seconds away from Blaze putting a bullet in him instead.

Fucking children.

Chapter Four

Blaze

Finally, everyone is dead, and I find the shipping container in the back with the victims inside. What should've been an in and out easy infiltration, turned into a fucking circus show. It took all my fucking willpower not to shoot both Selene and Santos dead along with the rest. Zander is looking amused, his mouth in a permanent upswing, and I have to admit it's better than the slump he'd been in since finding out his father was a filthy cunt a few years ago.

"I know they piss you off," he snickers as we guide the women and children to the waiting van, "but this is the best we've been. I know it feels chaotic, but it's an organized chaos. Santos isn't flying off the rails, Darius isn't taking brutal beatings, and I see your sneaking smiles, too."

We walk by said group only to find Darius once again pissing on the pile of bodies, Santos yelling at Selene about winning their bet, and Selene making the motion of jacking off her knife and rolling her eyes while Santos yells. I snort at the scene, and Zander nudges his shoulder against mine.

"See?" He looks back at them affectionately. "We're like a proper family now."

"Whatever." I growl, even though I begrudgingly agree.

"You need to get laid," he huffs. "What are you waiting for? Candles and rose petals?"

"I was supposed to fuck her this morning but Pepe fuckface showed up and we ended up here."

"That's your problem," he squeezes my shoulder, "you need Selene's magic pussy."

"Yes, he does." She purrs as she comes up behind me, wrapping her arms around my waist. "Just a little Mommy and Daddy time together."

I snort before I can stop it, and Zander falls into a fit of laughter.

"What's funny?" Santos comes up and wraps his arms around both Selene and I, "are we having a group Kumbaya?"

"Will you get your hands off me?" I growl as Santos' wandering hands find my chest.

"I'm hungry," Selene whines at my back, her hands heading south while Santos' rub over my chest.

"Ask Daddy nicely and maybe he'll take us for burgers," Santos adds.

I shrug out of both of their holds, shoving Zander into my vacated spot, and watching his eyes widen as they do to him what they were doing to me. I snort again and then chuckle as he looks down, finding Selene rubbing him through his pants.

"I'm so glad Baby Walton got Daddy Walton's genes." Selene coos, and I really lose my shit. My laughter rings out in barking waves, and as soon as I'm done, the warehouse is eerily silent.

All four of them are looking at me in shock, but Selene is the first to laugh, "Daddy Blaze knows how much of a daddy kink I have."

I chuckle again, and the rest look at each other, clearly thinking the end of the world is upon us, "I think that was deserving of burgers."

"I can't believe you laughed," Zander looks at me shocked, "that was a swift kick while I was down. I'm trying to make her stop talking about my fucking father."

"You can't be ashamed of your past, Zan," Santos cuts in, "Selene fucked you and your daddy, at the same time. That's like a milestone most don't get to hit."

"Thank you, baby." Selene nods.

"How about we ask Papi Loco to fuck her with you and see how you feel?" Zander growls, and I snort again.

"I wouldn't *consent* to that, fucker." Santos snarls, "if I remember correctly, you joined them? Right baby?"

"Mmhmm," Selene is grinning as Zander rolls his eyes and heads to his car.

"Whatever," he mumbles.

Watching Selene moan and groan over a burger with ketchup dripping down her chin is causing havoc in my pants. I really should've made time to fuck her this morning because now I have something building up inside of me, and it's fucking consuming.

We dropped the women and children off at the hospital, not giving anyone an explanation, then leaving before we were questioned. It's the way we've been doing it for years and it's always worked, but they must be seeing the rise in forced trafficking, and yet, nothing is changing. It's so frustrating.

Selene stuffs the last piece into her mouth, moaning around it, and then licking her tongue along her chin, trying to reach the ketchup. I scrape the chair back along the floor, making everyone look over at me, and storm off to the bathrooms. I'm pent up and about to explode. Between the frustration of not emptying my balls and the frustration with our justice system, I'm feeling slightly unhinged.

I lean against the counter and take a deep breath; I need to stay focused. I don't want to do this forever, stopping trafficking, shooting motherfuckers, running around, and avoiding being shot. I want to have a day to lie in bed, I want a quiet space, and I want to stop the craving for bloodshed.

The door opens and I roll my eyes shut, I can't even find peace in a fucking bathroom. I push off the counter, and then a soft, warm body pushes itself between me and the sink. I smell her before I look at her, knowing exactly who it is, and who she belongs to. My hands find her waist and I drag her in closer, just wanting to feel her.

"Something's wrong," she whispers.

"Yeah, there's always something."

"I know we're a handful," she starts, and I finally look down into her blue eyes, "and I know you get the brunt of that, but we're grateful, Blaze. I hope you know how much we all appreciate you."

I don't answer her because right now, in this moment, I don't give a fucking shit how annoying they all are. I want to sink my dick inside of her. I begin to undo her pants, shoving them down her legs, and she doesn't question me, just kicks them aside. She drops her panties to the pile as well, and hops up on the counter, spreading her legs wide.

She's wet, practically dripping, and I drop my hands to the counter on either side of her, my forehead hitting hers with a moan.

"This is probably going to hurt," I grit out as I begin undoing my pants.

"I know," she widens those milky legs further, "I'm counting on it."

My pants and boxers hit my knees, and I have my cock in my hand, stroking it and squeezing the pierced tip. I'm still considering getting the same piercings as that albino fucker had in Nevada, but I haven't had the chance yet.

I yank her to the edge, not even bothering to prepare her further. I need to fucking come and if I don't do it soon, I'm going to snap. I line myself up and slam it home, groaning while she screams. Her nails dig into my shoulders, the stinging bite sinking in beyond my shirt. I don't give her the time to adjust, I begin drilling into her tight, wet pussy at a punishing pace, watching as my dick gets coated with cream.

She begins to squirm, probably from being fucked to within an inch of her life, but I grip her hips, knowing there will be bruising, and hold her still. She whimpers with each one of my thrusts, but soon she begins to pant, and her little pussy begins to squeeze tighter as she nears her climax.

"Tell me what it was like to pull John's lungs from his body." She moans, and I look down at where we're joined. Her delicate flesh stretched to the point of pain, wrapped around my cock.

"Is that gonna help you get off?" I chuckle.

"Fuck yes," her hand snakes down between us and she begins to circle her clit, "I need details, Zander couldn't do it."

"Because he's a fucking pussy," I growl as I slam into hers.

"Please, Daddy." She moans, and I nearly explode, "tell me."

I slow down to stave off my impending orgasm and look down into her big blues. "I sliced through the skin and muscle on his back," she moans so loud at my words, "thick, warm blood sprayed out, and coated my hands. He passed out before I even began hacking at his ribcage, breaking them open one by one, and revealing his bright red lungs. They felt like velvety thin sponges, quivering as I gripped them in my fingers."

"Oh fuck," she pants, her pussy clamping down, "don't stop."

"I pressed into the soft organ and the blood pooled around my fingertips as I carefully lifted them out, such a vivid, red color. Then I settled them over the protruding rib bones, putting them on display."

That's when she fucking detonates all over my cock, and I watch in fascination, knowing this woman is my fucking equal in every sense. A warrior.

I follow soon after, filling her up with cum, and her pussy milking every last drop. Then I pull her closer, my cock still deep inside, and lean down to kiss her. It's slow, sensual, and fucking yanking on my cold heart.

"Is this where you tell me you love me?" She flutters her lashes as I pull out of her, tucking my wet cock back in my pants.

"Not today." I grin.

"Well, I'm not telling you either." She snaps and begins to put her pants back on, grumbling about my cum slipping from her pussy.

I will tell her, but it's not going to be in some dive diner's restroom.

Selene

The throbbing between my legs is now a sharp ache as I walk behind Blaze back into the restaurant. He can really tear a pussy apart with that weapon he calls a cock. I sit at the table and squirm in my seat, trying to alleviate the pain.

"Someone got the big daddy dick down," Santos snickers.

"Jealous?" I grin at him as he drags my chair closer to his.

"Always," then he moves closer to my ear, mocking a whisper loud enough for Blaze to hear. "One day I'll get that big daddy special, too."

"Like fuck you will." Blaze snarls, but his voice doesn't hold the same edge he had earlier. I grin knowing I not only milked him of his cum, but a bit of that grumpiness, too.

"Your phone keeps ringing," Zander nods to the burner I've had since Nevada. The one I stupidly left in the room while I went gallivanting my stupid self around with Henry's chauffeur. "It looks like a Nevada area code."

I yank it open, hoping to hear Aniyah's voice. "Hello?"

"Selly?"

I groan so loud right into the phone at the sound of my sister's voice, then I close the old-style flip and throw it back into Zander's lap. "Who gave her my number?" I screech as I look at each of them.

"None of us," Zander shrugs.

"Maybe your purple headed clit-licker did." Blaze says with a smug look on his face.

Oh. That makes sense.

"Shouldn't you talk to her?" Zander asks as he holds up my ringing phone, the same number flashing on the screen.

"No," Santos cuts in, "she doesn't have to until she's ready. Let's go home and figure out our next step."

By the time we get home, my phone has rung a total of sixteen times, and with each shrill noise, my anger rises.

"What if it's something important?" Zander asks as I stomp through the front door, ready to toss the phone in the toilet.

"She has a whole MC she can turn to," Santos snarls, completely understanding me in this situation.

"What if it's something she needs a sister for?" Zander counters.

"Then maybe the fucking cunt should've found her, no?" Santos once again comes back with the exact sentiment I'm thinking.

Yes, I forgave her for not trying to find me hard enough, and for giving up too soon. But that doesn't mean I'm ready to slip back ten years and forget everything that happened. I need time and she's not giving it to me.

"She left a voicemail," Zander calls to my retreating back, "at least listen to it."

I slam my room door and sit on my bed, silencing the seventeenth phone call. Once it's finished ringing, I open the phone and call my voicemail, settling in to hear what the fuck she wants.

"Hey Selly, it's me Jan, your sister." I snort because duh, "Loqi got a lead on where his sister might be, and I understand Santos isn't interested in a relationship right now, but I wanted to let you guys know since she's his sister, too. She was taken, like I was, and they think she's somewhere in Vegas. I was also hoping to find out a bit more about John Dempster, since it seems like he was the one who bought her. I spoke to Aniyah, and she told me as much as she could, but she said you were investigating him. Could you please call me back?"

I know Santos is pissed and rightfully so, but I don't think he knows about his missing sister. I really believe he would want to help, especially because she's innocent in all that's going on between the rest of his family. I run out of my room and slide into the kitchen. They're all sitting there, trying to figure out the next step in tracking down the fat-assed, no teeth having Mack Delaney.

"She does need something." I hold up my phone.

"I knew it," Zander nods.

"Loqi's little sister was taken a few years back, and she was sold to John Dempster." I look at Santos and watch as different emotions flint over his face.

"Little sister?" he finally says as he rises to his feet, "what little sister?" I can see the confusion making him start to lose his cool.

"I think we need to call Loqi," I say quietly, "we'll put it on speakerphone, and I can do the talking."

We gather around the table, and I plant my ass in Santos' lap, knowing he'll need me to keep himself under control. Darius grabs my hand and squeezes it, knowing exactly what it is I'm doing. We put my phone in the center of the table and listen to the ringing, all of our hearts clogging up our throats.

"Hey Reaper," Loqi's voice fills the room, "do you need help killing someone?"

I have a smart remark ready on the tip of my tongue, but Santos cuts me off, "tell me about her."

"Is that you Santos?" He gets a grunt in response and then continues, "our *hermana* was sweet, nothing like you and me. She was always trying to help people, and even when she was acting like a brat, she was still kind."

"What happened to her?" Santos asks, his voice low and filled with emotion.

"Papi and I took her to see a movie being filmed in Vegas. Her favorite actor was there, and we made a mini vacation out of it. We got VIP treatment on set and that's where we lost her. No one could find her; it was like she was gone without a trace. We emptied trailers, and movie sets, she was gone. We interrogated everyone there that day, and after two years, someone has finally come forward. She was the makeup artist on set, and she said she saw a young girl being forced into a large, white van. When she questioned a producer on set, she was told the girl was a troublesome actress being carted off to rehab."

"For sure that was our sister?" Santos asks.

"We believe so, the producer's name at the time was John Dempster."

A chill snakes down my spine, and I know without a doubt, Santos' little sister fell victim to John and his skin operation.

"But," Loqi continues. "John's dead, thanks to you guys. I won't be able to interrogate him. But we can go to his house and see what we can find. It's been closed and processed by the police in Vegas. Papi has paid for us to get in there for a day and see what we can find."

"Keep us updated if you find anything," I lean forward, "we'll come there if you need us."

"Thank you, Reaper." He sounds grateful. "And *hermano*," he says to Santos, "I'm not our papi, you and I should have a talk."

"Yeah." Santos grunts.

"Okay, I will be in touch." Then he hangs up the phone as I turn to Santos.

"Are you okay?" I ask him, resting my hand on his cheek. I wish we could go back to the version of Santos who woke up this morning.

"I went through most of my life thinking I just had my mami, and then when she died, I believed I was truly alone. Papi left us when I was nine, and Mami said it was because he didn't know how to be a husband or a father. Then she got really sick, she had a rare heart disease, and there was no cure, but I believe it was a broken heart. I was put in a foster home and even though the caregivers weren't bad, there were just so many of us. Darius showed up a few months later and we became unruly, running the streets and pushing drugs."

"Out of control," Darius hums his agreement.

"We began taking care of the prostitutes, ya know? Making sure they got to their locations safely, and then back to their blocks again. We charged a small fee but soon enough we had a bunch of them requesting the service."

"You were pimps." Zander snorts, and Darius hoots.

"Still are, little bitch." He sneers at Zander.

"Go on." I nudge Santos.

"A few of our girls went missing, and both of us," he points at Darius, "felt like shit. It was our job to keep them safe. We followed the trail to a house party and became acquainted with Los Diablos. We found out they dabbled in a bit of everything, drugs, weapons, and girls."

"That's where we met," Zander finishes it off.

"It's hard to comprehend I have any blood relations after this long. My brothers here were my only family, and now, there are others." Santos wraps his arms around my waist, tugging me in closer, "what if they don't like me, like Papi?"

"I'll stab each of them," I promise while kissing the top of his head. "No one, not even blood relatives have the option of hurting you, and Papi Loco will find that out firsthand."

That piece of shit has a fucking date with my knife.

Zander

We don't hear anything back from Loqi until a few days later, and our inside Diablo Pepe has also been a bit quiet. There are no upcoming shipments for Los Diablos, and I can see all the guys—including Selene—beginning to bite at the bit, needing something to calm our desires for blood.

That's why when the phone rings and we see Loqi's name, we all scramble over each other to get to it. I grab the little flip phone and open it, pressing it to my ear.

"Hello?"

"Which one is this?" Loqi asks, his voice filled with humor.

"The best looking one." I retort and the rest of the guys in the room groan, all too well acquainted with how much I love myself.

I put him on speaker just as he says, "you're not my brother."

"That's right!" Santos hoots, and I roll my eyes.

"What do you have for us?" Selene shoves me aside and sits in front of the phone.

"I have a few names we found here." He continues, "he had a ledger."

"They all have fucking ledgers," Selene spits, "your father's is still back in that Vegas apartment. We need to get back there and get my shit."

"What's in the ledger?" Santos asks.

"Tons of names, but we narrowed it down to three on the day she went missing, one being extremely familiar. I have an Earl Jr. —"

"Dead." Selene interrupts, "he's wrapped up in a tarp and buried in the desert." When I look at her in question, she shrugs, "Earl had to die."

"I watched her kill him," Blaze interjects and grabs his cock in his pants, "so fucking hot."

"Names," Darius cuts us all off.

"Okay, so we can scratch out Earl. Next one is Eugene Haynes, he bought about ten of the eighteen girls taken that day."

"He's dead, too." Selene cuts in, and I groan, "what? He was a bad man, but he had a nice castle for a home, horses, and paintings, and his staff called him King. I wanted to be Queen, but he was too furry, like a donkey."

"Yeah," Loqi snorts into the phone, "we knew he was dead, there are photos of him with a bloody scythe on his forehead."

"It was the only spot clear of fur." Selene nods.

"If he bought our sister, we need to know what happened to all the staff in his home." Loqi inquires. "So, we're looking into that."

Selene's face brightens and I can see her squirming with excitement, "Loqi! There were a few young girls when I was there, I do know one was arrested in suspicion for murder. Look into that!"

"Thank you, I will." Then he chuckles, "the third name will interest us both but won't be a surprise. Mack Delaney."

"He's the one who grabbed Selene," I inform him, "he's here in New York, still selling girls. We've been fucking with his shipments. You can leave him to us for now."

"Sounds good," Loqi agrees, "let us know if you need back up. Selene, thank you for the heads up, we're going to check out the girl who was arrested."

"Let us know." Selene says as we hang up the phone.

We're all quiet as we mull over everything we've just been told. Mack Delaney has been in the skin business for over thirty years and his end is coming near. I never knew he was this big or running this wide of a distribution. I always thought he was small compared to my father, but I was clearly wrong. He was always the big-timer.

"Let's try to get a hold of Pepe," I say, "we need some movement on Mack, we can't lose sight of him now."

"Agreed." Blaze nods.

"I'd really like to know where the fat fuck is staying," I growl, "I would like to have constant surveillance on him."

"If we find him there's no surveillance," Selene growls, "my knife is slamming into his forehead."

Santos groans and reaches for her, making her straddle his waist, "keep saying shit like that, baby." He moans as he slips his fingers up under my t-shirt she's wearing—the only thing she's wearing, "fuck, and you're so wet."

Blaze growls in frustration again but it's not as heated as usual, he's probably realizing there's no stopping them. This is just the way they are.

"We need to know who else he's dealing with, and if there's someone above him. We want to end this once and for all." I explain.

"I don't want to do this for the rest of my life," Blaze says, and everyone stops what they're doing to look at him. "I want to fucking relax."

I feel that. I want it too.

"Okay, Daddy." Selene whispers. "Let's do it the right way and take out as many as we can. Then we'll go on vacation."

"To where?" Blaze raises a brow.

"I say Vegas." She grins and gyrates her hips on Santos' hand. "I wanna visit Aniyah."

"I'm not too particularly keen on seeing that woman again," Blaze rolls his eyes, and I understand why. Him and the purple haired prostitute have a history.

"She's a friend." Selene tosses back, "and I'll see her if I want to."

That's the last of the conversation because Santos stands up and throws Selene over his shoulder, "come Darius," he grins, "I'm craving your dick and her blood."

Santos stomps his way down the hallway with Darius taking up their rear.

"You know, you're going to have to tell her what you did with Aniyah eventually." I say to Blaze, and he shrugs.

"Maybe."

"It might one day spill from the prostitute's mouth, and you know damn well Selene will lose her shit."

"Maybe." He says again, this time with a sinister grin, "I do like when she loses her shit."

We're all so fucked up.

Santos

My fingers flex against Selene's waist as I force her back onto the bed, my body pressing down on hers as I devour her mouth in a searing kiss. She whimpers as my fingers tighten against her skin, the small bite of pain urging her on.

The sound of Darius stripping behind me makes my cock harden more, and I pull back from Selene to watch him, his heated gaze already on mine. While I'm distracted, Selene takes advantage and flips us over, straddling my hips with a dark grin. She pulls her shirt over her head, grinding on me as Darius crawls onto the bed with a smirk.

"You going to get naked? Or do I rip the fabric from your body with your knife?" he murmurs, causing me to fly into action. Selene squeals as I buck her off, yanking my clothes off in record time. Darius tears what's left of Selene's clothes off, swallowing her curse as he kisses the hell out of her.

I love being with both of them. No jealousy or rules, just pure sex, and acceptance.

I grab the back of Darius' neck and yank him toward me, loving the groan of approval as he kisses me almost aggressively, a battle of tongue and teeth. He bites my lip, a hiss leaving me at the sting left behind, the taste of copper spreading across my tongue as I lick the tender skin.

"You want me to bleed, *amante*?" I grin, not giving a shit if there's blood in my teeth. He has no idea how good it felt when he called me his lover that day. He is more than my anchor, and the warmth in my chest has been a constant lately whenever I look at him. The same warmth I get when I look at Selene.

His eyes blaze in need, as I reach for Selene, pulling her to me and plastering her back to my front, biting her neck sharply. "Touch her, D."

Darius does as he's told, moving forward to press her between us, snaking his hand down her front to toy with her clit. She arches against him, dropping her head back on my shoulder with a breathy moan. "Stop playing around, fuck me."

I give Darius a glance, silently communicating with him to grab the shackles that are laying on the floor. She thinks I've forgotten about our little deal, silly woman.

The moment he climbs from the bed and the shackles clink, she stiffens in my arms and growls. "Don't even fucking think about it."

I run my tongue down her slender neck, my arms tightening around her as she tries to pull away. "You're such a sore loser, baby girl. May I remind you this was your idea?"

She snarls, thrashing against me as I restrain her while Darius threads the shackles through the headboard and grins at me. "C'mon, bring her here."

She fights me, just like I was hoping, my dick so hard it's painful. We manage to get her wrists secured, and Darius chuckles, waving the key in her face to taunt her. "Be a good girl, and I'll let you go."

"I'm going to kill the fucking pair of you!" she snaps, not bothering to yank on the shackles. She knows she isn't going anywhere until we let her.

I run my eyes over her naked body, leaning over to grab my knife from the bedside drawers to place it beside me. "You ready for me to make you bleed? You're going to look like a work of art against the bed sheets," I murmur, her eyes flashing with annoyance, but her body arches slightly in need. Our girl is desperate to bleed on my blade, I could sense it a mile away.

"You're in trouble when you let me go, *estupido*. You'll be bleeding too," she snarks, glaring at Darius. "I can't believe you're in on this."

"In on it? He's the one who grabbed the shackles from the floor," I chuckle, dodging her foot as she tries to kick me. I get on my knees and dip my head, burying my tongue in her dripping cunt, wanting to taste her more than anything. She moans, the shackles clinking as she tries to touch me, letting out a frustrated growl when she can't.

I startle as something wet touches my ass, relaxing as Darius' hand slides around my front to fist my length. If he wants to lick what was left of my soul out of my ass, I'm not going to stop him. It feels fucking good, for starters.

Selene watches us hungrily, wriggling when I slow down my attack on her pussy.

"Dammit, Santos! Eat me like you're going to starve to death if you don't, or let Darius do it!" she snaps, causing a wicked grin to spread across my face. My girl wants it rough? Then that's what she's going to get.

I suck her clit into my mouth and bite firmly, a surprised scream leaving her from the sudden pain. Darius groans, sending vibrations straight up my fucking ass and making me jump. Selene chuckles, eyeing me with amusement. "That feel good?"

I lift my head, pushing two fingers inside her without warning, her wet heat surrounding them as she clenches. "You're talking too much. D, how about you shut her up for me?"

"But I was…" Darius starts, but I cut him off.

"Do it. I promise not to cut her while your dick's down her pretty throat. I'd hate for her to bite it off."

"I might bite it off anyway," Selene grumbles, jerking against her shackles as I pull my fingers out to lightly slap her pussy.

"You bite it off, and I'll fuck your tight cunt with the sharp end of my blade," I threaten playfully, waiting for Darius to straddle her chest and jam his dick into her mouth, giving me five minutes of silence.

I thrust my fingers into her pussy again, leaning forward to bite Darius' butt. He flinches in surprise, choking Selene in the process, but after a second, he relaxes, letting me do whatever I want to him. I lift up on my knees, getting closer to shove my tongue in his ass, making it nice and wet before sliding a finger up and down his crack, easing it inside slowly.

"Fuck, do you want me to cum in minutes?" Darius grunts, moving in and out of Selene's plush lips, pulling back enough to sink over my finger more. I add a second finger, working both his ass and her pussy with ease, loving the sounds coming from them.

Selene clenches around me, her muffled moans becoming a cry as she comes hard, and my dick becomes jealous of my fingers. I pull away from them both, needing to be inside her right the fuck now.

I practically shove Darius off her, making him chuckle as I align myself with Selene's pussy, and slam inside, her loud moan music to my ears. I grab my knife and slow my thrusts, running the cool metal gently across her throat without marking her, loving how her eyes flash with heat. I press harder, the blade lightly slicing across her pretty throat and leaving a small red trail of blood behind.

Leaning forward, I lick across her skin, tasting the devilish, metallic honey and closing my eyes to savor it. She always tastes like Heaven in a sinful shell.

"Cut her here," Darius murmurs softly, running his fingers across her belly. "Make her bleed for me." Well, I can't exactly say no to that.

I do as he asks, watching her eyes as they stare into mine, the breath practically leaving her body as the bite of my blade cuts into her flesh.

Darius leans forwards, coating his fingers in her sticky blood before turning to me with a smirk. "You going to let me in, babe?"

I go to move back to let him have a moment with her, but his free hand stops me. "I meant *into* you."

"You want to fuck me, D?" I ask in a low voice, groaning when he nods. Selene looks ready to combust at the sound of me being nailed.

"Please, please let him fuck you," she begs, gasping when I smash my lips to hers and thrust harder into her while Darius moves in behind me. He uses his fingers to stretch me, grabbing more blood from our girl as he needs it, finally coating his dick in some and pressing firmly against my ass. He doesn't warn me, knowing I don't need it, slowly easing into me until he's almost all the way in, slamming the rest inside at the last minute.

I jerk forward, growling into Selene's mouth as he withdraws and does it again, slowly getting faster until he's fucking me into Selene almost painfully. I welcome the burn, letting it drive my hunger to inflict pleasurable pain, wrapping a hand around Selene's throat and feeling the drying blood under my fingertips.

"Oh, fuck," Darius grunts, leaning over me more as if he can't get close enough, something stirring inside me. I feel like I'm going to explode, and not out of my dick. I'd be lost without both of them, and I don't even think before I blurt out what I'm feeling.

"I love you."

Darius slows, while Selene's eyes widen a fraction before they soften. I stop moving, watching her with uncertainty. Did I just fuck everything up?

When she doesn't say anything, I glance over my shoulder and meet Darius' eyes, keeping my voice steady despite the fear seeping into me. Nothing scares me, but this? I'm fucking terrified. "I love you both."

He gives me a grin, dropping his lips to my shoulder, his words calming me. "I love you too, San."

Selene still hasn't said anything, and I turn my attention back to her and swallow the lump in my throat. It's like she's staring into my damn soul, a soft smile finally taking over her face. "You love me?"

"So much. I'd turn the town red for someone even looking at you sideways," I promise, scowling at the shackles. I want her hands on me. Sensing my thoughts, Darius pulls away from me and grabs the keys, unlocking the bounds on her wrists. She instantly throws herself at me, devouring my mouth as her hands run across my back, keeping me close.

"I love you too. You too, D," she breathes, the tightness in my chest vanishing and making room for the warmth I always feel when they're close. I drop onto my back, hauling her on top of me and sinking back inside her with ease, resting my hands on her waist with a smirk. "Prove it. Fuck the crazy right out of me."

"We could be here a while," she teases, reaching over to stroke Darius' length, his eyes darkening.

"I love you crazy fuckers, too," he growls, moving closer to kiss her hard, her moans filling his mouth as I thrust up inside her firmly. He finally pulls back and looks down at me, running his gaze over my sweaty abs and down to where I'm connected to our girl, his voice low. "You're both fucking perfect." Then he dips down to kiss me, his hand running along stomach until his fingers reach Selene's clit, making her gasp.

I've never cared about anyone like this. Selene and Darius are everything to me, keeping me steady when I want to explode, while Blaze and Zander were the brothers I never knew I needed. We are family, and nothing will get in the way of that.

If it does? I'll set the fucking world on fire and watch it burn.

Darius

I thought telling someone I loved them would feel different. There's no worry or confusion, just peace of mind as the words come from my mouth. Santos was worried about our reactions, but nothing felt so fucking right in my entire life.

I rub Selene's clit until she's screaming, grinding down on Santos until her body turns to jelly, but I'm not about to let her rest.

I hand her Santos' blade, loving how his eyes darken at knowing what I'm asking.

"Cut him."

Her eyes flare as his grip tightens on her waist, keeping their pace slow as she grips the knife and leans forward. "You want me to mark you as mine, baby?"

"Fuck yes, make me bleed so D can use it as lube, and then everyone will know who I belong to," he answers firmly, removing a hand from her waist to point at his chest, right where his heart is. "Right here."

He hisses as she carves into his skin, his eyes firmly on her as she works, the bloody S appearing vibrant against his tanned flesh. We never thought we'd find a woman who understood our need for blood and violence in the bedroom, wanting both of us for who we are. We hit the fucking jackpot.

Blaze and Zander probably wouldn't appreciate her brand being on them, but I love it. She's claiming us in ways no other women would appreciate as she does, and that causes something primal to burn inside me.

When she's done, she swipes her finger through the sticky liquid and pops it into her mouth, moaning as her eyes flutter closed. That snaps my control.

I grab her throat and turn her face to mine, forcing my tongue into her mouth to taste him, blindly rubbing my fingers against Santos' chest to gather the oozing liquid. I waste no time in coating my dick with it, not being gentle as I push myself inside her from behind, her scream of discomfort filling the room as I shove her chest down onto his, spreading his blood between them.

I fist her hair, making sure she doesn't move as I plow inside her tight ass, my balls rubbing against Santos' and urging me on as he starts to move in tandem with me. We work as one, chasing our pleasure while feeding each other's need for pain, the sound of flesh slapping and our grunts and moans bouncing off the walls like music.

The moment Selene clenches around us, Santos comes with a growl, his hand grabbing my thigh tight in his grip as if needing my touch to keep him from floating away. Selene's gasping for air as she comes down, lying there completely spent as I slam into her a few more times before following after them, my muscles bunching as I let go.

I slump over her back to catch my breath, reaching a hand out to run my fingers through Santos' black hair, my lips trailing across Selene's back to soothe her. I've never been the type to give a fuck about someone's comfort after sex, but it has always been different with these two. I want to comfort them, keeping their demons at bay while we enjoy the afterglow, not wanting to pull away from them.

"I need to pee," Selene mumbles, making me chuckle as I force myself to pull back, admiring the smeared blood that coats her ass and across her cheeks. I glance down to find blood mixing with my sweat on my groin and abs, calming something inside me.

Santos grumbles as Selene climbs off him, standing on shaky legs as she heads to the bathroom, giving us a moment alone. Santos glances at me, grabbing my hand and tugging me on top of him to kiss my neck. "I actually think my dick's gone to sleep."

I chuckle, running my hand down his body to find his dick soft, giving it a few gentle strokes. "Want me to wake it back up?"

"I've reached my limit. I'm spent," he groans. "You really love me? More than just friends?"

"I think we've been past the point of friendship for a long time, *amante*," I point out, a smile taking over his face and almost blinding me.

"This love thing's even better than the killing thing. To celebrate, let's go and murder some cunts."

My man sure knows how to flirt.

Chapter Five

Zander

I'm used to Santos and Darius' weird quirks, but it startles me to find Selene leaving the bathroom, blood smeared all over her. We all know they like to bring knives to the bedroom, but I'm worried they really hurt her this time.

"Jesus fucking Christ. Let me look at you," I scowl, marching over to her and taking her face in my hand, tilting her head to the side to inspect the small cut along her throat. That's a stupid place to play with luck. If it had been just a bit too deep, she could have bled out with no hope of saving her.

She takes my hand and gives it a squeeze, her eyes calm. "I'm fine, Zan. Most of this is Santos'." That surprises me. They don't make a habit of cutting themselves, not that I know of, anyway.

"Should I check on him, too? Fuck, turn around."

She huffs but does as she was told, obviously too tired to argue. Blood covers her butt cheeks, and my eyes widen. "You're bleeding out your fucking ass."

"No, I'm not. It's Santos' blood there, too," she chuckles lightly, glancing at me with amusement as I cringe. They had a fucking great time, apparently.

"You need to clean up before Blaze sees you. C'mon," I sigh, dragging her into the bedroom to find Darius and Santos snuggled up together, blood all over them too. "You fucking crazy bastards."

Santos grins like the psychopath he is, but Darius shrugs. "You're being dramatic."

"Dramatic? Have you looked at yourselves? Is that a fucking S on your chest?" I snap as I notice the angry wound on Santos' chest, making Selene beam.

"I marked him!"

"I can see that. All of you get cleaned up. And Santos?" I growl, waiting for him to give me an innocent look to prove he's listening. "If you ever cut her throat again, I'll kill you. I don't give a shit what kind of kinks you share with each other, but that is downright stupid. What if you'd gone too deep?"

"I went really deep. Pretty sure my dick hit the back of her tonsils from her pussy," he cackles, pushing Darius off him to stand, my eyes catching on Darius' blood covered dick. I shake my head, deciding they are all bat-shit crazy. I mean, we know it, but this cements it.

"I'm going to clean Selene up, then you fuckers can meet us in the kitchen."

Santos grumbles his annoyance, but I ignore him as I grab Selene's clothes from the floor and drag her back across the hallway to the bathroom, locking us inside and ushering her into the shower. I strip down and climb in with her, grabbing the soap and lathering it over her body once the water heats.

She eyes me silently for a while before finally speaking. "I love them."

"I know. Doesn't mean you all need to cut each other to pieces every time you fuck," I grunt, a frown taking over her face.

"I know it's not your thing, but I like it. I wouldn't let them if I didn't want it, you know that. They'd never kill me," she answers, making me snort.

"Not on purpose, but you know they both get carried away, especially Santos. The thought of you bleeding out wrecks me, sweetheart. I don't like them risking it."

Her arms wrap around my middle as she presses her chest to mine, peering up at me with a small smile. "I promise I won't let them kill me. If they manage to, I'll come back and haunt you all. Sleep naked, I'll fuck you in your sleep."

I can't help the chuckle that leaves my lips, giving her a smirk. "That's creepy. You know you're starting to sound like Santos way too much, right? Little psychopath."

"Where the hell have you been? I've been like this from the start. Face it, you like me crazy," she grins, standing on tip-toe to kiss me. She's lucky I love her because I know exactly where her naughty little mouth has been.

Blaze

Selene's old school phone rings on the table and I see her sister's name flash on the neon green screen. She's been calling a lot and even though Selene is closed off, shutting her out, the girl keeps trying. I respect the tenacity.

I grab the phone from the table and flip it open, "hello?"

"Um... "she clears her throat, "I think I have the wrong number."

"You have the right number," I lean back on the couch, crossing my ankle over my knee.

"Which one is this?"

"The sane one." I fire back.

"Zander?"

"Fucking seriously? You think he's sane?" I retort.

"Um, shit." She curses under her breath, probably afraid to fuck this up further. "I don't know any of you really."

"It's not us you need to work on," I relax, "start with your sister."

"I'm trying," she exhales her frustration, "it's not working."

"Because you're not doing it right."

"Any advice?" I like that she's asking, it really shows she's invested.

"Actually, yes." I scrub at the scruff on my chin, "your sister is not the average woman, she doesn't care about gifts or anything like that."

"Shit." She hisses.

"What did you send?"

"Flowers and a teddy bear, when we were growing up she didn't have many toys, but she loved stuffed-"

"She's grown now." I cut her off, "she likes other things. She had to grow up fast and her interests have changed."

"Right." She sounds a bit defeated.

"She has a penchant for knives, large, serrated hunting types. We know she likes dicks; she has four of them."

She snorts on the line, "lucky girl."

"But I think what she's craving the most is a family she thought she lost. She's tough, her skull even tougher, and it's not going to be easy. You have to somehow show her you're here to stay."

"I've been calling-"

"I know," I cut her off again, "anyone can call someone. That shit's easy, but the hard part is proving you're sticking around."

"This is Blaze, right?"

"What makes you think that?" Curiosity killed the cat.

"You seemed the most serious of the group, or maybe the most mature."

"You're not wrong." I say with a shake of my head.

"So, I need to pull up my big girl panties and face my seriously intimidating sister." She says, her voice trembling with nerves.

"Bring a knife too, make it a pretty one." I hang up the phone and place it on the table just as Zander comes into the room.

"Those three are going to fucking kill themselves one day." He huffs as he falls on the couch beside me.

"Who's suffering from blood loss?"

"All three of them could be at this point," he pinches the bridge of his nose, "I had fun with it in Nevada, but I couldn't do that often."

"Because you're you, and they're them. They're big boys, and Selene is a big girl, they can handle themselves." I flick his hand off his face, "stop stressing, you're not their father."

"I know," he narrows his look onto my face, "what if something bad happens during one of their kinks?"

"We'll deal with it. But you can't judge them for what they like," I stand up, "let's go see what we can find out from the new hookers on the street. I need to do something instead of waiting around for intel."

"Sounds good," he stands and stretches, "make sure you're not sampling the product this time."

"Hey, if that's what it takes to get the job done, then so be it. Selene does the same."

"She will never open her legs for another person outside of the four of us again." He snarls.

"You guys spoke about it?"

"No." He gives me a confused look.

"It's her job," I shrug.

"It was her *technique* to find her sister, which she did, so she's done." He shoves by me, and I chuckle at his back.

"I think we should have a family meeting to discuss it, I really want to hear that conversation."

He shoots me a dirty look over his shoulder, and I chuckle again. No one tells our Little Reaper to do anything, I can't wait to watch as she hands Zander his balls.

Selene

Santos and Darius are sleeping off our sexcapade, Zander and Blaze aren't home, and I'm bored to shit. On the plus side, my sister has finally fucked off with the phone calls. I don't like the way my stomach falls with the thought of her giving up. She's done that plenty already.

I lie on the couch, without a stitch of clothing on, and turn on a serial killer documentary on Netflix. All of these fuckers are seriously psychotic, and I don't know how the people around them didn't see it. Like hello? I'm clearly certifiable and *everyone* knows it. I watch the first episode and laugh as the cops fumble through crime scenes, their incompetence documented for all to see.

I just start to get into it when the doorbell rings, making me groan as I get up off the couch. Who the fuck would be here? I stride over and swing it open wide, only to find my Jesus humping buddy.

"What would Jesus do!" I yell, raising my hand in the air.

"Why don't you have any clothes on?" He stares at me wide eyed, but I don't miss his tremble of fear, which still strikes me as strange.

"When I first met you," I tweak the nipple that seems to have caught his attention, "you were tough, saying you wanted to kill me." Once the nipple is nice and hard, I move to the other, his eyes following the motion, "but now, you're acting like a little boy who has to spend one on one time with a priest."

"Because I had no idea who or what you were, I was recruited a week before, and when I saw you, I thought you were a helpless… person."

"You wanted to say 'woman'!" I point at his face with shock.

"It's not in the way you think." He holds up his hands, his eyes still darting from my tits and back to my face, little deviant. "The women in my family are strong, *mi abuelita* is the strongest. But none of them kill like you do." He almost sounds revenant, and that makes my pussy warm, "you killed everyone in the house that day."

"Not everyone," I bop his nose and hold the door open, "we still got time though." I give him a wink and watch as he swallows, his eyes roaming down lower. "Come in, you must be here for more than to stare at my pretty pussy." My fingers spread it open for him, and he nearly chokes on air, "or is that actually what you came for?"

"No! I have info on another shipment." His brow dots with sweat as he struggles to keep his eyes on mine. "You're injured. Was that from the fight at the warehouse?"

"Booo." I slap his face with the hand that was just toying with my pussy lips, then I run it down over his mouth, "I thought this was going to be a fun visit, and no, the blood from the cut was what my boyfriend used as lube to fuck my other boyfriend."

I move out of the way so he can come inside, and then I follow him to the kitchen as he sits at the table. I sit in the chair beside him, dragging it in closer, and giggling when he leans away from me.

Santos comes shuffling into the kitchen next, still half asleep, and his juicy cock swinging back and forth. "Did I hear the doorbell?"

"Son of Jesus is here with an update." I coo, and grin when Santos' eyes darken on my equally naked body.

"That's blasphemous," Pepe exclaims, then drops his face to his hands, "why is everyone naked today?"

"Because we fucked like Adam and Eve." Santos deadpans, and I squeal with laughter.

"*Santa Maria,*" Pepe gives himself the sign of the cross, "I need to get out of this place."

"Why *are* you here, boy?" Santos turns with a tired grin, "do you want to call me *Papi* and tell me your sins?"

"I know when the next shipment is coming in, and it's supposed to go to Nevada." Pepe groans, but that has me straightening in my seat.

"Nevada? Did you hear for whom?"

"No names, just an MC." Pepe looks between Santos and I, trying hard not to glance at our fun bits.

"It has to be for Papi and Loqi," Santos murmurs while I nod my head.

"When is the shipment leaving for Nevada?" I ask Pepe as I cross my legs and play footsies with his pant leg. "I also need the address."

"Tomorrow night." He digs into his pocket and pulls out a piece of paper, handing it to me. "The container is already there."

"Alright," I nod, "you can go." I snap my fingers, and Pepe jumps from his seat, running for the front door. "Do you think he's a virgin?" I ask Santos.

"Why do you care, baby girl?" He leans on the table, his swinging cock slowly growing hard. "Do you want to play with him?"

"A little," I grin, "I wouldn't mind bleeding him dry and then fucking you over his Christian body. A gift from God no doubt."

He snickers as he leans in, kissing me sweetly on the forehead, "what are we doing about this shipment?"

"Do you want to take a trip to the MC?" I grin at him. "I need to grab my stuff from that apartment."

He looks caught between a yes and a no, and I know it's because he's not ready to see his family yet, but he won't let me go alone.

"Maybe we can send Blaze with you." He smirks, "Darius, Zander, and I can try to pump little Pepe for more info."

I respect his wishes and give him an eager nod. Besides, I haven't had my fill of Daddy's big cock yet.

"Is this a good idea?" Darius asks from his spot beside Santos. They're holding hands, and I can't help but feel giddy inside at the sight of it. "What if it's not the Afilados who's picking up? There are tons of MCs in Nevada."

"I'll be with her." Blaze shrugs. "This would be the best time to see if there is another MC selling skin, we could put Afilados on to them."

"My mind is set," I stand, "I already purchased our plane tickets with the *new* Mr. Walton's credit card, and we need to catch that flight in two hours."

Zander groans at my admission.

"You were just going to leave again?" Darius' eyes narrow on me.

"No, *amante*," Santos squeezes his hand, "she sat here and told us her plans. She's not leaving us."

To hear the trust Santos has in me, burns my chest with love, and I step forward to curl up on his lap. "Thank you."

"Be careful." He says as he nuzzles my hair, "make sure you check in with us."

I nod, and find Darius looking at me with sadness, "I promise to come back, I love you, remember?"

He gives me a small smile, but I still see the worry in his blue depths. There's nothing I can do about the mistrust I've caused in him; all I can do is come back and show him I'm here to stay.

"What are we doing in the meantime?" He asks Zander.

"The three of us are going to cause some mayhem with the Diablos. Blaze and I tracked down some of their new hookers this evening, with the right amount of money, quite a few were talking."

"They have infiltrated into our town and have taken up four residences, well three now since we figured out the one they were keeping Selene in." Blaze adds.

"So wait," Santos stills underneath me, "are you saying we get to blow some shit up?"

"Yeah, man." Zander snickers.

Santos hoots, slapping Darius on the chest. "Kaboom, baby!"

Darius' eyes meet mine and I see the excitement brimming in them, "we haven't *kaboomed* anything in a long time." His grin slowly grows.

I'm chomping into the small packet of roasted peanuts in my lap, smacking my lips together, and clicking my tongue off the roof of my mouth, but I don't get a reaction from the stone man beside me. He continues to watch the boring movie on the small screen, which makes sense with how boring he's being, as well.

I wiggle around in my seat, but I can't seem to stay still. I'm fucking bored. It's a five-and-a-half-hour flight and we're only an hour in. I'm going to end up hauled off this plane in cuffs, because I'm about to threaten the thing with a bomb if something interesting doesn't happen soon.

"Fuck it," I stand, Blaze's eyes finally swinging my way, nothing but apathy in the dark irises, "I'm going to the bathroom. Ask the attendant for more nuts."

I shove his big legs out of the way, and he grunts with irritation as I block his screen. I saunter down the aisle, grinning maniacally at babies, and then winking at their daddies. The mothers all give me nasty looks but that just makes it all the more fun.

I get to the small bathroom, and lock myself inside, sitting on the tiny toilet. I don't need to piss or anything, I just needed a change of scenery before I killed someone. Preferably the boring asshole sitting next to me. I couldn't bring my pretty knife onto the plane and even though Blaze has promised me a new one, I want to carve my name into the walls right now.

The sound of the sliding door opening is the only warning I get as Blaze stuffs his big body in this small room with me.

"Wait," I stare at the door stunned, "I locked that."

"I know how to unlock just about anything, now get up."

"Couldn't you have waited your turn?" I huff at him as I stand, my skirt still up around my waist. I didn't wear panties because I was hoping for an intrusive pat down by one of the hot security chicks.

"You weren't even using the toilet," he points into the empty bowl.

"So?"

He drops his pants and maneuvers us around, sitting on the toilet seat. He leans back so his hard cock is practically poking me in the eye, and his balls are hanging outside.

"You asked for nuts." He motions to his saggy ass balls.

"Oh!" I grin, "we're joining the mile long club." I drop to my knees between his long legs.

"You mean high." He rolls his eyes.

"Well, it looks long to me." I retort as I grab the fucking monster and suck it deep down my throat.

"Fuck," he hisses when I drag my teeth along the velvet surface, and then tug on the piercing in the tip. "Make it quick," he growls, "I want to eat that asshole."

Well damn.

I continue to stroke his cock as I bend my head and suck his balls into my mouth. His legs tense beside me as I suck on one and then the other. Once they've had enough attention, I move back to his cock, the head a deep purple and the shaft jerking. I work his length, the sounds of sucking and gagging filling the small room, and when his fingers grip my hair, I know he's close.

"Right there," he grunts, and slams himself down my throat, his hot cum spurting in thick, salty ropes. He groans out my name, loud enough for the plane to hear for sure, and then he's making me stand.

"Put your hands on the sink and bend over, I want your asshole right here." He points at his mouth.

"Yes, Daddy." I grin, and do as he demands.

He spreads my cheeks wide, lands a quick, sharp slap to my pussy, then seals his mouth around my asshole, just like he promised. He licks the tight rim, and then shoves his tongue inside, thrusting in and out.

His large fingers begin to work my clit with rough, tight circles against the sensitive nub. Then he forcefully shoves three fingers inside my pussy while his tongue fucks my ass. I'm so wet, I can bet everyone outside of this door can hear the sounds my pussy is making alone, not even including the breathy moans and whimpers coming from my mouth.

Blaze is rough, unforgiving, and so fucking delicious.

"You need to come now," he growls as he bites into the tight ring of muscle at my ass.

"Make me, Daddy." I dare retort.

And just as I figured, he gets rougher as a form of punishment for my disobedience. His hand cracks loudly against my ass cheek and then he's back to fucking my asshole with his tongue. His fingers slip into my pussy juices to spread it over my clit, giving it a hard pinch.

I lose my breath on the intensity of my orgasm. My legs shake, and my mouth gapes open on a silent scream. It's too much, and Blaze doesn't let up, draining me of every spasm, claiming each one with his mouth. Then just as quick as he started, he pushes me up, and stands, dragging his pants up.

"Hurry back out and shut the fuck up for the rest of the flight," he grips my face in his hand, devouring my mouth with his.

Then he slams open the door, not bothering to close it, and heads back to his seat. I look up and find a lineup of people, all looking equally shocked as I pull down my skirt to cover my ass.

"You won't be getting the same experience as me but enjoy your nature's calls." I give them all a curtsy and rush back to my seat, a giggle escaping as people shoot me dirty looks.

I shove by Blaze who's once again engrossed in the screen as if nothing happened, and squeal when I find another three packs of nuts on my seat.

"Stuff your mouth and shut up," he growls, but I see his scar twist with a ghost of a smile.

"Oh, look! Just as shriveled as yours." I crack into a crunchy nut loudly.

"You better watch your mouth before I fill it again."

"Promise?"

Darius

Santos is practically bouncing out of his fucking seat, glancing at Zander, and grinning every few minutes as we drive toward one of the houses the Diablos have claimed. His energy is seeping into me, excitement coursing through my body at knowing we're about to start taking back what's ours.

"Are we there yet?" Santos asks Zander for the millionth time in ten minutes, causing Zander's knuckles to crack on the steering wheel.

"For the love of God, no!" he growls, glancing at me in the rear-view mirror. "If you want to make him choke on your dick right now, I won't stop you."

"I'm pretty sure my balls are one-hundred-percent empty at this point in time," I reply dryly, making him grunt. Santos, on the other hand, smirks at me over his shoulder and winks.

"I bet I could find more in there. It's not the explosion I was chasing today, but I won't say no."

Zander rolls his eyes, but the corner of his lips lift into a small smile. He secretly loves our relationship. Seeing Santos so happy and carefree after he'd been down for so long is like a breath of fresh air, one we all appreciate. He might not be built big like Blaze, but my man can pack a punch, just ask my fucking face.

"Focus on the task ahead, not my junk. I say we blow shit up and ask questions later," I answer, and Zander chuckles darkly.

"That's the plan. We know there's no innocents in there, so go crazy. Send them a message they can't ignore," he grins, and I swear Santos squeals like a girl.

"I don't have to hold back? I can take them to pound town with my fists and I won't get yelled at?" he beams.

"Pound town? That's probably not the best way to describe it," Zander snorts.

"Why not? They'll be completely fucked once I get my hands on them. Seems pound town is fitting after all," he shrugs, turning his attention out the window to watch the scenery. Most people would think he's zoned out, but he likes assessing his surroundings. If things go south and we get split up, he remembers every dark corner to run to. He's probably thinking about jerking off to the image of setting the whole damn neighborhood on fire.

"The only rule I have is to not blow us up in the process. I haven't forgotten the last time I let you loose," Zander adds, giving him the side-eye. "You burned my goddamn eyebrows off."

"And you looked so pretty, like a damaged little fire beetle!" Santos exclaims without looking away from the window. Zander shakes his head and scoffs.

"That doesn't even make sense."

"Does anything make sense?"

"Not when it comes from your fucking mouth," Zander mutters, pulling over one street over from our target. The neighborhood is quiet, half the houses being abandoned over the years as gangs started taking over, so if anyone sees us walking down the street with arms full of explosives, they won't do shit.

Santos bails from the car like lightning, not wasting time as he starts grabbing his toys from the trunk, while Zander runs through the layout of the property one more time, as if Santos is listening. Once the crazy bastard gets in destruction mode, his ears are usually turned off.

We lock the car and walk to the next street, seeing the house instantly, noticing one man standing on the front porch smoking a cigarette.

"You think I could get a bullet between his eyes from here?" I mumble, earning a scowl from Zander.

"Play it smart, D. Just because you have a silencer, doesn't mean you have to start the party early."

"You're becoming boring like Blaze. Besides, you said no rules, so that's on you," I throw back before lifting my gun and lining up my shot. Zander sighs but doesn't say anything, knowing I'm right. He let us out to play without setting boundaries, not that Santos or I listen when there are rules involved anyway.

I fire my shot, the bullet sailing through the air and hitting the guy straight in the eye, his body falling to the ground instantly.

"You missed," Zander informs me, making me chuckle.

"Doubt it. He went down, that's all I give a fuck about."

"Anyone inside could have heard his body hit the deck."

"Good, they can all come running outside and get riddled with bullets," I shrug, but Santos starts running toward the house, a deranged laugh leaving him.

"Leave some for me, baby cakes!"

Zander watches him run, turning to glance at me after a moment. "Baby cakes? Why does his sweet side freak me out so much? He's a psychopath and it's weird."

I grin, loving all of it. "Leave my cutsie poopsie alone." Then I take off after Santos, leaving Zander behind to fake a gag.

I catch up with Santos who instantly unloads his armful of explosives into mine, taking pieces as he needs them. "You think they know we're here yet?" I ask, amusement filling his eyes.

"Nope. But they're about to. Gimme that," he states, motioning to a bunch of wires. I frown, handing it over to him.

"Don't you need a power source? C'mon, San. I think you're losing your brain cells finally."

"Leave that to me. What happens when things are wired wrong?" he asks, humming to himself and reminding me of Selene, causing a smile to tug at my lips.

"Electricity is a dangerous thing. Either nothing happens, or a hell of a lot happens. Are you asking me because you don't know?"

He peeks through the closest window, answering quietly as he cracks it open when the coast is clear. "I was just making sure you knew, that's all."

He makes his way around the house, distributing everything from my arms around it, then we make our way back to the window he opened where he hauls himself up onto the ledge and climbs inside.

"San!" I whisper yell, but he ignores me, fucking around with something on the wall before coming back out.

"When I say run, run," he says casually before turning on the little device in his hand. "Maybe start moving now so Zander knows to stay back. His fat ass can't run as fast these days."

I snigger but turn to see Zander leaning against the fence further away, motioning for him to stay put. He gives me a look as if I'm crazy, already aware it's best to stay back. After the eyebrow incident, he doesn't trust Santos with explosives in the slightest.

Santos chuckles to himself, pressing a button before his eyes dart up to mine. "Oh, shit. I meant to say 'run' first."

I grab his hand and yank him behind me as I start to run, his loud psychotic cackle filling the air, seconds before the house blows, shaking the ground under our feet, the force of the explosion knocking us down.

He lands on top of me, mischief taking over his face. "You wanna fuck right here? You little devil!"

"Get off me!" I laugh, pushing him away just as Zander runs over to help us up. Shouts fill the house as smaller explosions sound, making me frown.

"Do they have a meth lab in there? What's that sound?"

Santos can't wipe the smirk off his face as he eyes me. "I possibly plugged a device into their power inside. It sends a current through the entire wiring system and slowly burns away inside the walls. There should be another big boom any minute now and…"

I stumble as the next big explosion hits, the shouts getting louder, and a handful of people spill from the house, their eyes instantly finding us.

"You pieces of shit!" someone yells, but Zander blows out a breath and fires a shot over my shoulder, taking him out.

"You couldn't put explosives near the front door? You could have blown the entire thing up without any hassle."

Santos frowns, cocking his head slightly. "Where's the fun in that? I like playing with them."

"Go play then, because they look pissed," he grumbles, eyeing the men left who seem to all be armed now that the confusion has worn off. Wonderful.

I follow Santos as the guys start running toward us, firing shots that miss us by a mile. “Fucking hell, who taught you to shoot? A blind man?” Santos calls loudly, aiming his own gun at one of them to take them out. I watch the man I love as he skips toward the mayhem, talking to himself about wannabe gangsters, and I can almost feel the eye roll behind me from Zander. There are only seven people total in the house, so it doesn't take long for us to clear it out and head back toward the car, our next target on our minds.

Fuck, I miss Selene.

Santos

I didn’t enjoy the first house as much as I thought I would. The explosions were cool, and it felt like a scene out of an action movie, but my dick didn’t get hard over it. Maybe we’ve been fucking too much after all and my mini-me has finally had enough.

I try to stop thinking about my comatose dick as we arrive at the Diablos next house, my mind made up on how to approach it already. I jump from the car and open the trunk, pulling out a machine gun I hid in the spare tire compartment, the fabric of the trunk covering it up.

Zander glares at me, motioning to the trunk with his hands. “Where the fuck’s the spare tire gone? And where the fuck did you get that?”

“Found it,” I grin. “Hidden with a bunch of other cool shit.”

“Where did you find it?” he demands, glaring at Darius as if it’s his fault. I shrug, but I can’t help the smile on my face.

“You know where Blaze hides stuff so I can’t find them?”

“Yes,” he grunts, groaning when I continue.

“Well, there. That’s where I found it. I assume it was a surprise for my birthday and that’s why it was hidden, I’ll have to thank him later. I love it!”

"He hides that shit from you because it's meant to stay hidden. You should not be in control of this type of weapon," he snaps, putting his hands out. "Give it here."

"Finder's keepers!" I declare, clutching it tighter and accidentally firing a bunch of shots into the air. "Whoops!"

"Dammit, you *loco* piece of shit!" Zander barks just as the front door of the house flies open and men run out to see what's happening. Darius is laughing so hard I'm pretty sure he's going to piss himself, not seeming to give a shit that bullets are quickly being fired our way.

Zander curses at our cover being blown, but I let out a whoop and run headfirst toward them, swinging my new kick-ass toy in their direction, and holding down the trigger. Bullets rain across the front yard, my dick getting hard at the glorious view. *That's more like it.*

"San!" Zander shouts. I turn to look at him, chuckling as Zander and Darius dive for cover, and I realize I forgot to take my finger off the trigger.

"My bad!" I holler, hearing Zander curse me out colorfully as he gets to his feet to glare at me.

"This is why you don't get those kinds of toys, asshole! It's not your dick, you can't just swing it everywhere!"

"I don't see why not. Look, weeeeeeee!" I exclaim as I turn to fire more shots at the remaining men who've been trying to hide from my outburst, spinning in a circle as I go, causing Darius and Zander to duck for cover again. Seeing me almost kill my own guys probably has them wondering just how crazy I am. I'm not crazy, I'm passionate about my job. I should add that to my resume.

"No one would hire you, you stupid fucker!" Zander bellows over the sound of the gunfire, making me pause to look at him.

"You can read minds?"

"You said it out loud, you idiot!"

"Oh, thank fuck. You scared me, brother," I exclaim as I let out a breath, feeling his eyes burning into me.

"I'll scare you in a minute! Give me that!" he shouts, darting over to me and snatching my baby, making me pout.

"You're not fun!"

"Aren't I? I wonder why the fuck that would be?!" he snaps, holding the weapon tighter as I reach for it. "Don't even bother! Get in the car!"

"Yes, Mr. Walton," I mutter as I go.

"I wish I'd gotten a receipt for you. Some days I want to return you," he growls, turning to Darius so the pair of them could make sure the house was clear. Darius rigs it and blows it to pieces, leaving nothing behind. The Diablos need to know whose town this is.

It's ours.

Chapter Six

Zander

Santos can pout at me all he likes; we are done for the day. We drive in silence all the way home, his eyes drifting to me every so often to sulk. I told Blaze ages ago we can't hide anything from Santos, but he seemed to think it would be fine. Turns out, he was wrong.

Darius glares at me for most of the drive, annoyed at me for upsetting his boyfriend. I don't give a fuck; Santos should never have an automatic weapon in his grip. Ever. And this is why. Both Darius and I could have easily been killed today, but I seem to be the only one who gives a fuck about that.

I usually don't mind when I pull the short straw to play babysitter, but I've been doing it a lot lately and it's starting to burn me out. I love Santos and Darius, they are family, but fuck they drain the energy right out of you.

Once back at home, Santos climbs out and slams the car door, making me snort. He can throw a tantrum if he really wants, but he isn't getting his toy back. Imagine if he had it in the house? Selene and Blaze would come home to Swiss Cheese Avenue in their living room.

Darius runs after him, taking his hand silently to let him know he's on his side, leaving me to clear out the trunk and stash the weapons. Fine by me, I don't want them anywhere near it.

I make quick work of it, heading into the house once I'm done to find Santos lying on the couch, making the most annoying sounds possible. It's like a child sulking crossed with Selene's singing.

"For fuck's sake. Would you shut up?" I groan, but he just makes the noise louder, the wailing noise grating on my nerves. "Either you shut up or I shut you up, what's it going to be?"

He goes silent, and I think I've won until he sits up to let me sit, only to sprawl across my lap with a sly smile on his face. "How would you shut me up? A gag? A punch to the face? Your dick? I mean, I'm not opposed to any of those."

"Get off me."

"Get you off? Alright. Dick treatment it is!" he states and acts like he's going to unzip my pants. I move fast, flipping him off me and pinning him under me with a snarl.

"Stop it! Is that all you think about? Dick and violence?"

His tongue runs across his lips before he speaks. "No."

"What else do you possibly think about?!"

"My baby girl's heavenly pussy on my face. I think about that a lot, actually."

"I'm close to losing it with you. I really am," I warn, but he just chuckles and leans up to kiss my cheek because he's a dick.

"I'm close to losing control too, Mr. Walton. I can't explain it, you just do it for me."

When I said I loved them, I didn't mean I wasn't considering killing them.

"Oh, I do love a gang bang," Darius drawls as he wanders in, plonking down on the other couch, where I should have sat in the first place.

"Keep your boyfriend off me before I beat his ass," I grit out, glaring at him when he laughs.

"Let him torment you. He's bored without Selene."

"He'll be bored when he's bedridden and I'm not here because I'll be in a cell for attempted murder," I hiss, his eyes narrowing.

"Fine. Come here, *amante*. I'll occupy you," Darius claims, patting his lap. Santos raises an eyebrow at me, telling me silently to get off him, then he switches to the couch with Darius, sprawling contently across his lap. The happy sigh he lets out simmers some of my temper, and I can't help but smile as Darius runs his fingers through Santos' dark hair to calm him.

"I'm sorry. You just drive me crazy sometimes," I mumble, and Darius snorts.

"Sometimes?"

"Regularly," I correct. "How about we all shower and have a lazy afternoon while we wait to hear from our girl and Blaze?"

"You want to shower with us? Alright. I'll allow it," Santos jokes, and I let out an exasperated sigh.

"Lord, give me strength."

"You've been hanging around Pepe too much. You seem to be praying a lot lately," Darius teases.

"I like that little shit. He's my favorite pet I've ever had," Santos says absently as he stands to stretch, and I can't help but laugh.

"He's your pet?"

"Yep. I want to keep him," he decides, finalizing the subject. Pepe has no idea what he's in for if Santos has claimed him. I can't wait to see how that plays out.

Blaze

"Are we there yet?" Selene asks me for what must be the millionth time. We only just got into the rental ten minutes ago. It's like having Santos here.

"Knock it off," I growl at her. "Call your sister and tell her where the rendezvous point is."

"Fuck her and the cunt she was shoved out of."

I snort because fuck, she's a clever little shit. "We need the guns and the extra help."

We found out the MC meeting up for the shipment is not the Dientes. Pepe texted Selene while we were on the plane, and we received it when we got off. It's another MC called The Highway Knights. They're known for their brutality and constant turf wars with Dientes.

"I know." She huffs, "that's why I'm calling Papi."

I don't argue with her because I understand what she's feeling, and I'm not going to push her to talk to a sister who gave up so easily on her. Especially when Selene never gave up, even when the odds were slim that Jan was even alive.

"*Hola, Reaper Pequena*." Papi's voice purrs into the phone, and my teeth crack with irritation.

"*Hola, culo* eater." Selene retorts, and a startled laugh breaches my lips. Fucking little shit is on another level today. "We're in Nevada running a lead on a skin drop off today."

"We're not picking anything up today," he replies, his voice sounding suspicious.

"It's for The Highway Knights. We also learned they're your rivals. Wanna help me kill some people?"

"Yes, we fucking do!" I hear Loqi in the background, his hoots sounding eerily similar to Santos'.

"I guess we'll meet you there, send us the location." Papi Loco snarls before hanging up.

"Santos got the best out of that asshole's saggy balls." She growls as she tosses her phone in the cupholder.

"That's not saying much." I grumble.

Selene declines her seat all the way back and begins to hike up her skirt.

"What the fuck are you doing?" I ask, trying to keep my eyes on the road and not the slow exposure of my favorite pussy.

"All this talk about saggy balls and Santos has me needing to get off," she groans as her fingers dip into her pink flesh. "Besides, it'll help keep me focused when I need to take fuckers out."

I try to ignore her tiny mewls. I even try to ignore when they grow into loud moans for Santos, but the scent of her arousal has me snapping, quickly cutting the car to the side of the road, making other motorists lay on their horns.

"Get out of the car." I snarl, and her head quickly turns to look at me.

"What?"

"Now, Selene, before I choke you to death and fuck your warm pussy until it turns cold."

She slowly pulls her skirt down and opens the door, stepping out into the stifling Nevada heat, fuck I miss New York already. I'm out of the car soon after her, and we meet at the hood.

"Are you making me walk the rest of the way?" Her arms cross over her chest.

"No," I grab her hair and drag her into me, slamming my mouth to hers in a bruising kiss. We part, and I throw her on top of the hot metal of the hood.

Her hands hit the metal, and she hisses through the heat, but just like I thought, she endures the pain as I flip her skirt up. I undo my pants in record time, and slam into her already prepared cunt. Horns honk as the cars pass, and I continue to punish this little brat until she comes all over my cock.

"Fuck, yes." She screams as I feel her begin to tighten. My hand cracks down over her ass and I grab her hair, yanking her back to my chest.

"Stop with the disobedience, or I will redden your ass at each turn off on this highway, am I understood?"

"Yes, Daddy." She whispers as I shove her back down.

"Now, have this pussy creaming all over my cock before I shoot at these honking fuckers."

She listens like the good girl I know she can be, and we come simultaneously, our moans getting eaten up by the traffic around us. I pull out of her, slap her ass one more time and do up my pants.

"Now your cum is going to be all over the seat." She snickers.

"It's a rental, what the fuck do I care?" I turn on my heel and snap my fingers at her. "Get in the car, put the fucking seatbelt on, and behave for the rest of the way."

"Okay, Daddy." She smirks as she walks bow-legged back to the passenger side door. I don't know what it is about her calling me *Daddy*, but I kind of want to drag her back to that hood and this time, fuck her asshole raw.

I pull back out into traffic, and grin when she does indeed put on her seatbelt, settling in for a nap. Finally, fucking peace and quiet.

"The last time I was fucked on the hood of a car, I had Zander's dick in my mouth, and his daddy's in my pussy."

Well, as close to peace and quiet as I can get.

Selene

I feel rough fingers brush against my cheek, and I sleepily look to my left, finding Blaze giving me a rare soft look.

"Are we there yet?" I croak out, and his scar tugs on his mouth as he smiles.

"Yeah, baby." He looks out the windshield and then back to me, "no sign of the shipment, but I see some bikes rolling up. I just can't tell who they are from here."

I follow his gaze and see that he's parked us up on a cliff, overlooking the meeting spot down below. It's discreet and we can sneak up on them when we're ready. There are about ten bikes rolling in, and as they get closer, I see the Dientes logo on the helmets. You can't miss the large shark teeth they have designed around the visors.

Blaze taps his horn four times in quick succession, and I see the lead bike point up at us. "He has a passenger." Blaze mumbles. It's Papi's bike and I know who's there holding on to his waist.

"I see that." I can even hear the deep tenor as my voice changes, I'm working on my anger toward my sister. I'm slowly coming to the realization she's not me, and her need to find me was doused when she found our bloody, ransacked apartment. But the operative word is *slowly*. I'm not one to be forced into anything and that includes a relationship with her.

"Ignore it and let's kill some fuckers, yeah?" I turn back to Blaze with a large grin, loving how he used my line.

"Hell, yes." I squeal and throw open the door when I hear the bikes' roar coming up behind us.

I lean against the trunk of the car, my arms crossed over my chest, and watch as they all kick down the stands, their bikes lined up in a perfect row with Papi in the center. I want to kill the old fucker for what he's done to Santos, but I won't take that away from my man. He may just want to do it himself.

They cut out the bikes and all of them stand one by one. As they take off the helmets, I start to recognize them. Kho and Kaine, Perc and Vico, Loqi, Papi Loco and my sister, Hook, and three other older men I wasn't introduced to. They must be Papi's men.

"Reaper!" Loqi exclaims as he strides forward. "We meet again!" I bump his fist with my own, and he gives Blaze a nod.

"Let's distribute weapons." Papi says as he drops a bag down on the sand. His hand goes up and each biker comes forward with bags of weapons.

"This must be how Santos feels when he sees guns." I squeal through the excitement. At the mention of his son's name, Papi's jaw locks, but he's smart enough to keep his mouth shut.

"Selene?" I turn to look at my sister as she timidly comes forward, "I have something for you."

"Is it a fuck?" I watch as her eyebrows come together, "because I can't seem to find my own." Blaze's elbow digs into my ribs, and I growl. "Sorry," I give her a fake smile, "what do you have for me dear sister of the east?" I lean into Blaze, "get it? Like the Wicked Witch of the East?"

He snorts again and nudges me with his shoulder, "give her a chance, *Dorothy*."

"I figured since you had to fly out, you wouldn't have your pretty knife belt. So, I had you one made by our very own forger, Hammer." She holds out a pretty metal ornate belt and tucked into the buckle is a gorgeous knife with the words Reaper Incarnate engraved into the handle. The blade itself is black, but a large silver scythe is etched into the surface.

I stare at its obvious beauty, completely speechless.

"You've somehow found a way to shut her up." Blaze snarks as the guys laugh, but I can't move my eyes from my new toy. Even after all these years, after how much I've changed from the little sister she knew, it's like she still gets me at my core.

"I hope you like it." She says nervously.

"I do," my voice cracks, and my eyes begin to fill, surprising the fuck out of myself. Am I really going to cry over a blade?

“I think it’s more over the blade your sister got you, which is very much in your tastes.” Blaze says as he whistles at the design.

“I said that out loud?” I feel the first tear fall over my cheek. Thank fuck all the bikers are laughing and not paying attention to my weak moment, I’d hate to have to kill any of them.

“So, you like it?” Jan wrings her hands.

“Yes,” I nod, and finally my heart sheds its icy exterior. “I like it so much, It’s perfect.” I step into her and pull her in for a tight hug, feeling the tension leave her body at once.

“I’m so sorry, Selly.” She whispers into my neck.

“I know.” I tell her as I give her a final squeeze. I release her and for the first time, I feel lighter. “Let’s focus on killing some assholes.”

“I’m gonna stay up here and watch you guys,” she chuckles. “I’m not a fighter, I just had to come see you.”

The distant rumble of bikes sounds in the valley below, and everyone stops their chatter.

“This is it.” Loqi grins as he bounces on the balls of his feet. He has a fully automatic machine gun strapped across his chest with multiple rounds of ammo, and once again, I’m struck with how similar he is to Santos.

“We don’t do anything until the shipment shows up.” Blaze steps forward, “which should be at any moment. Then we piss on their parade.”

“Like actually piss?” I look at him, “that’s not fair, I don’t have an extension hose like the rest of you.” I pout.

Loqi bends over laughing as Papi Loco fights to stop the grin crawling over his mouth and failing. He distributes the guns and I end up with a handgun I tuck into the waistband of my skirt. The bikes park down in the valley, and we count four bikes and a large cargo van.

“Should be any minute now,” Blaze says, “let’s start creeping down closer.”

"You stay here, Henny." Papi grabs my sister around the waist and kisses her breathless, "stay safe."

"Okay, Papi." She murmurs as her hand settles against his cheek, "I love you."

Watching them makes my heart hurt, I miss my boys, and I can't wait to get them all back together again. As if sensing my thoughts, Blaze puts his phone in front of my face and I watch a video of Santos skipping into a group of Diablos and spinning while shooting a machine gun, his maniacal laughter pulling one from me as well.

"He's getting knocked the fuck out when I get home." Blaze mutters, a ghost of a smile coating his lips. "I hid that shit from him for that very reason."

The video ends as Zander screams, a bullet whizzing by his head, and I laugh again, loving every second of it and wishing I were there.

"Here comes the truck," Papi says, and we look down at the valley.

"Let's move." Blaze brushes by me to lead us closer.

"Selly," Jan grabs my hand as I move to follow Blaze, "please be careful."

"Can't promise that, but I promise to stay alive." I grin at her. "I get to kill Gingivitis if he's here." I call dibs on Mack.

"Fine," Blaze concedes as we make our way down the steep incline. "No shooting until the shipment is safely boarded into the van."

Everyone murmurs their assent, and we continue down. To my great disappointment, Mack is not present for this drop off, but that doesn't mean I won't have fun shooting holes into the rest of these scumbags. We watch the exchange happen and I snarl when I see a few young kids among the group, crying and being slapped around for it.

"I wish I'd kept Walton's strap-on," I growl. "I'd be fucking some assholes."

Loqi chokes on his laugh, and Papi slaps him on the back of the head with a stern warning to be quiet. Once the victims are all safely inside the van, I aim my gun, and shoot the closest biker to me, watching as he drops like a sack of shit to the sand.

"Dientes!" One of them yells just as we come running out of hiding.

The valley becomes a battlefield as bullets rain down around us and shouts of distress and the cries of death become overwhelming. I take out four men before I turn and find Blaze mowing down three in a row. Without panties to reign it in, I flood my fucking thighs. My man is a hot motherfucker.

When we finally kill every last piece of shit, I look around us, letting out a whoop when I find we've had no casualties.

"That was like taking candy from a baby." I holler.

"Only because they weren't prepared for us." Loqi calls out as he opens the van, "I need to see if my sister is here."

My heart hurts once again for him, knowing the feeling all too well, and seeing his desperation. When he steps out of the van, my stomach sinks with his long face, she's not here.

"Hook," Papi calls out. "Drive the van back to the compound, Henny will drive your bike back."

"On it, Boss." Hook heads for the driver's side of the van.

"Loqi, call the scrappers to come for these bikes."

"You got it," Loqi nods at his father and pulls out his phone.

"You two can come back to the compound. We'll get you some food and you can rest. We'll return your car to the rental, and you can take one of ours back, unless you want to leave that shiny new knife here." Papi nods to my waist.

"Hell no," I shake my head.

"Let's get out of here." Papi heads back up the hill.

The compound is buzzing with excitement when we get there, and soon enough a party is underway. I sit at the bar in front of Licker who gives me a wide smile in return.

"Deadly Reaper!" He exclaims, "welcome back!"

He drops a whiskey on ice in front of me, and I hum my approval at his memory.

"How was the shootout? Did you get any?"

"You know it," I grin, "killed those motherfuckers dead."

Blaze snorts as he sits on the stool beside me, "that she did."

He gets a whiskey pushed in front of him, and I grin seeing he drinks what I do. He ignores my look with a roll of his eyes, and drinks in silence.

"I wanna get back." I tell him.

"Same." He nods, "we take a few hours to relax, and we can head out. It'll take a few days to get home."

Loqi appears to my left, and signals for Licker to grab him a beer.

"Still haven't found your sister?"

"No," he shakes his head sadly, "the police station won't release the info on the woman they have in custody, yet. It's just a waiting game."

"What is her name?"

"Cara."

My glass pauses in its path to my mouth as the name washes over me. I know that name. I wrack my brain and when it hits me, my glass drops to the floor, shattering.

"Loqi," my voice is a coarse whisper as the people around me stop and stare at the commotion. "I know your sister."

Santos

Zander is still pissy with me for my machine gun merry-go-round incident, but at least he's stopped glaring at me. I had so much fun, I passed the fuck out with my head on Darius' lap half-way through the first movie.

I wake up to someone shaking my shoulder gently, fingers tracing up and down my spine, and the scent of Darius surrounding me.

"San? Wake up."

I groan, cracking my eyes open and blinking against the bright light from the TV, finding Darius peering down at me with a soft smile on his handsome face. "Why? I'm tired after all the fun I had today."

"I know, babe, but Zander wants to take out the other house now, it's dark. There are more people there than the last two, and we're hoping they've all congregated there, licking their wounds. Let's go cause some mayhem," he replies, chuckling when I bolt upright with excitement.

Zander walks in as he's shoving a gun down the back of his jeans, his eyes landing on mine immediately. "No machine guns hidden in my fucking car this time."

"I wouldn't have had to hide it if you weren't such a stick in the mud, Zan. Didn't you see how many motherfuckers I gunned down?" I frown.

"I did see. You almost gunned us down in the process. You use your handgun and your knife, got it? Pepe is in there so don't start blowing shit up unless you want us to use him as collateral damage," he warns, my eyes going wide. I don't want my pet to die, I like him.

"I'll be good!" I promise, making him roll his eyes as he walks toward the door.

"Sure, you will. Let's go and get your pet then, shall we?" Don't have to tell me twice.

I get to my feet and follow Zander, letting Darius lock up as we head toward the car. I consider bringing fireworks to scare them, but I have a feeling Zander wouldn't find it as amusing as I would, so I leave them at home.

I miss Selene, she would have loved playing machine gun merry-go-round with me, and she definitely would have found the fireworks hilarious. I hope whatever they're doing in Nevada is going smoothly. I worry about her sister fucking with her emotions, but my girl can handle herself.

"I'm setting rules this time," Zander says as we drive, dragging me back to reality.

"Why? We had so much fun last time without them!" I huff, earning a side glance in return.

"Did we?" he deadpans. "I don't recall enjoying that. We stick together, no splitting up to do dumb shit, and don't blow anything up until I say so. You don't want to hurt Pepe, do you?"

"I'd never hurt Pepe!"

"Stick to the rules then. Stay by me, this is a stealth mission until I say otherwise. *Comprende*?" he asks firmly, making me grin. Of course, I understand, but I like fucking with him.

"*No comprendo, otra vez, por favor*?"

"I won't say it again! If you don't understand, I'll turn this car around and drop you at home! Did you need me to repeat myself, or do you fucking understand?" he snaps, and I roll my eyes at his dramatics.

"*Si*. You need a strong coffee or a tight pussy to bury your dick in. How long will our tight pussy be gone? I can't deal with you like this for too long," I sigh, but he ignores me and turns the conversation to Darius.

"We check around the house for guards, try and locate Pepe before they know we're there, then somehow get his holy ass out before the gunfire starts, alright? Keep an eye on Santos and don't let him do anything stupid."

Darius grins, giving me a wink. "If he steps out of line, I'll punish his ass."

"Am I getting a daddy kink like our girl and daddy Blaze? I wouldn't mind one of us bending the other over and…"

"You don't have a fucking daddy kink, you have a *piss Zander off* kink," Zander growls, giving me the evil-eye before turning his attention back to the road ahead. He has zero humor, I swear. Selene needs to come home and fuck the stick right out of his ass.

We drive the rest of the way in silence, and the moment we park, Zander presses the button to lock all the doors, stopping me from bailing out. "Hey!"

"Tell me the rules," he demands, and I flip him off.

"How does go fuck a donkey sound?"

"It sounds like you're going home?" he offers, making me scowl.

"No explosions, no machine gun, not letting my dick out, no stupidity, and do as I'm told," I state.

"Sounds like you're ready then," he nods and unlocks the doors.

"Sounds like a fucking downer of a party and I'll die from boredom. If anyone shoots at me, I'll let them take me out. Has to be more fun than this," I grumble, climbing out to stand beside Darius who ruffles my hair playfully.

"C'mon, once we don't have to be stealthy, we'll have some fun. Let's get Pepe out and paint the walls in blood, *amante*," he declares, and nothing sounds more damn romantic than that.

Zander grumbles about us being idiots, but he's smiling, so that's a start.

We head toward the house and sneak around the back, peering in windows to try and locate Pepe. We find him in one of the back rooms, talking to someone on the phone. I tap on the glass quietly, ignoring Zander's growl, and Pepe turns to look at us with wide eyes. Someone enters the room, and we duck, not wanting to be seen yet.

"What are you looking at?" The person asks, his footsteps coming toward the window. We crouch down further, managing to stay hidden until the footsteps retreat.

"Nothing. I'm just paranoid after those other attacks," Pepe replies, finishing his conversation on the phone as the other man leaves.

I peek through the window again, huffing when I realize he's left the room. "How do we get him out then? I was going to drag him out the window."

"Why don't you try knocking on all the other windows and find him? Maybe one of the Diablos can help you," Zander deadpans.

"Well, that's a dumb idea. They'll know we're here then," I snort, making him roll his eyes. "Oh, you're being funny." Asshole.

We make our way around the house until finding an open window, and before Zander can tell me not to, I climb inside. I can hear his muttered curses, but Darius follows me, not wanting to miss out on any action.

Zander soon does the same, giving me a dirty look as we sneak through the house, coming to a halt when we find Pepe in the kitchen with some of the Diablos. The floorboards creak under our feet, drawing eyes to us instantly.

"Shit," Zander mutters, so I figure that's permission to end the stealth mission.

I dart into the room, throwing Pepe over my shoulder and turning toward the hallway. "I'd wondered where I left this! Pretend I'm not even here, guys!"

"That's not yours!" someone shouts, as I start running, speaking over my shoulder.

"Finder's keepers!"

Footsteps pound through the house after me, gunfire sounding as Zander and Darius cover for me.

"Put me down!" Pepe screams, making me laugh.

"Like fuck, you slippery little sucker! I'm keeping you! Boss said I could!"

"You're going to get me killed!" he snaps, swatting at my butt. "Put me down!"

"Calm down, at least buy me dinner first before spanking me! What would Jesus say? You little minx!" I cackle, ignoring his protesting as I find a back door and run outside.

I put him back on his feet and motion to the car further up the road. "Go get in the car and hide. I won't let them hurt you, but I want to go back and play with them."

Surprisingly, he does as he's told, leaving me to turn some Diablos into *Pinatas*.

Best day ever.

Darius

Zander's cursing about Santos as we cover for him, taking out anyone who tries to chase after him. I know he'll be back in a second, he hates missing out on all the fun.

I back down the hallway, keeping my gun in front of me as I wait for any of the Diablos to follow, but I freeze as an arm wraps around my neck from behind. "Nice try."

Zander's further up the hallway, but with the dim lights, he might miss and shoot me by accident instead. I stay still, but the man is suddenly ripped off me, and Santos jumps on his back, clinging on as he smacks my attacker in the head with his gun multiple times.

"Pinata! Pinata!" he shouts, and I have to smother a laugh at the sight. Zander comes up to me and nods to make sure I'm okay, then he keeps an eye out while Santos has his fun. The guy's nuts, and I fucking love him for it.

"Get off me!" the man slurs, his brain being rattled around by the hits.

"The only person allowed to choke D, is me! Keep your slimy hands to yourself, heathen!" he barks, jumping off his back before grabbing his knife from his pocket and fisting the man's hair, yanking his head back to expose his neck. "*¡Adiós, pendejo*!" then he stabs him in the throat, dragging the blade down sharply.

The man's gurgling for air, and blood spills, slowly choking him to death as he drowns, but Santos is done playing with him as he moves toward me, taking my face in his bloodied hands to inspect me. "Did he hurt you? I'll kill him again if you want?"

"Since when do you care if I'm hurt?" I tease because he's being softer than normal. He scowls, glaring at the dying man before meeting my gaze again.

"I care because the only person allowed to make you bleed is me."

"Can you two have your foreplay later?" Zander asks dryly as car tires squeal out front, signaling the arrival of more Diablos. "We have things to do."

Santos grins manically before kissing me hard, not looking back as he turns on his heel and runs toward the threat like a cat chasing a ball of yarn. Zander sighs, his expression tired, but he follows to make sure he doesn't get himself killed.

Shouts and screams sound as the men enter the house, and I keep an eye on the surroundings as Zander and Santos gun them down one by one, then I join them as more Diablos arrive. *How many of these fuckers are there?*

"Zan, duck!" I bark as someone runs for him, and he does as he's told quickly, giving me a clear shot to the man's skull. Zander gives me a thumbs up before charging across the room at someone, unloading two bullets and knocking them down instantly.

I find Santos drawing Tic-Tac-Toe on one of the body's faces with his blade, seeming deep in thought, ignoring the chaos around him as usual. He curses, somehow losing against himself, then he stands and puts three rounds in the man's face with annoyance. "Stupid game." Then he takes off to jump on someone's back as they try to sneak up on Zander, pretending he's a cowboy riding a bronc. "Yee-fucking-haw!"

Two Diablos make a break for it, deciding against messing with my psycho man, leaving three behind which we gun down pretty fast, leaving the house in silence. Well, other than Santos' panting from burning all that fucking energy.

"We good?" Zander asks as we check ourselves over for damage. "Good. Let's rig this place up and get out of here."

It doesn't take long to fill the house with explosives, and once we are half-way back to the car, I give Santos the button to blow the place to Kingdom Come. He enjoys it more than I do, so I figure he'll appreciate the gesture.

"Pepe?" Santos sing-songs, jogging toward the car to peek in the windows, seeming satisfied to find the shaking man in the back seat. "Oh, good! Let's go, my pet looks hungry!"

Santos climbs into the back with Pepe, letting me sit up front. I'm surprised when Zander silently drops the keys into my hand, climbing into the passenger seat and shutting himself inside.

I don't question him as I slide in behind the steering wheel, starting the engine and driving off toward home, smirking as Santos babbles on to Pepe about all the fun he just had. The poor man is whispering prayers under his breath, wondering why God put such demons in his path.

Back at the house, Zander mumbles about needing a shower and takes off for some peace and quiet, leaving me to deal with Santos and Pepe.

"You should have seen me! I smashed his skull in!" Santos exclaims, his hands waving around as he gives Pepe a play-by-play of the evening's events. Pepe silently sits on the couch, looking out of place as his new best friend keeps talking, and I figure I'll break the ice a little and get the fucker to relax. He doesn't seem to understand he is one of the safest people in the damn house right now with how much Santos likes him.

"You want a coffee? Or a beer? Santos needs to go shower all that blood off," I offer, and Pepe lets out a breath of relief as he nods.

"Coffee, please."

"Oh! And get those little cheesy puff snacks! They look like fingers!" Santos grins, giving me a kiss on his way past to the bathroom.

Once Pepe has a coffee in hand, and the cheesy puffs on the coffee table in front of him, Pepe looks at me with a frown. "Have you heard from Selene and Blaze? I hope they're okay."

I shrug. "They'll call when they're ready. They're probably neck deep in body parts right now. They can handle themselves, trust me."

"She's scary," he admits. "She doesn't seem to have a filter, either."

"Our girl's one of a kind. You'll get used to her antics eventually," I smirk, sipping my coffee and watching him, trying to see what Santos sees in the little weirdo. We make small talk until Santos comes back, instantly sitting beside Pepe and stuffing his face with the cheesy puffs, sucking the flavor off his fingers in the process. It's hot, and it shouldn't be.

"You know, you have blood on your face," Santos says to me, stating the obvious.

"I'm aware. You put it there. Can you two play nice while I shower? If Zan comes back out, give him some space. He's fucking tired and has had enough of our shit today," I grunt, knowing he deserves a rest. It can be hard trying to be the sensible one out of all of us, and Santos especially is probably giving him grey hairs.

Santos drops an arm around Pepe's shoulders, making him jump. "Me and Pepe will be fine! I'll put a movie on. You like slasher movies?"

I leave them to it, despite Pepe's panicked squeak, knowing they'll be fine.

I quickly rinse off the blood, scrubbing myself clean, and I'm not surprised to find Zander sitting on my bed waiting for me. He looks exhausted.

"You good?" I ask as I head toward my drawers and drop my towel, yanking some boxers on. He groans, dropping back on the bed.

"I'm so fucking tired, man. Santos is worse than a toddler, and you're not much better some days."

I find some sweats and put them on before sitting on the bed, looking down at him with a raised eyebrow. "Santos has a lot of energy, and he sees the world differently than you do. Let him be crazy and stop getting so uptight with him. You know why you're tired? Because you spend so much time and energy trying to control things you can't. Let him have fun, we'll always get out alive. You saw him today; he was having a blast."

"I know, but earlier today was ridiculous. He could have shot us. I like spilling blood like the rest of you, you know that, but he's out of control," he replies tightly, scrubbing his face with his hands. "We can't rely on luck being on our side forever."

"Selene and Santos both like to handle things the same way. Let them. Stop stressing yourself out over things that don't matter. Selene and Blaze won't be gone for long, then we can fuck the hell out of her until we pass out. Things will be back to normal, just hold out a little longer," I mumble, his hands lifting from his face to look at me.

"The fuck does normal look like? We've never been normal."

"It's our own normal. There will always be violence, sex, and frustration. It's who we are. You need to learn to roll with it, old man," I tease, sliding back from him as he swats at me.

"I miss them," he sighs, and I pat his shoulder as he sits up.

"Me, too. They'll call and fill us in soon. You want a coffee?" I offer as I stand, waiting for him to follow.

"Fuck, yeah. Where's Santos?"

"Playing with Pepe," I grin, chuckling as we walk into the living room to find Santos and Pepe on the couch, watching a horror movie and sharing the cheesy puffs.

I don't know what Zander is worried about. Things seem pretty normal to me.

Chapter Seven

Zander

The exhaustion is bone-fucking-deep. I'm tired of having to always be the one who makes sure we all stay alive, and more times than not, I'm left with these fuckers who enjoy flirting with death. I want to retire from blowing up houses, shooting down cunts, and saving little altar boys. Speaking of, I find our little altar boy relaxed on the couch beside Santos—of all people—and watching a bloody slasher movie.

I sit down across from them and take the offered beer from Darius, settling in for the night. I place my phone on the table between us, hoping to hear from Blaze or Selene soon, and begin to drink my beer.

I'm deep into the movie, the spray of blood, suspense of who the killer is, and females running for their lives, when the shrill ring of my phone interrupts us at a suspenseful part. Pepe shrieks like a cat in heat, tossing the bowl of cheesy puffs in the air, and Santos joins in, fear coating his features as he wraps his arms around the altar boy.

Darius slides off the couch with roaring laughter, and I can feel my own bubbling up in my chest.

"Are you serious?" I glare at Santos, his arms still around a panting Pepe.

"Why is your ringtone set to? *Pig slaughter*?!" Santos roars as he releases his arms from around Pepe.

I answer the phone with a chuckle when I see it's Blaze and put it on speaker. "Brother."

"Tell me you all got out with your balls intact."

"Daddy Blaze is very concerned with our balls even though he doesn't care to play with them." Santos explains to Pepe, and I laugh.

"Fuck's sake." Blaze growls, and I lose it again, "will you all be quiet, we have some news. You'll want to pay attention, Santos."

The tone of Blaze's voice has us all sitting up straight, this isn't a check-in. "Go ahead." I tell him once I see we're all listening.

"Santos, we think we've located your sister, her name is Cara. Selene believes she met her here in Nevada when she was on her *solo* mission." We hear a scoff in the background, clearly coming from our girl. "We were going to stop off at the apartment she had here for rental before the lease is up to grab her things, and maybe get a bit more info. I need you guys to be prepared to fly out."

I glance over at Santos and find his face pale, a look of terror coating his eyes. He's only ever looked to us as his family and now he's being bombarded with multiple siblings.

"Okay," I clear my throat, "did everything go okay over there? Did you get the shipment sorted?"

"Yeah, we took out a few bikers from the rival MC to the Dientes. Thanks to Pepe for his intel."

"Pepe is here with us now, looks like we're keeping the little fucker." I snicker.

"Great, maybe he can cleanse Santos' soul." Blaze retorts.

This would be the point where Santos would have a snarky come back, but he's sitting there with his hands in his lap, looking lost. Darius glances up at him, and hauls himself off the floor, shoving Pepe aside to sit by his man. He takes his hand, and Santos finally reacts, looking into Darius' face.

"I need to save my little sister." He whispers.

"Hey, Blaze." I call down to the phone.

"Yeah?"

"I think we're going to hop in the car and start on our way to you. That way we can bring some toys, Santos should be there." I keep my eyes on Santos.

"Sounds good," Blaze consents, "we should have more for you when you get here."

He hangs up the phone, and the room falls silent. Santos is staring down at his and Darius' joined hands, and Pepe is glancing between all of us.

"Let's go pack a few bags." I say as I get up to stretch. "Pepe, since all your stuff was destroyed, you can borrow some of my shit. We'll grab you more clothes on the way."

"Can we leave now?" Santos asks, his face one of complete torture.

I'm so fucking exhausted, my eyes are screaming for sleep, but I won't let him down, "yeah."

"I'll take the first leg so you can get some sleep," Darius says as he passes by me, his hand landing on my shoulder.

"Thanks," my shoulders deflate.

I really wouldn't want us dying because I fell asleep at the wheel, I'm pretty sure all of our fates are sealed to Santos with bullets from his Merry-Go-Round.

Selene

Being in this apartment again feels so surreal. I can't believe it was only a few short weeks ago I was chasing down leads and trying not to kill John Dempster prematurely. Blaze comes striding through the front door, and I scoff, "maybe you should've taken the window," I thumb over my shoulder, "for old time's sake."

He chuckles as he falls onto the couch, "or I can spray cum all over this table again, or better yet, go cut off another dick?"

"Gross." I shudder with a grin. I begin packing up my clothes and toiletries into the one duffle bag. We're waiting for Loqi to get back to us, and then we're going to devise a plan to free Cara. When Blaze told me the rest of my boys were on their way here, I felt immediate relief. I want Santos to have a part in saving his sister.

I go back out to the living room to see Blaze watching one of the three channels I had here. It's the local news station breaking that they found a woman's dead body, she was believed to have been a prostitute.

"What the fuck?" I mutter as I sit on the couch. Thoughts of Aniyah fill my mind with worry. She wasn't at the compound when we were there, and the guys said she left to come back home. Something about being homesick. "I need to go to the bar."

"Good Times." He mutters, and I nod. "Let's go then."

"Wait," I put my hand on his arm, "you can't be seen with me. I'm going to see what I can find out, and no one will talk to me if I'm with you."

"Does my Little Reaper want to go hunting?" He gives me a sly smirk.

"Mmhmm." I smile.

"And she's not going to need her daddy's help?" My thighs immediately clench at the deep tenor of his voice.

"No," I shake my head slowly, "but Daddy can watch."

The bar is filled when I walk in a few hours later, and I spot a frazzled looking Colleen behind the counter. I shove a dude off my stool, and when he turns to fight me on it, I growl in his face. He has the right idea to turn away because I'm ready to stab a cunt.

"It's not nice to be a bully." A girl snickers from beside me.

"This is my seat." I say loudly and grin when Colleen's head snaps around to look at me.

"Selene?" She rushes over and grabs my hand, "thank God you're alright."

"Sorry I haven't checked in; it's been a crazy couple of weeks."

"It's okay, Aniyah filled me in." Colleen smiles as her eyes roam over my face.

"She's been here?" Hope soars in my chest.

"A few days ago, we celebrated the demise of the guys who were taking the girls." She leans in, "but now we have another problem."

"I saw." I nod, "and you haven't heard from Aniyah?"

"No." Worry clouds her eyes, "I'm afraid she's been caught up in something. She was trying to become a caregiver to the girls on the streets, teaching them how to spot trouble. And now I'm afraid she might've found some."

"Tell me everything you know."

"She told me what you are," her eyes widen when she leans in, "I'm so glad you're back."

"Not for long though." I grin when she pours me a whiskey. "I live in New York."

"She said that, too. She looked a little sad about it."

"She had her chance." I shrug. "Now, tell me what the rumblings on the streets are."

"The girl found dead was a veteran on the streets, she knew the ins and outs, and this is screaming more than just a random kill. Her body was found mutilated, riddled with stab wounds."

"Sounds more like a passion killing." I muse.

"Yes. Almost like a scorned woman." She nods.

"Who could've possibly caught her husband straying." I tap my chin, "what else?"

"Aniyah found out who her last few clients were, and I'm worried she's gotten herself in trouble."

"Who were the clients?" I lean forward.

"I don't know," she shakes her head, clearly frustrated with herself, "but I know she found out from a few girls who work the corner." She lists off the street names, and I quickly down my drink, then get up out of my seat.

"Wait, you're going now?"

"The longer I wait, the worse it could be. I'll try to come see you again, Colleen, but with so much going on, I can't promise it. I will send you word that I'm okay though." I reach over the bar and hug my friend, committing her scent to memory. I will miss the fuck out of her.

"Be careful." She says, and I give her a salute as I head out the door.

He's following me, those familiar tingles on the back of my neck alerting me to the fact, and I can't believe I never figured out it was him the whole time. I grin knowing he has my back as I walk down the darkened streets, whistling another nursery rhyme.

"Slow, slow, slow will be your death, I can't wait to hear your screams. Merrily, merrily, merrily, merrily, your blood will make me cream." *Fuck, I really did miss my calling.*

A group of girls are huddled together at the next intersection, and I hurry over to them, not liking the fear I'm sensing. They hear my heels as I approach and slowly break apart, looking at me suspiciously.

"What's happening?" I ask as I come up next to them.

"Who are you?" One of them asks, and I grin at her, happy she has some sense.

"My name is Selene, and I'm a hunter. I like the flesh of men who hurt working girls." I give them a wink. "I'm here to help."

I give them a few moments to absorb my words, and finally one of them says, "we were just approached by a man, he asked us to come back to his hotel room. He said he and his *wife* were looking for a bit of fun."

"What happened?"

"We declined, none of us are interested in playing with a married couple, we know the risks of what could go down if the wife becomes jealous." Another girl pipes in, "he became angry and called us filthy whores."

"Did he say which hotel?" I can feel the excitement creeping up on me. They nod and tell me the name, pointing just further up the street. "Do you three know a woman by the name of Aniyah?"

"She was just here!" The last girl says, "she's headed toward the hotel." She points ahead again, and I sigh with relief.

"Thank you." I give them a nod, "from now on, arm yourselves. Pepper spray, a switchblade, fuck get a Pitbull out here, but don't continue on these streets unarmed."

Once they all give me a nod, I rush by them, and run up the street, hoping to run into Aniyah. I reach the hotel without sight of her and rush inside. There are two women at the desk, and both give me startled looks as I quickly approach.

"Did a woman come in here just now? Purple curly hair and hot as sin?"

"Yes," the first answers, "she just got on the elevator, she's headed to the tenth floor, room ten-fourteen."

"Thank you!" I call out as I run for the elevators. I am going to kill her when I find her. This shit is dangerous, and Aniyah is not trained to take out anyone.

Finally, the elevator door opens with a ding, and I scramble inside, slamming my finger to the number ten over and over until the door closes.

"Come on." I begin to pace as the fucking thing crawls up the floors, and then I curse when it stops not once, but fucking twice before getting to the tenth floor. I squeeze my body out as the doors slowly open and run down the first corridor, hooking a right to another one that brings me to room ten-fourteen.

I stand there, listening for ten seconds, and when I hear nothing, I knock on the door. No footsteps, no noise, nothing. I knock again, a little louder, and my heart rushes up to my throat. "Fuck."

"No room service," a small voice calls out, and I grit my teeth at its familiar tone.

"Aniyah, you Purple Headed People Eater," I snarl, "open this fucking door."

"Selene?" I hear her gasp, and the door opens. She rushes me in a mass of purple curls, and I hold her tight, so fucking glad she's alright.

"What the fuck are you doing here?"

"I could ask you the same thing!" She says excitedly. "I couldn't stay at the MC's compound; I knew I needed to be here and help the girls." She leads me back into the room. "Luckily, I returned when I did. These two," she points to two passed-out people on the bed, "are hunting women and killing them."

It's indeed a woman and a man, and both are snoring loudly. "What's wrong with them?"

"I drugged their drinks." She shrugs. "I found out they were the ones who killed that poor young girl. Stabbed her over a hundred times, all because the husband wanted to fuck other girls, and the wife liked to kill them after." Her eyes tear up, "they're not from around here, they could have hundreds of victims, and no one would care about murdered prostitutes."

"Tell me," I cross my arm over my chest as I look at the passed-out couple, "what were you going to do next?"

"Stuff pillows over their faces." She nods.

Not bad.

"But now you're here," she claps.

"Indeed." I grin.

Blaze

It's been ten minutes since Selene ran into this fucking hotel, and she has yet to contact me or come out. So, it looks like I need to get my ass in there and look for her. I'm going to redden *her* ass later for causing me worry.

I stride inside and see two girls standing at the desk, they each give me frightened looks, unabashedly staring at my scar.

"Blonde chick, just came in ten minutes ago," I tap the counter's surface, "where did she go?"

"Room ten-fourteen," one of them blurts.

"Thanks." I nod and bypass the elevators. This place is old as shit, those elevators are probably like molasses on a winter day.

I take the stairs—three at a time—and reach the tenth floor barely winded. Luckily, where the stairwell is, room ten-fourteen is right across the hallway. I stride across and lift my leg, kicking in the door with one blow. A female screams, and I know it's not mine. I round the corner and find Selene standing beside the purple-haired hooker. Selene is looking at me with a grin as the other one is wrapped around her, clearly terrified.

"I was wondering how long it would take you." Selene grins at me. "You remember Aniyah?"

"Yeah," I decide to let it all out, "she sucked my dick once while I was here watching you. I was pissed you were with these guys, and she was offering."

Aniyah backs away from Selene, clearly scared for her life, and I wait for the shitstorm to begin.

"I figured something happened," Selene waves me off, "you're both lucky I love you or else you'd be bleeding out. Let's not do it again, yeah?"

"Not a chance in Hell." I agree.

"I didn't know he knew you… he was a random…"

"Aniyah," Selene huffs, "I know. It's all good. Anyways, we got it from here," Selene points at the people lying on the bed, drugged out obviously. "You need to go see Colleen and tell her you're alright, she's worried."

"Okay," she nods and walks by us, giving me a wide berth. "Am I going to see you before you go?"

"We'll swing back by the bar." Selene smiles at her, and then the hooker disappears. "I can't believe you stuck my daddy dick down my friend's throat." She shakes her head, "I should cut it off."

"I was missing you," I shrug, "and you were out humping everything."

"I know." She walks up the side of the bed, grabbing the woman's bright orange hair in her fist, "this is the one who killed the girl. Stabbed her over a hundred times."

I whistle and look at the guy, "what about him?"

"He's fucking them and letting his wife take out her anger on them after." She snarls, dropping the frizzy head back to the pillow.

"How do you want to do this?"

"How can we wake them up from such a deep slumber?" She gives me a mischievous look, "I kinda want them awake when I begin the torture."

"I'll grab some ice." I head back out through the door that's hanging off its hinges and find the ice machine on this floor. I fill up a bucket and head back to the room.

I find Selene slapping the guy's face, and his groans sounding as he slowly starts to wake up.

"The bitch isn't responding," she growls, "but this one is."

I head into the bathroom and fill the bucket of ice up with some cold water, making sure it's filled. Then I head back out to the bed and carefully tip it over the woman's face, holding it in place. Finally, she stirs, and then she begins to sputter around the ice and water.

Selene's face becomes radiant with excitement, and my cock hardens, pushing painfully against its confines. I want this done quickly and then I want to fuck the shit out of her. I lift the bucket off the frizzy, orange head, just as the guy opens his eyes, and they widen as he looks between Selene and me.

"What's going on?" He asks groggily.

"I'm the girl you ordered to diddle your little dick while your wife watches, remember?" Selene coos. "Let's see what we have here." She begins to undo his pants while the guy struggles to fully wake up.

"You don't look like a prostitute," the wife tries to sit up and fails, "why am I being drowned?"

I snort at their stupidity, "you passed out on us before the fun began."

Finally, her eyes connect with mine and her mouth drops, "we only deal with women."

"Shame," I begin to undo my pants, "your husband promised me a turn inside your ass."

"What?" The husband begins to understand what's happening, but Selene's fist to his jaw shuts him up.

I pull out my hard cock, giving it a few long, leisurely strokes. Her face pales, and I chuckle as her mouth falls open. "Her husband must be small."

"Let's find out," Selene says excitedly as she yanks his pants open, reaching down inside. He's too afraid to do a single thing, still unsure of what's going on. "Found it!" Selene begins to pull him out and laughs, "he's like a hairless mole rat!"

A strangled laugh leaves my throat as she points down at the man's hard dick, definitely looking like a hairless mole rat.

"Your wife should be the one getting the dick while you watch," Selene tsks. "That's shameful. Now, let's watch her ass get laid with that pipe."

"No," the wife furiously shakes her head, her eyes never leaving my cock.

"Oh, come on!" Selene begs, "if I can take it, you can, too. It only feels like a burrowing beaver digging his way to your bowels for ten minutes, tops!"

I can't help it; I bellow out a laugh as the woman continues to beg me to not touch her.

"Well, you're no fun." Selene pouts then pulls her fancy new knife out of her belt, "I guess I'll have to make my own fun."

She grabs the guy by his hair as I tuck myself back into my pants, and the woman's gaze finally leaves my crotch. He's struggling trying to get out of Selene's grip, but he's still sluggish from the drug. Selene looks up at his wife and tosses her a wink, "I heard you like to get stabby, well, so do I."

Then she quickly begins to stab the guy repeatedly in the neck and throat, the blood spraying all over his wife. She begins to scream when his head starts to come away from the body, and I wrap my hand around her mouth, forcing her to watch as Selene fully decapitates him. *Savage.* If I hadn't decided to keep her yet, I would've done it right in this moment.

"I love you." It flies out of my mouth before I can stop it, and Selene looks up at me with shock, still holding the guy's severed head.

"Really?" She stares at me, her eyes wide.

"Fucking completely, you own me."

She tosses the guy's head into his wife's lap as the wife's muffled screams sound against my palm. "I love you, too, Daddy." Her eyes fill up with tears, "so much."

I pull my hunting knife out of the holster around my waist and slice into the wife's throat, her blood spraying out in a beautiful arc across the bed. I drop her gargling body as Selene crawls up onto the mattress and slowly comes toward me on all fours, "take that pipe back out, I want the beaver burrowing deep."

"Fuck," I groan at her words, my cock once again solid.

She begins to take me out, then slurps me down her throat, her hands full of blood, and her outfit completely saturated. "Let's make sure he's nice and wet."

She spits down my length, thoroughly soaking my cock, and then she flips around, pulling her skirt up over her ass. "Love me, Daddy."

I stare down at her asshole, pink and tight, and I spit down onto it, sticking one, then two fingers deep inside. Her moans are loud, and I'm about to combust just listening to her. I press the head of my cock to her hole, and begin to push in slowly, not wanting to hurt her—this time. But she has other ideas.

"Ram me," she pushes back. "I want to feel it for days."

Fuck.

I pick up the pace, but I'm not fucking ramming her, I love her, I want her holes intact for future pipe laying. Once I bottom out, her pants are loud, and she grabs the dead woman's frizzy, orange hair. "See bitch? That's how it's done."

I plow into her ass, knowing I won't last long, "baby, play with your clit."

"Okay, Daddy." She coos, and I have to stop or else I will fill her ass with cum right now.

She furiously rubs her clit, her hips moving against my cock. Then she surprises me again when she grabs up the husband's bloody head, placing it in front of her on the bed. "Take notes into Hell with you, I expect a show when I arrive." She tells him, and I come so hard into her ass, with her following not too far behind me. I pull out, watching as my cum pools out of her hole and slips down to her pussy. "You're welcome," she tells the head, and seals it with a kiss to its mouth.

Yeah, I found my perfect match.

Santos

I'm a ball of emotions, more than usual, and I know Darius is worried about how I'll react by the way he's glancing at me in the rear-view mirror. Going from no blood family to finding my father and brother really started pushing me over the edge, but now we were off to save a sister, too? I really need a fucking drink.

I sit in the back with Pepe, thinking it will give me some time to brood on everything, but Pepe seems adamant to pull me out of my own head for some reason after being on the road for a while. I guess my pet likes me after all. He doesn't really know what's going on with my family, but he must sense my inner turmoil.

"I'll pray for her," he says firmly, closing his eyes and whispering words under his breath in the quiet car, asking Jesus to look out for my sister and bring her home to me. I want to tease him for it, because I'm not a believer in prayers being answered, but the fact that he wants to, makes me feel warm and fuzzy.

"Thanks," I mumble, surprising Darius with my grown-up approach. He's expecting me to make jokes.

Pepe finishes his prayer and looks over at me with a smile. "It's obvious you care about her."

"I don't even fucking know her," I grunt, but he shrugs casually.

"So? She's still your family. I think it's good you're going to help her. Will you bring her back with you and get to know her?" Good fucking question.

I have no idea what to do when I find her, but a part of me wants to have her in my life. Papi is one thing, but Loqi and Cara are another. They didn't know I existed, so I can't exactly hold a grudge against them. Doesn't mean I'm ready to face the reality that I have a family yet.

"She might hate me. Or run home to Papi Loco. I can't be around him right now. I just can't," I admit, chewing on my bottom lip in thought. If she's a nice girl with a different upbringing, she might be terrified of the man I've become. If it was anyone else, I wouldn't give a shit about their thoughts about me, but the thought of my own sister despising me? It's starting to eat away at me like a flesh-eating poison.

"C'mon, who wouldn't like you and your murderous antics and scary bomb skills?" he laughs dryly, making me snort.

"Normal people?"

"I have a feeling if she shares the same blood as you, she will be anything but normal. Try not to think about it until we get there. Let's play I Spy," he suggests, making Zander scoff from the front passenger seat. His eyes are closed as he tries to nap, but he never misses anything.

"It's dark out."

"So? I spy with my little eye, something beginning with A," Pepe continues, not giving a shit when Zander growls about us being children. I grin, loving the idea of playing some games to pass the time, especially if it annoys Zander.

"A? Alright, let me see," I hum, peering out the window into the darkness around us. I can't see shit, so I turn my attention back to the inside of the car, thinking hard. "Air Conditioner?"

"Nope!" he grins.

"Radio?"

Darius chuckles, not taking his eyes off the road. "That doesn't start with an A, San."

"Who gives a fuck, it has an A in it!" I throw back, making Pepe laugh.

"Keep guessing!"

I frown, deep in thought, trying to think of anything else in the car that starts with A. I like the challenge, and the way Pepe is practically bouncing in his seat tells me it's probably funny.

"You want a clue?" he finally asks, grinning when I nod. "It's grumpy."

"Zander? That doesn't start with A!" I exclaim, but he cracks up laughing, slapping his knee in his excitement.

"No, but asshole does!" he wheezes, and I can't stop the cackle that leaves me. Darius is sniggering, but Zander glares over his shoulder at us.

"Watch it, or our threat to help you meet Jesus early will be added to the calendar."

Pepe's in hysterics, feeding my amusement and causing us both to laugh until our stomachs hurt. The little weirdo has a sense of humor, good to know.

"My turn! I spy with my little eye, something beginning with W!" I grin.

"Window."

"God-fucking-dammit!" I snap. "How did you guess that so fast? You cheated!"

"How do you cheat at I Spy?" Zander groans, but Darius snorts.

"He can't cheat, babe. Do another one."

I give Pepe the evil-eye, trying to think of something harder. "Fine. Something beginning with C."

"Car?"

"No."

"Chassis?"

"You can't see that from inside the car!" I growl. "C is for *cheater*. Because you cheated!"

Darius and Pepe burst out laughing, and Zander jumps, glaring at us again. "Can you play the fucking silent game or something? I need some sleep, or I won't be held accountable for my actions when I lose my shit."

"What's the silent game?" I frown, his voice lowering with annoyance.

"It's when you all shut the fuck up and see who can go the longest without making a sound. It's my favorite fucking game in existence."

"That sounds boring. How will I irritate you if I'm quiet?" I question, making him growl and turn around to face the front, shuffling down in his seat to try and block us out.

"Hey! I have something fun to do!" Darius announces, drawing my attention. "Let's do car karaoke!"

Zander lets out a loud groan, cursing out Darius and his first-born child, but I sit up straight with glee. "Yes! Put on Zander's favorite song and we can sing along. What Does the Fox Say by Ylvis!"

"I fucking hate that song!" he barks, but Darius ignores him and finds the song, putting it up nice and loud.

"Sorry, can't hear you!" he says, giving me a wink in the mirror.

Despite the murderous glare from Zander, I think I sing it perfectly well. Pepe seems impressed, anyway.

Darius

We pull into a hotel for a night and finally let Zander sleep, knowing he needs to rest. I felt like an ass for torturing him with terrible songs and games most of the trip, so he deserved his nap. Pepe had fallen asleep too, leaving Santos to stare at him as if trying to figure him out.

But today is a new day, and Zander is driving while Pepe and Santos watch YouTube videos on Santos' phone. I barely slept last night, worrying about Santos and how he'll react when he meets yet another one of his siblings.

I must've passed out because I'm awakened by Zander giving me a shake, "you've been out for twelve hours. Think you're good to drive?"

I sit up and quickly look into the backseat, empty fast-food bags are scattered, and Pepe is sleeping, Santos though is not. He's looking out his window with a forlorn expression on his face.

"We have about ten more hours of driving," Zander says, "I just need a few hours and then I can take over for the last bit."

"No problem." I nod.

"We got you some food," he points to the bag at my feet, "it's probably cold but we didn't want to wake you."

"Thanks," I give him a smile.

We switch seats, and I pull back out onto the road, snorting when Zander falls into a deep sleep almost at once. Santos falls asleep next, and I let out a breath of relief, he needs to rest.

Eight hours later, and both Zander and Pepe are still out, but Santos stirs awake.

"You good?" I ask, feeling grateful to Pepe for cheering him up so much. The last thing we need is Santos having an emotional melt down inside the small car space.

He glances up at me in the rear-view mirror, a frown on his face. "I don't know."

"You want to talk about it?"

"I don't know how I'm supposed to feel," he admits quietly.

"There's no wrong way to handle it. You're confused, which is okay. Are you prepared to see Papi and Loqi again? Loqi seems nice," I state, remembering the similarities between them.

"I don't like dealing with Loqi because of Papi. I'm not mad at Loqi, just confused by it all. I want to get to know him and my sister, I think. What if they hate me?"

His voice is tight, telling me he's starting to freak out a little. I sigh, reaching back to rub my hand on his leg. "They won't hate you. Loqi and you are similar. He's crazy, loves the chase as much as you do, and he's been blindsided like you about all of this. If you can get to know him without Papi Loco around, I think you two would hit it off."

"I always wanted a brother," he murmurs. "I know I have you guys, but as a kid, all I wanted was someone to play with. And my sister? What if she's nothing like us? What if…"

"Relax. For all you know, Cara is as crazy as you two. If you want to stick around and get to know them, I'll stay with you. If you need more time, we can come back another day," I promise, his eyes filling with defeat.

"Yeah?"

"Yeah, San. I've got you. Pepe seems fun," I smile, changing the subject. Santos' face lights up and he grins.

"I like him. He's funny."

I chuckle. "Yeah, he's alright. Selene and Blaze will scare him to death if he sticks around."

He gives me a horrified look. "What do you mean *if he sticks around*? I'm not letting him go anywhere." Didn't think he would.

"You know what I mean. I'm glad you've made a new friend."

"He's my best friend," he declares, scowling as if I'm insulting him.

"What about me?" I fake pout. "I thought I was your best friend?"

"You don't count. You got promoted to boyfriend. Best friends don't usually enjoy each other's dicks in their asses," he grins. "And I *really* like yours."

"I love hearing that," I smile, making him laugh.

"What? That I love your dick in my ass?"

"That too, but I like being called your boyfriend," I shrug, starting to feel like a little bitch. If Santos grins any wider, his face will crack.

"I like hearing it, too. Never thought I'd have a girlfriend or a boyfriend, let alone both. I can't wait to cut you both again. I want a big S on your chest like mine." He's such a romantic sometimes.

"You want some good news?" I ask lightly as I pull over. "We're here."

His eyes widen as he glances outside into the dark, the sun starting to rise in the distance. "Our girl's here?"

"Yep. I think…" I don't get to finish my sentence before he places his hands on the window and smacks his head against the glass in his excitement, trying to catch a glimpse of our blood queen. I chuckle, leaning over to shake Zander awake. "Brother, we're here."

"You drove the whole way?" he mumbles half asleep, sitting up properly to glance around. "You were supposed to let me drive halfway."

"Yeah, but you needed the sleep. We kept you awake half the drive, so it was only fair," I reply, and he doesn't disagree with me.

We climb from the car and head toward the apartment, and the moment the door swings open, Santos barrels past Blaze and almost knocks Selene over with a hug. Pepe hangs back, unsure of our crazy girl and the big brute blocking the doorway.

"What's Bible boy doing here?" Blaze grunts, looking the man up and down with a frown. I go to speak, but Santos darts over and drops his arm around Pepe's shoulders.

"Leave my bestie alone! Pipi is staying with us!"

"It's Pepe," Pepe says dryly, making Santos grin.

"Yeah, I know."

Zander's hugging Selene tight, kissing the top of her head and whispering something dirty in her ear, no doubt. The nap must have done him some good.

"What do you mean, he's staying?" Blaze growls, not impressed by the decision.

Santos huffs, hating to explain himself. "He's staying with us permanently. He's my best friend and I don't care what you say. My pet stays with me."

"You banging him too?"

"Bite your tongue," I scowl, glaring at Pepe as if it were his fault. "Santos is mine."

"Ours," Selene teases, coming over to stand in front of me, wrapping her arms around my middle. "Missed you guys."

"Missed you, too. Pepe played games with Santos the entire drive," I smile, knowing Selene will soften at knowing he cares for Santos. She smiles brightly, bouncing on the balls of her feet.

"What games did you play?"

Zander snorts, firing off everything that's happened since we left the house. When he gets to car karaoke, she squeals loudly. "Oh my god! You played that without me?!"

"Sweetheart, no offense, but your voice is too much for that small car," Zander cringes, and she blows him a kiss.

"I guess you're right. It's too good for a car ride. Maybe I should see if a record label wants me?"

The look of horror on Blaze and Zander's faces are hysterical, and I can't help but laugh. "Yeah, babe. I have a feeling you'd be too big of a star for them, too. I think you should stick to murder and bouncing on our dicks with that tight pussy of yours."

"You're right. It would be hard to calendar all that in while on tour. I guess we'll never know if it was meant to be," she sighs, turning to Pepe and crossing her arms. "So, what are your intentions with my man?"

I think we're in for a long fucking day.

Chapter Eight

Zander

I can feel the tension wafting off Santos as he paces the small apartment. We have the phone on the table in front of us, and Papi Loco is telling us what they've found out about Cara.

"She's being held in a small police station because she's only nineteen. They don't have enough evidence to convict her, but she also refuses to tell them who her family is. Our guy who works there can't be sure if she's *our* Cara, and I can't see why she wouldn't say who her family was if it even is her."

"Maybe she's forgotten?" Blaze asks as he leans forward.

"She was taken when she was twelve, it's only been seven years," Loqi pipes up, "she would remember us."

Selene tosses me a look from across the table and I can read it loud and clear, maybe she doesn't want to remember.

"We're gunning down the place tomorrow night, we're thinking around two in the morning. They have a guard shift change at one and then there's only two cops in the building until six." Papi continues, "gives us enough time to pump the place full of bullets and get her out."

"Yeah, sounds good." Blaze cuts in, "we'll meet you there." Then he abruptly ends the call and looks at all of us. "There's no need to pump the place full of bullets, two cops?" he scoffs as he leans back.

"I think we need to get to her before they do," Selene chimes in, "she'll recognize me and if she's Santos' sister, there may be a reason she's not giving them Papi's information."

"Do you think my father hurt her?" Santos' voice is deadly calm, and I can see the vein in his neck pulsing.

"I'm not sure, but there has to be a reason she doesn't want them to know where or who she is." Selene stands and walks over to Santos. "We'll get to her first. Let's make our own plans and then we'll go from there."

Santos drags her in for a hug, but I can see the stiff tension all over his body, he's still struggling with accepting his blood family. Even so, I know he would never want to put his little sister back into harm's way.

"Is this really a good idea?" I'm whining like a bitch because I left the planning up to the others and I'm questioning every bit of it.

"I'm a hooker, Zan!" Selene exclaims, "it's going to work perfectly."

We're sitting outside of the small police station, waiting to see if the shift change will happen as Papi said, and then we're heading in there ourselves, an hour before the Dientes arrive. I'm not feeling comfortable going against the MC, they could take us out in one fell swoop, regardless of Santos' blood relation. It's not like Papi actually cares about him.

"You're worried about retaliation." Blaze states.

"Obviously!" I throw my hands up, "they have their way of dealing with shit! Why are we getting in their way? We're just asking to have ourselves executed in the fucking desert at this point."

"If she's my little sister," Santos finally pipes up, "I will go in and get her myself. Maybe she'll hate me for it, but I think Selene is right, she's holding back information for a reason."

It's the most sensible I've heard him in a while, and I turn my head to look at him in the backseat. He's been quiet and inside his head, so unlike the man I'm used to. Usually, he acts out in violent outbursts when his emotions overflow.

"I think you should be the first one she sees." Selene agrees.

"I'll come with you." Blaze adds, and we all look at him with a bit of shock.

Santos nods and I look to see Darius' reaction, he looks a bit relieved. "You and I will cover the front, with our new friend Pepe watching the car." I nod at Darius.

About ten minutes later, two new cops pull up, and head inside, just like Papi said. Then in the next five minutes, three cops leave to go home. Looks like the shift change is complete.

"And the new cops were men!" Selene squeals, "it's like it was meant to be."

"What if they're gay?" Blaze asks her, his mouth tipping up into a grin.

"Then you would have to take one for the team." Selene fires back.

"The fuck I would," he growls as he gets out of the car.

"Santos," Pepe says, "I will pray for you and the safe retrieval of your sister. God will be watching you tonight."

"Hopefully, not all night." Selene cackles, and I can't stop the grin on my mouth.

"Thank you, Pepe." Santos says as he gets out of the car next.

"Is he okay?" I ask Darius, "I'm waiting for the explosion."

"I think he's nervous." Darius mutters and gets out of the car.

"Pepe, as soon as you see us coming for the car, you start it up and move to the backseat, got it?" Pepe nods, his eyes wide. "If you see any other cop cars coming up the street, you text me or Darius."

He nods again, and I get out of the car, following Darius to the front of the station where Santos and Blaze are leaning against the wall, their heads pulled together in quiet conversation. I watch as Selene fluffs her long, blonde hair, the ends touching just above her ass, and she yanks down on the leather mini she's wearing. Her legs go on for fucking days, and her strappy heeled shoes are hot. I'm going to ask her to leave those on later.

"Let's go give these cops a good time." Selene claps her hands.

"If you even think of opening your fucking legs to them, there will be mayhem, Reaper." Blaze growls, and Selene tips her head back and laughs. Not at all affected by him.

"He's saying that because he loves me," She coos and blows him a kiss.

I look at my boy with shock, "did you tell her?"

"She decapitated this dude, and she was covered in blood, you'd have said it too." He crosses his arms over his chest.

Fucking right I would.

Selene

I haul open the doors of the station, and saunter inside. Two cops sit with coffee cups and a box of pastries, both looking at me suspiciously. I look every bit of the hooker tonight, and I am fucking hot. I stride up to the desk they're sitting at and hold out my wrists.

"I've been a naughty girl, y'all need to cuff me."

"Pardon?" His name tag says *Duey*.

"Yes, Deputy Duey. I have been sucking and fucking cocks all night, and I can't take another moment of it. I'm tired and I need a bed, this was the first place I thought of."

"Are you turning yourself in for prostitution?" The second one asks; his name is Darryl.

"Yes, Darryl. I need you two to lock me up because if I go anywhere else, cocks will sniff me out like Bloodhounds."

They both give me a slow perusal and then look at each other.

"Don't even think about cavity searching me, my pussy allure will have you both chewing at the bit, and like I said, I'm too tired. Double penetration just cannot not happen tonight, D-Squared."

Deputy Duey stands abruptly from his seat, grabbing the cuffs from his belt, and opening them. His face is one of incredulity and he gives a startled look to his partner.

"Darryl, is this not the oddest shit to happen here?"

"Indeed," but Darryl isn't looking at his partner, no, his eyes are still all over my body. I can work with that.

"Darryl, is it?" I shimmy my ass onto his desk, scattering papers to the floor. "I think you're cute, want to share a cell? I don't think Deputy Duey would mind."

"Are you soliciting an officer for sex?" Duey astonishes from behind me.

I look at him over my shoulder, "why? Would that get me in more trouble?"

"You're darn right it would!" Duey sputters, red-faced, and shocked.

"Well then, yes." I turn back to Darryl with a wink, "I think I am."

"That'll get you processed and in the cell for at least a night," Darryl winks right back.

"Processed?" My mouth curls up further, "are you teasing me with a good time?" Duey slaps a cuff to my right wrist, and I squeal, "I love a good pair of shackles. I have a set at home."

"I don't think she needs to be cuffed," Darryl snickers, "she brought herself here, after all. We do need to bring you to the processing room, though."

Darryl stands and motions for me to follow him as Duey removes the cuff. I walk behind Darryl, and Duey takes up my rear, as they lead me into a back corridor and then into a room with a single table.

"Take a seat," Darryl says. "We're going to need to ask you a few questions."

I sit down, Darryl sits across from me and Duey to my right, this couldn't have worked out any more perfectly. Duey still has the fucking cuffs in his hands, so fucking eager to see me shackled, I get it, it's hot.

Just as he sits his ass to the chair, I reach over the table and slam his face down into the hard metal surface. I hear a crunch, and before Darryl can react, my knife is out of my belt and pressed to his throat.

"Silly pigs," I snicker, "did you think you were safe against a little girl?"

The cuffs are laying on the table, abandoned by Duey as he moans over his broken nose. I grab them with my free hand, and secure it around Darryl's wrist, looping it underneath the large metal pole down the center of the table.

"Give me your gun," I hold out my hand, when he doesn't move, I press the tip of my blade into his throat and watch as a bead of blood pools out. "The gun."

This time he does as he's told, and I take it from his outstretched arm, tucking it into my belt. "Good boy. Look I'm not here to kill you, we're just springing someone free." I give him a saccharine smile, "Cooperate and you'll be just fine."

He settles into his seat with a shrug, and I grab the other side of the cuffs, hauling him into the table. I grab one of Duey's wrists and secure them together. Now they're trapped at the table underneath the pole. They can move from side to side, but they can't get up at all.

"There we go," I fire off a text to Blaze. "Now, what do y'all wanna do for the next ten minutes? I know a few good nursery rhymes."

Blaze

"She's got them occupied." I say to the others as I open the front door, "she says the keys for the cells are hung on a corkboard."

Santos is following quietly behind me, his nervous energy clogging the air around us. I'm not going to bug him about it or question him, this can't be easy. Besides, we need to be in and out before other cops or the MC show up.

I find the keys easily enough and I head down a corridor that I hope leads to the cells.

"Do you hear that?" I stop at the sound of screeching.

"That's our angel," Santos chirps in, "she's singing somewhere in here."

"Jesus," I mutter and keep going down the hall, "she'll kill those cops, make them deaf at the very least."

Santos hums along to whatever it is she's singing, I don't know how he can even decipher it, and we turn into a large space, occupied with three different cells. Two appear empty while one has a small form curled up on the thin, narrow bed.

"Cara?" I call out, and a dark head pops up from the pillow. "Is your name Cara?"

She turns on the bed and sits up, her face obscured by her messy, matted hair. But even from here, I can see the resemblance in her face to Santos, and there's no doubt in my mind, she's his sister.

"Who are you?" She calls out.

"My name is Blaze-"

"I'm your brother," Santos steps forward, quickly coming out of his stupor when he sees her, "my name is Santos."

"I don't have a brother named Santos," she shakes her head, confusion heavy in her deep, brown eyes. Eyes so similar to her brother's standing next to me.

"That's because our dick-of-a father left me and my mom when I was young."

Her eyes narrow as she looks him over closely, standing from the bed and coming closer to the bars. "You have Papi's eyes." She says quietly.

"So do you." Santos nods. "And Loqi, too."

"I don't want to go back with Papi and Loqi." She whispers, and I come up closer to her.

"Why not?"

"They sold me." Her mouth begins to tremble. "The man they sold me to told me. I was sold because Papi never wanted a little girl."

"If that were true," I say softly, "they wouldn't have been trying so hard to find you."

"Regardless," Santos growls. "They failed to take care of her."

"You're really my brother?" Her hand wraps around a bar.

Santos wraps his hand around hers and swallows, "yeah, let's get you out of here, and if you don't want to go back with those assholes, you can come with me."

"Really?" Her eyes brighten, and I swallow my groan. Another one in the fucking house. My home is turning into a zoo of strays.

I unlock the door and open it; the young girl flies out and into Santos' arms. Too trusting, that's what probably got her into this mess to begin with.

"Let's get out of here." I tell them and lead them out the way we came in.

Selene meets us in the hallway, and when Cara lays eyes on her she gasps, "you're the prostitute who killed Eugene!"

"Sorry you got in shit for that," Selene grimaces, "I did tell you to run."

"I know," Cara huffs, "but I was looking for more money. I knew that hairy dog had more stashed around the place!"

"I wish I knew who you were then," Selene shrugs, "maybe I could've helped more."

"It's okay," Cara waves her off and slips under her brother's arm, "I am starving, and I need a shower. How did you guys get me out?"

"Sounded like our girl here sang the guards into a deep sleep with her lullabies." Santos says.

"You heard me?" Selene's eyes brighten, and I grumble as I brush by them. I don't want to be here in case she starts off again.

"You sounded like an angel." Santos tells her.

"Is this your wife?" I hear Cara ask, but they're silenced when we all hear the sound of rumbling bikes.

"Fuck," I growl, and head out the door.

I see about four bikes pull up and Papi is at the head, Loqi to his right. They kick down their stands and take off their helmets.

"Why are you coming out of the fucking station?" Papi bellows.

"Watch your fucking mouth, old man, before I fill it with my fucking knife." I stride forward. Guns are cocked and aimed at me, but I don't give a fuck. I know how this cunt treats his oldest son, and I won't hesitate to take him out, even if I go down in the process.

Loqi holds up his hand, "stop. What happened? Did you guys get Cara?"

"Yeah, she's inside with her *brother*. She has quite the story about her father and brother *selling* her."

"What?!" Papi jumps off his bike and rushes me until we are standing toe to toe and nose to nose. "Move aside, asshole. I want my daughter."

My hand itches to grab my knife and stab it through his eye, but I stay still, letting his hot breath hit my mouth. I don't move my eyes from his, I don't back down.

"Aw, look Cara, big, bad boys are out here fighting," Selene's voice hits my back, "all we need is a pool of mud and some popcorn."

Papi looks over my shoulder, and his body softens when he sees his daughter, "Cara." His voice cracks and I can hear the genuine emotion. Judging by his reaction alone, I don't think he sold his own daughter, but that'll be up to him to convince her.

"Cara!" Loqi jumps off his bike. "It's really you."

I step aside so Cara can have a clear view of her father, if she wants to go to him, who are we to stand in her way? Cara looks between the two of them, her brother and father, and when Loqi begins to get closer to her, she holds up her hand.

"No." She says firmly, "I don't want to go back with you guys."

"What?" Loqi lets out a strangled sound as Papi scoffs.

"You can't mean that."

"I do, you both sold me!" She screams as Santos' arms wrap around her.

"No, baby," Papi shakes his head, "we would never."

"How did it happen?" Cara cries out, "how did I end up here? And you're only here seven years later? SEVEN!"

"Come back to the compound where we can check you out," Papi's voice is pained.

"I'll only go if Santos goes." Her little body curls into Santos' side, and I watch as my brother glares down at his father.

"She needs medical attention." Papi says, trying to convince Santos. "I know I treated you terribly, and we have time to figure that out, but we have to do what's best for her."

"Just to get checked out, then we're leaving." Santos snarls.

"Cara," Loqi stands beside his father, "please rethink this. You should be home with your family."

"Santos is my family." She says and looks up at her brother, "Can I ride with you? I never want to be on a motorcycle again."

"Yeah," Santos says as he leads her to the car.

"We'll come to your fucking compound, your fucking doctor can check her out, but when it's time for us to leave, you will let us." I grit out to both Papi and Loqi, "if either of you try anything, I'll blow your shit to the fucking sky."

"Kaboom." Selene whispers, her hands spreading out over her head.

I watch as Zander, Selene, and Darius walk back to the car and I turn to look at the men next to me, "don't start a war you can't win."

Santos

I'm going to kill someone, many someones, if Cara's out of my sight much longer. She reluctantly let me go to get checked out, and the look of confusion and betrayal on her face is eating me alive. If Papi and Loqi had sold her like she claims, I'll kill them.

"Breathe," Darius murmurs beside me as I lean against the bar in the MC's compound, his fingers brushing my arm lightly to relax me. I meet his eyes and nod, but my jaw is so tight, it's starting to hurt from clenching my teeth. I know I haven't known Cara for more than five-fucking-minutes, but the need to protect her is waging a war inside me, the confusion from earlier being completely taken over by pure rage.

"You look like you need a beer or six," Licker chuckles as he moves up to us on the other side of the bar, not waiting for a response before pushing two beers in our direction. Selene is talking to her sister, Zander and Blaze standing close by in case she explodes. Selene isn't smiling, but she isn't stabbing her either, so that's good.

"Thanks, Licker. How have you been?" Darius asks lightly, not taking his eyes off me. Giving me alcohol while my emotions are so messy probably isn't the best idea. I don't need to get on the bar and reenact my pirate incident from last time I lost the plot. I doubt we'll get out alive, but fucking hell, it's tempting.

Licker doesn't seem fazed by my grumpy attitude; he simply leans on the bar and grins at us. "I've been good. Maybe you should take your man into the bathroom and fuck that look right off his face. Man's going to chip a fucking tooth soon." He isn't wrong. My teeth are aching, but I grind down on them harder, giving him a dirty look.

"Mind your business."

"Oh, testy today, Santos? C'mon, I'm just playing with you. Drink your beer. Cara won't be long," he states with a softer smile. "She's stronger than she looks."

"Of course, she's fucking strong! Who wouldn't be after that piece of shit…" Darius slaps a hand over my mouth, his other hand resting on my waist and giving it a firm squeeze.

"Let's go sit down, hmm? Thanks for the beer, Licker," he says before letting me go to grab our drinks, leading me toward a table in the back. I sit down heavily, glaring at him as he sits beside me.

"I want to kill him. He…"

"I know. If Papi did do it, I'm one hundred percent starting a war by your side. We can't take on the entire MC without facts though, alright? I'm channeling my inner Zander right now. We need to do this with a clear head," he cuts in with a low voice, running his hand along my thigh and leaving it there. "I promise. Whoever hurt her will fucking pay."

That eases some of my anger, and by the time Zander and Blaze join us, I'm not so fucking murderous. Still a little stabby, but I'm less likely to go for a main artery.

"You two behaving?" Blaze grunts as he sits opposite me.

"Always," I snort. "Selene and Jan okay?"

Blaze glances at them as they chat away, now at the bar with drinks in their hands. Selene has the tiniest smile on her face, and it settles me to know she's starting to let her sister in. I'm jealous she can forgive her already, wondering if I could ever be the same way with Loqi. Especially because it isn't exactly his fault our father is a piece of shit.

"They're talking about knives, so she's in her element. Figured it was safe to give them some space," he shrugs. Zander looks at me seriously, concern swimming in his eyes.

"We're more worried about you. You look ready to gun the place down, and we can't afford…"

"I know, Zan. I'm cooling down, don't worry," I scowl, placing my hand on Darius' under the table, linking our fingers and giving it a gentle squeeze. I need his comfort and calming words, otherwise I'm likely to detonate and take everyone else with me.

He squeezes back, not giving a shit as he leans closer and presses a kiss to my shoulder. "Yeah. We were just talking about playing this smart."

"Well, fuck my ass and call me Susan, you two are learning," Zander deadpans. "It's about fucking time."

I'm way too tired and emotional for his teasing, so I keep my mouth shut and glare at him, ignoring his chuckle.

We sip our drinks silently for a while, but I bristle when Papi Loco joins us, his eyes firmly on me. "We need to talk, boy."

"You need to turn your ass around and leave me alone," I snap. "I have nothing to fucking say to you."

"Hear me out. I'm an asshole, I get it. We need to talk, and I'll drag you if I have to," he grunts, causing Darius to tense beside me.

"You can try, old man. I'll flatten you," I bite back, but I stand and shuffle past Darius, not wanting a brawl to break out. We're severely outnumbered in here, I'm not completely stupid.

He smirks, almost looking proud of my answer as he motions for me to follow him, and Darius grabs my hand, giving me an unsure look. "You want me to come, too?"

Papi Loco mutters something about us being pansies, but I give Darius a tight smile. "I'm good. This won't take long. Then we can grab Cara and get the fuck out of here."

I follow Papi into his office, not bothering to sit. I don't want him to think I'm going to sit around, chatting for hours. He gives me a look, but he doesn't say anything as he sits behind his desk, eyeing me seriously.

"You're not taking Cara with you. She belongs here with her family."

I clench my jaw, glaring at him. "She doesn't want to be anywhere near you, asshole. Besides, I am her fucking family."

"She doesn't even know you."

"Who's fucking fault is that, *Papi*?" I snarl. "You running off and abandoning me was one thing, but not letting me know I had a brother or a sister? That's another. How does it feel to know two out of three of your kids hate you right now? I'm glad you left because you're the worst father anyone could ask for."

His palms slam down on the desk in front of him, his eyes blazing with anger. "Don't fucking speak to me like that!"

"Why not? You don't deserve my respect!" I shout. "You fucking abandoned me! You sold your own fucking daughter! You…"

"I didn't fucking sell her! I love that girl more than you could ever know!" he bellows, and he's lucky I don't stab his stupid fucking face.

"Of course, I don't know how you could love your own kid. You never loved me, so why would I know any different? If she says you sold her, then I believe her. It's about time someone stood by her side."

He glowers at me for a moment before calming himself, sudden sadness washing over him. "Cara was—still is—my baby girl. We have spent years looking for her. Whatever she's been told is a lie. We've spent our lives saving women from the clutches of that kind of evil, so why the *fuck* would I do it to my own daughter? My own flesh and blood?" he asks firmly, waiting for me to respond. He has a point, not that I admit it. They seem adamant to protect women from slavery and the sex trafficking ring, so it doesn't make sense to do it to his own kid.

If he did, I doubt Loqi was involved. I saw the relief on his face when we walked out of the station with Cara. No one can fake that kind of happiness. Well, maybe Papi could, but Loqi has been genuinely worried about her.

When I stay quiet, Papi stands, moving across the room to stand in front of me. "I know you won't believe a single thing that comes out of my mouth, but I'd never hurt Cara like that. I was devastated when she vanished. Loqi and I have been trying to find her from the moment it happened. You don't have to like me, hell, I don't blame you if you don't, but I swear to you someone else took my baby girl and sold her."

"Until Cara says otherwise, I'm not changing my opinion on it. Right now, she's the only family I care about. The only blood family who exists to me. You'll be smart to drop it. Let me go to her before I lose my shit, and your men find you splattered from one wall to the other," I hiss in a low voice, his eyes narrowing.

"You're too much like your Papi, Santos."

"When you find him, tell him I said *hey,*" I snark, turning on my heel and leaving the room, just as Cara walks out of one of the back rooms. She practically runs toward me, throwing her arms around me and clinging on as if I'm the only person alive who can keep her safe.

I hug her tight, keeping an arm around her as we walk toward where Darius and the others are all sitting, relief obvious on Darius' face to see me in one piece.

I sit down, putting Cara between Darius and I to keep her protected from both sides, and she gives me an appreciative smile. "So. You want to explain why I didn't know you existed? The resemblance between you and Loqi is kinda freaky."

"Like I said, Papi's a piece of shit and bailed on me and Ma when I was a kid. Didn't see him again until we got caught up in the sex trafficking shit."

Her eyes go wide in horror, and I rush to correct her thoughts. "Shit, not like that. Selene has been looking for her sister for years. She followed a trail out here, and when we got called out to join her, we found her sister."

"Where is she?" she asks softly, making me scowl. Selene, on the other hand, joins us with a teasing smile on her face, telling me she's about to be rude.

"Under Papi. Turns out, my sister likes old man dick." Jesus Christ.

"Where's Pepe?" My eyes widen as I fly to my feet.

Blaze rolls his eyes and motions toward the bar. "He's fine. He's been talking to Licker for the past ten minutes. He's been hiding in the car like a little bitch since we got here, though."

Cara's watching me with confusion, her brows pulling down. "Who's Pepe?"

"The guy who prayed for you all day and night, then again when we got you in the car," Zander snorts.

"The weird guy who kept mumbling under his breath the entire trip?"

"He's not weird!" I growl. "Leave my pet alone, Zan. I'll fight you."

"Shaking in my boots, brother," he chuckles. "I suppose the little Bible boy isn't that bad."

Darius grins, reaching over Cara to grab my hand and tug me back into the seat. "No one's going to hurt him, babe. You really need to work on your breathing exercises. It can't be healthy to be so high strung all the time."

Cara's eyebrows almost fly off her face when I blow him a kiss. "Yes, baby cakes. You're right. Want to help me with that later? I find I focus a lot better when you're naked though."

"Yeah, on this dick," he grins, sitting back in his seat, narrowing his eyes on Cara who's appearing stunned. "What? You have a problem with queers like your Papi?"

"Wait, what? No! You two are together? Aren't you with the crazy blonde lady?" she sputters as she turns to me. I chuckle nervously, suddenly feeling terrified of her hating me.

"Uh, yeah. I'm with both of them, and all four of us are with Selene."

"That's so fucking cool!" she exclaims, jumping up and down in her seat, all anxiety seeping out of me as a smile hits my face.

"Yeah?"

"I would love to find someone after everything I've been through. I will say, I was luckier than most. I wasn't a sex slave, and I've remained, you know," she leans in, "untouched, Mr. Haynes just liked to see me strip every now and then, but the other girls," Her face grows sad, "they had to do things."

After knowing what she's been through, I don't want another man touching my sister. She will remain pure until the day she dies, and then we'll bury her with the nuns at the cathedral in New York.

As if sensing my thoughts, she groans. "Not you too! Papi and Loqi always said I couldn't have a boyfriend!"

"That's because men suck," I reply tightly, her eyes narrowing to slits and looking a hell of a lot like Papi.

"You're dating a man."

Darius chuckles, amusement filling his eyes. "Yeah, and trust me, I suck real good."

Everyone bursts out laughing, but Cara gives me a dirty look.

"You're lucky I like you already, or you'd get a fork to the eye, and I'd yank it right out of your socket to make you choke on it."

Well, what do you know? Turns out she is just like Loqi and me, after all. The rest of my panic melts away after that, knowing I have nothing to worry about.

Darius

Watching Santos and Cara is awesome. They tease each other relentlessly, and by the time Pepe joins us—apparently deciding Licker is too scary to keep as company—Santos makes him sit down and tells him all about his cool sister. It's kind of cute if I'm being honest. He looks so fucking happy.

Pepe keeps glancing at Cara, not sure about her as she discusses how long they can torture a person before they die, and I have to bite back a grin. It's hilarious. Even Blaze seems to be amused by the whole thing.

Loqi wanders over, looking lost, his eyes on his sister. "Cara? Can…"

"No. Fuck off," she hisses. "I'm not talking to you. You and Papi sold me to those pieces of shit. They told me so. I hate you."

Pain fills his eyes as his shoulders droop, but surprise takes over his face when Santos points to the chair close by. "Don't stand around. Sit down or fuck off."

Cara looks ready to protest, but Santos drops a protective arm around her shoulders, his voice gentle. "Let him sit. I don't think he had anything to do with it. Papi can go fuck himself though." That surprises the rest of us. Santos must have done some fucking deep soul searching to come to that conclusion and be okay with Loqi's presence.

Loqi grabs the chair and drags it closer, sitting without a word, not wanting to be sent away. Selene starts a conversation with him about the sex trafficking ring and how we're going to deal with it, and after a while the two of them are deep in discussion, easing the tension around the table. Zander gives me a *what the fuck* look, but I shrug. If Santos is giving Loqi an olive branch, I'll roll with it. It has to be better than the alternative of them killing each other.

After a while, we're all talking about it, and Cara is loudly voicing her opinion on the situation, causing both Loqi and Santos to fume at the thought of their sister going through anything like that. I keep my eye on Loqi, trying to catch even the smallest sign his love for her is full of shit, but I find nothing. He's pissed that she'd been taken, and we can all see what it means to him to have her back. Speaking of which.

"So, when do you guys want to head out?" I ask, and Loqi's eyes dart to mine.

"You're going to leave already?"

I shrug, but Selene sighs. "Yeah, we have shit to do. Besides, Santos doesn't need to be around Papi any longer than necessary. It's asking for trouble we don't need right now."

Loqi's eyes go to Cara next, pleading silently for her to stay, but she curls up against Santos and smiles sweetly at Selene. "I can't wait to see where you all live. Do you have a big house? Do you all share a bed? Oh, ew! Am I going to hear you fucking all the time? Please tell me I have my own room!"

Selene sniggers. "You'll probably see it if you aren't careful. We like to walk around naked, just a heads up."

Cara fakes a gag, but I chuckle lightly. "Don't worry. You can have my room. I usually bunk in with Santos anyway. That way, you get your own space, and your eyes won't burn from the debauchery."

Santos' eyes soften, and he gives me a smile, grateful I've accepted his sister so fast. Of course I have, it's his sister. I'll do anything for him, so she gets the same treatment by default. She's my family now too, whether she knows it or not.

She turns and hugs me, surprising the shit out of me. "Thank you. I'm sure it's nice, but I really don't want to see your poo covered peen after it's been in my brother. I'm fucked up, but that's crossing a line."

Zander chokes on the drink he's sipping, and Blaze scowls. "Great, just what I need. Another one of you."

Selene giggles, reaching across the table and taking Cara's hand in an unusual show of acceptance. "It might be cool to have a girl around. Do you like knife throwing? I have targets set up at home for practice. Maybe we could find some moving targets and have a girl's day?"

Cara moans. Literally moans at the thought of throwing knives at a human being.

"Can you ditch these guys and be my girl instead? You're kind of perfect, even if you're a little scary."

Selene cackles, giving Blaze a wink over her shoulder. "Hear that? You guys are fired."

"Like fuck, you cheeky wench. Speak like that again and I'll spank you until you remember who owns you," he growls, her eyes filling with heat.

"Yes, Daddy." Good lord. Why does that make my dick hard when it isn't even aimed at me?

Cara laughs, but it dies down when Papi approaches, a no-nonsense look on his face.

"I don't want you leaving the compound. You belong here. We've looked for you for years, Cara. We…"

"I don't want to hear it. I'm leaving with Santos, and that's final. You can't make me stay, I dare you to try," she spits, looking ready to lunge over Santos and claw her dad's eyes out.

Pepe's eyes are wide, waiting for the shit show to go down, but Papi scowls and gives Santos a filthy look. "If anything happens to her, I'm taking my pound of flesh from you. You got that?"

"You mean something like what happened when you were watching her?" he answers dryly. "Don't worry, I actually give a fuck about my family. Well, some of them."

I'm sure Papi is going to explode, but he simply grinds his teeth together and stalks off, slamming his office door behind him.

Loqi hesitates as we all stand, getting to his feet and saying goodbye, but he turns to Santos and gives him a nod. "Keep her safe?"

"I will. We'll be in touch," Santos replies, seeming conflicted before offering his hand to shake. The move surprises me, and everyone else is silently waiting for Loqi's response. Relieved sighs go around the table as Loqi shakes his hand and gives him a small smile.

"Yeah, we will. I have a feeling we won't be waiting too long to run into each other again." He isn't wrong. I have a feeling we'll be running into each other again soon, too.

Chapter Nine

Blaze

Santos, Darius, Pepe, and Cara are taking a flight back to New York so as not to put Cara through the stress of a long drive. Two days of steady driving in a packed vehicle is stress enough, but with all of these fools, it would be torture.

Zander, Selene, and I are taking the car back home. But, before we leave Nevada, Selene wants to pop in to see Aniyah and Colleen. I could go the rest of my life without seeing the purple-haired hooker again, but I don't want to cause a fight with Selene, I'm just happy she didn't take my balls when she found out what happened.

"Aniyah?" Zander snickers from the backseat, "that should be interesting, huh Blaze?"

"Selene knows, asshole." I give him a look in the rear-view.

"I can't hold him to a different standard than I hold myself," Selene says, "but now things are different." She turns in the passenger seat and looks at Zander, "the five of us are in this together and if I even catch a wayward glance at another female, I'll begin taking trophies, starting with your ballsack."

"Jesus," I squirm in my seat and then a startled laugh escapes me when I see the look of complete horror on Zan's face.

"Glad we understand each other," Selene claps and turns back around.

I pull up to the bar and we all get out, stretching our legs. "We'll stay at the apartment tonight, and then get back on the road tomorrow."

"Sounds good," Zander nods. "Now, let's go get a few beers, we deserve it." He strides for the door, and Selene goes to follow but I grab her long, blonde hair and yank her back to my chest.

"You will not be putting your mouth anywhere on that purple hooker either, or I'll start collecting trophies," I press my mouth to her grin, "starting with your pretty little clit."

"I hear you, Daddy." She whispers and licks the scar on my lip.

I release her as she giggles and jogs to the front door. I look up at the sign *Good Times* and groan, I fucking hate doing people shit.

I get inside and find Selene at the bar sitting beside Aniyah, both of them speaking to the bartender and laughing. I find Zander at the old-fashioned jukebox, his face a mask of confusion. I head his way, not really wanting to be around the women, and come to stand beside him.

"It looks like you're trying to figure out how to put your little dick into a pussy hole."

"Will you fuck off?" He snaps at me, "my dick is well above average, asshole."

I chuckle and lean against the jukebox, "what are you trying to figure out? It's not Rocket Science."

"I put my *little* quarter in the *slot* but nothing's happening." I snort at his attitude and shove him aside.

"It's not digital fucker," I roll my eyes, "this green light means it's ready for you to pick your selections. You get five songs per quarter, which ones do you want?"

He lists off a bunch of songs I don't know, and then we head to a booth, giving the girls space to fucking squeal and shit. As soon as we sit down, a waitress comes over and takes our order for a pitcher of beer. The selections Zander picked starts to play, and I groan into my hand.

"You love some emo sounding music, dude."

He's tapping his fingers to the beat and tosses me a smile, "it makes my dick hard."

"What the fuck?" I give him a raised brow, "you're sitting here with me, you sick cunt. You've been around Santos too much."

"Yes, I fucking have," he leans forward, anger in his tone. "It's time I have a vacation from babysitting."

"Stop fucking complaining, those are your brother husbands now," I chuckle, "till death do us all part, brother."

"Which will be sooner than we think with Santos helicoptering a machine fucking gun."

"You survived." I shrug.

"You would've lost your shit and killed them all." He scoffs.

"Which is why you are the most suitable for the job." I grin at him. "Look, I know it's tough with them sometimes, and I'm hoping when we finally get our paws on Mack, things will calm down."

"I need them to calm down." He huffs as he drinks his beer.

I leave it at that because I'm no therapist and I'm tired of his whining. I watch Selene laughing at the bar and I check the time on my phone, wondering if it's nearing time to leave.

"Chicks can talk for hours," Zander gives me a knowing look, "we'll have to entice her to leave."

"I'm not making out with you." I glare at him.

"Was that a joke, *Daddy*?"

"Call me that one more time, and I'll beat you exactly how your actual daddy used to." I spit out.

"Damn," he whistles, "you're heartless. But no, I'm not in the mood to kiss your ugly face tonight," he leans across the table, "there are a few chicks at the table behind you, they're giving us the eye. How about I give a subtle wink and entice them over?"

"You're really not that attached to keeping your balls, huh?"

"Hey!" he holds his hands up in the air, "it's not our fault if they approach us, right?"

"Does Selene come off as a rational female to you? Are we with the same woman?"

"Look, you're either in, or a big, fishy pussy." He leans back with a smirk.

"Fishy pussy? Seriously?"

"PH all out of whack, pussy." He nods.

"Jesus, maybe you have been hanging around those silly assholes too long."

"What is that?" He sticks his nose up in the air, taking a long inhale, "oh!" he waves it off, "just Blaze and his yeasty pussy."

"Are you done?"

He does indeed throw a wink at whatever chicks are sitting behind me, and then nods. "Yep."

I groan as I hear chairs scrape along the hardwood floor, knowing exactly what will evidently go down. Three girls appear at the end of the table, and when one attempts to sit in the chair beside me, I shove her off. Her ass hits the floor with a loud thump and draws the attention of those around us.

"I didn't ask you to come over here, sit somewhere else." I say as I drink my beer.

Zander is laughing as the chicks congregate around him, and it's then I feel a sinister energy. Like the moment before a thunderstorm shoots its bolt of lightning across the sky, or the thick, damp air before a downpour.

"You're about to die of blood loss." I smirk at Zander's wide eyes, he must feel it, too. "I hear it's a long and painful death to endure from the loss of your balls."

"What's this?" Selene comes up behind Zander, placing her hands on his shoulders. "Looks like a small gathering of chickens. What are y'all clucking about?"

"Not me," I gulp down the rest of my beer, "chicken's not my thing, I've always been more impartial to *fish.*"

"I know, Daddy." Selene smiles at me as she rubs Zander's shoulders. "I know."

"I think you *chicks* should skedaddle," I grin, feeling the shitstorm that's about to ensue. They get up quickly, darting back to their table and Selene continues to rub Zander's shoulders.

"Should we leave?" Her voice is too sweet, too laced with sugar.

"Yeah," I lift my nose in the air, "Can you smell that, Zan?"

His jaw is clenched and his eyes tight as he glares at me.

"I thought it was fish for a second there, but no, it's more like someone shit themselves." I get up out of my seat and head for the door, chuckling to myself when I hear a scuffle behind me.

"Selene, fuck." Zander growls, and once I'm outside I look behind me. Selene has Zander in a pressure-point hold at the back of his neck, and his back is contorted with pain.

"What the fuck was that?" She screeches as she shoves him forward.

Zander's face nearly kisses the pavement before he rights himself, and swings around to ward off any incoming attacks.

"It was him." I point at him, and he throws me a shocked expression.

"You wanted to leave!"

"True," I nod as I rub at my chin, "but I was willing to wait it out."

"I don't make idle threats, Zander." She tsks as she walks to the car, "those balls are mine."

My balls clench up tight at her threatening tone, and I follow close behind her, not wanting to miss a single second of the action.

Zander

I'm dead.

I really thought my best friend and brother would have my fucking back, but I was wrong. He's a sellout and clearly dropped me for the psychotic female we're all in love with. Now, I just have to remind her I am in love with her.

Fuck, why did I have to push it?

"You drive, Blaze." Selene sings out, "I want to sit in the back with my favorite boy."

I stop in my tracks, a few feet from the car, and vehemently shake my head. Nope, I'm not getting in there.

"Either get in, or you're a big, fishy pussy," Blaze calls out, the fucker somehow finding his funny bone that's been lodged somewhere up his ass his whole life.

"Nope." I shake my head, getting dizzy from the constant motion, "not until I know my balls are staying firmly attached."

"Seems like he wants to walk back," Selene rests her ass against the car. "That sounds sweet, a midnight stroll through the strip? Lots of alleyways to explore, and dark crevices to traverse."

"I'm not doing that either."

"I think he's scared." Blaze chuckles as Selene begins to saunter over to me. If I could run without looking like a complete pussy, I would.

"Are you scared, Zander?" Her head is tipped to the side, her eyes looking every bit as deranged as she is.

"Yes." I nod, deciding to go with the truth.

"Tell me why."

"Because you're looking like you want to kill me." I point out.

"You're right," she stops, folding her arms across her chest, "I want to kill you for provoking me and thinking there would be no consequences. Now, I really don't want to take your balls because I know you weren't going to do anything with those girls." I let out an audible breath of air, "but," my head quickly snaps back up to look at her, "I can't let such bad behavior go unpunished, right Daddy?" she looks over her shoulder to a manic looking dickhead.

"Absolutely not."

"So, Zander, tell me, how should I punish you?" She asks so fucking sweetly.

"Smother me with your pussy." I nod. "I will die a happy man."

"See? That's good and all, but you're not supposed to enjoy the punishment."

"I think he needs an ass spanking." Blaze calls out. "You have a few toys left over from your fun with the purple hooker, is there a whip?"

Her eyes alight with excitement, and I groan into my hands. Is it the worst punishment? No, I can take an ass whipping, I guess.

"I love ass play." Selene squeals, "so Zander? Will you let me punish your ass?"

I nod, sulking.

"Say it." She demands, "Blaze needs to be my witness."

"Yes, punish my ass." I throw my hands up and stomp to the car like a petulant child. Blaze has no idea what's coming to him. There will be a time he needs me to take his side, and I will gleefully throw him to the fucking wolves.

"You look mad." He snickers as he gets behind the wheel.

"He's going to be even more so when he realizes he likes it later." Selene cackles as we drive to the apartment.

Of course I'm not going to like it. I roll my eyes as we pull up to the apartment, but my girl is crazy and if I don't give her something, it's a very real possibility I will be missing my balls when I wake up.

Walking up to her apartment door feels like the longest trip of my life, I don't know why I'm so apprehensive, it's just a whipping. Fuck, my father did a hell of a lot worse. I guess what it boils down to is the fact that my girl is a certifiable lunatic. Hot, but still loony.

We get inside, and she tosses her trench to the couch, Blaze takes a seat beside it.

"Let me freshen up," she calls out as she walks to the bathroom, "I'll call you in when I'm done."

"Scared?" Blaze asks.

"Fuck you," I grumble.

"I warned you." He chuckles.

"You sold me out."

"Nah, she would've known right away what you were up to. Should've listened to me."

I don't answer as I sit on the other end of the couch and sulk, waiting for when I'm called to receive my punishment. It doesn't take long until I hear her call out our names from the bedroom, a slight giggle escaping her at the end.

She loves me. I remind myself as I get up off the couch, and a sore ass will be worth fucking her for after. I walk into the bedroom, Blaze hot on my tail, and find a naked Selene, stroking herself with a black, leather riding whip. The small, flattened end slips through her wet folds, and I groan as my cock expands.

Yeah, I can handle that.

"Take your clothes off." She demands, "both of you."

"You're not whipping me with that," Blaze grunts as he throws his shirt on the floor.

"No, Daddy," she smiles. "But you can whip me."

He's the next to groan as we both follow her instruction, tossing our clothes to the side. Selene rolls off the bed and comes toward us, slapping the whip against her thigh.

"Bend over the bed, Zander."

I groan as I do what she says, waiting for the crack of the whip, but when I don't feel it, I look at her over my shoulder. She's standing there with a tube of lube and coating her finger.

"Ass play, Zander." She winks.

I stand up straight away, my ass cheeks clenching, and my heart pounding.

"No." I shake my head, "no way."

"Please?" Her eyes widen innocently, "I want to be inside of you while Daddy is inside of me." Why my cock jerks at those words

I'll never know, but she catches it. "You'll like it." She nods, "and then all will be forgiven."

I look at the lube coating her fingers, and then her other hand tweaking her nipple, then groan.

"It never leaves this room." I point at both her and Blaze.

"We won't tell," Selene shakes her head, and looks up at Blaze, "right, Daddy?"

"I won't utter a fucking thing; not like I want to be an accessory to Zander losing his ass virginity."

Selene holds up a strap-on, and I almost pass out. It's already coated in lube, glistening in the room's dim light.

"No," I shake my head and back away, "no way."

"Your cock says otherwise." Selene points down to the fucking traitor standing straight up between my legs. "It's a small one, Zander." She holds it out, "see?"

I close my eyes and let my mind relax, I'm still turned on because it's Selene, not some dude. It's my girl, her big bouncy tits, toned stomach, and tight, sweet pussy. *It's my girl.*

"Okay," I exhale. "Fine."

"Bend over the bed, Zan." Blaze demands, "I want to be inside my woman."

I walk back to the bed and bend back over; how bad can it be? I like a finger in the ass every now and then when I'm getting head, it doesn't mean I want dick. Just like my girlfriend coating my ass with lube, completely normal.

"Step in here," I hear Blaze instruct, and I know they're putting that strap-on on her.

I begin to sweat with apprehension, I hope Selene knows just how far I'll go for her and realizes this is only happening because I love her.

"Ready, baby?" Her soft fingers skim down my spine, "open up for me."

I spread my legs wider and feel her step up between them, her fingers gripping the globes of my ass. I'm so fucking hard, pulsing as she spreads me further. The blunt end of the dildo presses to my ass, and I nearly jump out of my skin when I feel the slight vibrations.

"Shh," Selene continues to dig her fingers into my ass cheeks. "That's for me," she moans, "it has a built-in vibrator for my clit, I thought it only right I get fucked in the ass right along with you."

I hear Blaze groan and relax, feeling her push into me slowly, the tight rim of muscle slowly stretching to accommodate her. It burns, and when I think I can handle it, it gets worse. Until it isn't. Once the burn subsides, I can feel the dildo rubbing against a part of me I've never had explored.

"Fuck, Zander," She groans, pushing my shoulders down further to the bed, "you have such a pretty asshole."

That's a first.

This is all a first, but I'll admit, it's not a bad first.

"I really want to fuck you hard," she pants, the vibrator pressing into her harder as she works the cock into my ass. "Can I?"

"I can help you with that," I hear Blaze, then I feel Selene's chest hit my back.

"Daddy's gonna fuck me right into you." She whispers.

I don't know what about that sets me off, or why it makes my hand slip between me and the bed to grab my rock hard, aching cock. I begin to pump it as the cock in my ass begins to slam into me, hitting a spot with each thrust, making me see stars.

Selene is a panting, screaming mess behind me, her sweat coating my back, and Blaze is cursing about her tight asshole. The sensations become too much, too intense, and my balls tighten painfully to my body. This is it, the most explosive orgasm I've ever had, I can feel it.

"Zan," Blaze grunts, "what does it feel like?"

"Good." I groan as Selene slams in again.

"Describe it." Blaze demands.

"Fuck," I moan, "forbidden but so fucking good."

"Fuck," Blaze groans, the noise long and deep as he comes.

I'm not too far behind as I shoot my load all over the bed, then our girl between us is screaming our names, and grinding herself into the cock in my ass. Everything feels like it's too much, and when I look down at my cock, I find it still hard, covered in my cum.

I feel the second Blaze pulls out of Selene, it's like a pressure is lifted, and then she's next, slowly withdrawing out of my ass, the hole sensitive from her brutal fucking. I collapse onto the bed, my stomach hitting my cum, and yet, I can't move to save my life.

A sharp slap hits my ass cheek, and I peek an eye open.

"All is forgiven, baby." Selene giggles as she drops onto the bed.

"Bring that thing home with us." I tell her as I lose the war with my eyelids.

Yeah, I like my girlfriend owning my ass, literally.

Selene

I just fucked my boyfriend in the ass and now I can die, I've lived a completely fulfilled life. *Satan, come get your girl.*

"Why are your hands in a prayer position?" Blaze asks as he lies down beside me.

"Because that's what I'm doing, I'm praying."

He snorts and pulls me into his chest, his chin landing on top of my head, "I love you." He mumbles and my heart soars.

"I love you too, Daddy."

"But you love me more." Zander mutters sleepily behind us, "I let you fuck me in the ass."

Both Blaze and I chuckle, and I turn in Blaze's arms to face Zander, leaning over to kiss his sweaty cheek. "I love you so damn much." I whisper into his ear.

The next morning, we get on the road early, and I'm curled up in the backseat with Zander. He's been quiet, and I'm worried he's feeling embarrassed about what we did last night. I hope he doesn't think we're judging him and if Blaze bothers him in any way, I will break his fucking neck. I'll send him off with a kiss first, of course.

"Tell me what you're thinking," I murmur.

"Just tired." He lets out a long breath, "I want to be home; I miss the guys."

"The ones you were complaining about needing a vacation from last night?" Blaze smiles in the rear-view.

"Yeah," Zander chuckles, "I guess being away from the assholes puts things into perspective."

"We're a family." I say into his chest, "there's never judgment, no matter how hard we razz on each other."

"I know." He says quietly, "I guess I'm slightly questioning my sexuality after last night, as well."

"What?" Blaze nearly takes us into oncoming traffic at Zander's omission and quickly rights the car, "what the fuck do you mean?"

"I was fucked in the ass, and I enjoyed it."

"By your woman." Blaze scoffs, shaking his head. "Lots of men love ass play."

"Love it with a dildo?"

"Sure," Blaze shrugs, "why not?"

I'm shocked at Blaze's nonchalant attitude, and I feel my chest swell with pride. He's so accepting even though he comes off as the most hard-assed.

"But-"

"No buts, Zan" He growls, "and what the fuck does it matter, anyway?"

"Yeah," I feel him start to relax, "yeah, you're right."

He tips his head back and tucks me in closer to his side, his breathing beginning to level out. When he let me fuck him last night, I was shocked. I knew he would fight me on it and in all honesty, I didn't think it would happen. I would have never forced it on him, but I had a feeling there was more to Zander than what meets the eye. My most straight-laced, level-headed, even-tempered boyfriend likes to get a little crazy in the bedroom. My eyes meet Blaze's in the rear-view and he gives me a smile, his dark, brown eyes shining with love.

"You came in like a fucking blizzard, Little Reaper, cold and harsh. You ripped through all of our defenses and settled inside our frigid hearts."

I'm rendered speechless, my heart beating so hard against my ribcage.

"Now look at us, completely vulnerable and absolutely at your mercy. You've healed something different in each of us, and we've come out stronger in the end."

"You each give me something different, too." I whisper as I look up into Zander's sleeping face, "I could never live without you, any of you."

I rest my head against Zander's chest and listen to the steady beat, the first heart to reveal it loved me. The first person to ever tell me they loved me outside of Jan.

"What's happening with Aniyah and Colleen?" Blaze asks.

"Aniyah is stubborn and wants to stay in Vegas. She wants to make sure no more girls fall victim to prowling men. As much as I understand the feeling, I can't help but worry about her. Colleen promised me to look out for her, since they'll be rooming together."

"At least there's someone watching her, she's a big girl, you can't tell her what to do." He shrugs.

"I know." I sigh, "I was getting some weird vibes from them, though."

"What vibes?"

"I think Aniyah and Colleen are together." I grin. "I think they're dating."

"Good." Blaze growls. "Keeps her away from my woman."

"There was a moment," I admit to him, "I wanted her. I wanted her to be with me."

"I know." He looks at me through the rear-view, "It worried me. I was afraid we were losing you."

"No matter how hard I tried to forget you guys, I couldn't. The four of you were always meant to be mine."

The connection I had with Aniyah was intense, but it burnt out fast, and in the end, I knew it was nothing more than lust. And maybe, I was trying to fill a deep settled loneliness from missing my guys.

My soul's mates are all their own brands of crazy and it just so compliments mine.

Darius

The plane ride went smoothly, and Santos, Pepe, and Cara talked non-stop the entire way. I napped for most of it, taking the chance to regenerate myself. We've hardly had any sleep lately, so even five minutes of rest was bliss.

We take an Uber home, and our relaxing time period ends the moment we get there to find a note stuck to the front door with a knife in it. I march up to it, yanking the blade out, and I take the note in my hands, reading it with a scowl. I don't like being threatened, especially not on my own fucking property.

"We are watching you. Every move you make, everything you plan, and every time you fuck your whore. We see it all. Watch yourself, you won't be around much longer. Give us back Pepe, he's ours. You take something from us, we'll take something from you. Bet your girl screams real pretty." I growl, turning to face Santos. "Who the fuck do these cunts think they are? Threatening our girl like that?"

Santos snatches the piece of paper and glowers, his eyes angrily running over it. "I'll kill them. No one touches my baby girl."

Cara eyes us silently, assessing us as we fume, but Pepe pales.

"They're going to kill me," he squeaks. "What if they're watching us right now?"

I grab the back of his neck, unlocking the door and shoving him inside. "Then we act like you're here by force. But don't think for a second, we'd let them get to you. You're one of us now."

I let him go, and Santos instantly picks him up in a bear hug, jumping up and down. "I told you we weren't letting you go!"

Pepe chuckles, his eyes bright. His friendship with Santos is awesome, and I know it'll grow even more over time.

"I thought that was because you're crazy."

"That's a big part of it," I smirk. "San, put him down before you make him hurl."

He does as he's told, putting Pepe back on his feet before turning to me with a serious expression. "So, what do we do now?"

"We sweep the house then call the others to let them know, but we need to keep our eyes peeled. They might try to attack us now that we're home, and not all of us are here. We don't go anywhere alone, got it? That means you too, Cara," I inform them, turning my attention to Santos' sister. "They might see you as the weakest link in our group, and if they find out you're family, they'll definitely try something."

She grins, the same way Santos does when someone threatens him. "They can try. I'll gut them like a fucking pig."

Pepe's watching her with wide eyes, but I see the flicker of interest. *Oh boy, things could get interesting around here.* Especially, if he starts chasing her around like a lost puppy.

Santos doesn't notice, he's too busy beaming at his sister with pride. "Damn fucking straight. Let's practice your shooting skills later. I wanna see what you got."

"I'll slaughter you if you make it a competition," she answers. "I'm a pretty good shot, we all had to train to be a part of King Hayne's court."

"You're the coolest sister ever," he groans, her face lighting up at his praise.

"Yeah? You're a pretty cool brother, too."

I let them bicker about who's better at using different weapons while I check every room in the house for an intruder, then I sit on the couch and pull my phone out once it is clear. "Time to call Blaze. You two can continue this argument later."

Santos sits beside me, his hand resting on my thigh casually. "Selene's going to be pissed."

"We're all pissed. I can't believe they walked up to the door and stuck a note on it," I scowl. "I'll check the cameras in a minute too. Make sure they didn't actually get in."

Santos is instantly on his feet, jogging up the hallway. "I'll check now. We need to check the place for bugs before we talk to the others. For all we know, they've planted bombs here." Shit, he's right. I must be tired if I didn't think of it first.

I follow him, leaving Pepe and Cara to occupy themselves while we investigate, relief rolling through me at seeing two guys leave the note on the door and that's it. At least we know we can talk freely.

Santos is muttering under his breath once we rejoin the other two on the couch and wait for Blaze to answer the phone.

"You're on speaker," he says the moment he answers, his voice gruff as always.

"Hey. We found a note on the front door when we got home," I say immediately.

"What kind of note? Are girl scouts doing their cookies again? Be more fucking specific," he barks with irritation.

"Diablos. They're watching us, and they want Pepe back," I grunt, reading the note out loud to them. They're quiet for a moment, before Selene talks.

"I'm going to fucking kill them. They can watch us fuck if they want, but they aren't joining in. Did they get inside?"

"No, they put the note on the door then left. They didn't even try to get inside the house."

Pepe excuses himself, and we wave him off. I have no idea why the Diablos want him, he's a scaredy cat. If he's going to stick around, we need to toughen him up a little.

"We'll try and get there as fast as we can. Let us know if anyone starts snooping around, alright? I know you can look after yourselves, but you have Pepe and Cara to look out for too," Zander warns, making me snort.

"Pretty sure Cara can look after herself, right Cara?" I ask and look up, finding her gone. Santos frowns, not realizing she left the room either, but we continue chatting on the phone for a while before deciding we needed to find her. "Hey, we'd better go. How far away are you?"

"We'll be home the day after tomorrow. Don't fuck on the couch," Blaze grumbles, making me chuckle.

"You won't know if we do."

"I'll fucking know," he snaps before hanging up, leaving us to track down Cara.

Santos

My sister is silent and sneaky, I'll give her that. I didn't notice her leaving the room, which concerns me slightly. I can't relax like that or someone else might slip by me who isn't supposed to.

"Where the fuck did she go?" Darius asks as he stands, glancing around the room. "It's like she vanished into thin air."

"No idea. Maybe she went to lie down?"

"In a house she's never been in? C'mon, we haven't shown her around yet," he snorts, following me as we start searching. We don't have to look far, because we find her in the hallway, pressing Pepe against the wall as she kisses the hell out of him.

"Well, well, well, what do we have here?" Darius says with a grin, and Pepe pushes Cara back with a gasp, panicking at being caught out.

"We, uh…"

"What are your intentions with my sister?" I demand, eyeing them both. I'm angry at him touching her, but I'm also confused. They hardly know each other, and they couldn't be more opposite if they tried.

He gulps at the glare I send his way, darting his eyes between us and Cara. "I didn't… I wouldn't…"

"You're trying to fuck my little sister," I state, stepping closer. "I don't like that."

"No! I'd never do that!" he insists, my eyes narrowing with annoyance.

"Why the fuck not? Is she not good enough for you?"

Darius is smothering a laugh, but I can't help it. I don't like him touching her, but I don't like him not wanting her, either. I'm giving *myself* whiplash.

Cara leans back against the wall opposite Pepe, a grin on her face, but she leaves him to sputter more answers, enjoying this as much as Darius.

"No! She's perfect! I don't want to have sex until I'm married! It's nothing against her, she's really pretty, I swear!" The way Cara had him against the wall tells me she started it, but I'm not done interrogating him. It's starting to amuse me.

"Wait, you're going to marry my sister?!" I exclaim with a grin, happiness seeping into me.

"I'm not marrying anyone, I was just trying to get laid," Cara says dryly, but I ignore her and focus on Pepe.

"So? You're marrying her?"

"That's not what I meant!" he cries, "I just meant I wouldn't have sex with her unless I married her!"

Cara smirks, moving up to him and running her hand down his stomach, stopping just above his groin. "Sure didn't seem like that a minute ago."

His panicked gaze meets mine, and I grin. "Oh my God. We'll be brothers! Like, for real! Marry her, or else I'll kill you."

Darius loses it, laughing his ass off while Cara scowls at me. "I'm not getting married."

"You are now. Pepe said so!" I whine. "You can't take my brother away from me!"

"Can't I just fuck him? It's easier," she throws back, making me growl.

"No. My brother's not a piece of meat, Cara."

"He's not your brother, we're not married!"

"Whose fault is that? Pepe, I'm sorry. I don't know why she's saying these mean things!" I exclaim, grabbing him and pulling him in for a hug. He flinches back as his hard dick brushes my leg, and I smirk. "Is that for me or my sister?"

"I need to go and pray," he rushes out, running to his room and slamming the door, and Cara turns to me with a glare.

"Look what you did. Do you want me to stay a virgin forever?"

"I don't want to think about it. What's wrong with Pepe? He'd be the best husband. Oh! We can all live here and…" Darius grabs my shoulder, wheezing from all his laughter.

"Stop, you're killing me. They don't have to get married, San."

"Yes, they do, Jesus says so," I snort. "Isn't that right, Pepe?! Jesus says you have to marry her if you want to fuck her!"

Cara huffs, giving me the evil-eye. "You're not married, and you fuck all the time, apparently. Jesus claims homosexuality is a sin too, but you don't care about that."

"No, but I'm not into Jesus like Pepe is. He's gotta respect that shit," I grumble, crossing my arms tight over my chest. "Speaking of homosexual fucking, it's good to be home. D, let's fuck."

Cara scrunches up her nose. "I'll leave you guys to it then. I'll bunk in with Pepe, I assume?"

"I'd better not hear any noises from that room unless I see a ring on your finger!" I holler, and she flips me off before sneaking into Pepe's room, leaving us in peace.

Darius grins, ruffling my hair. "Stop teasing them."

I slam his back against the wall and kiss him hard, my fingers biting into his skin as I hold onto his waist. He groans into my mouth, his hand running through my hair and firmly yanking on it. I hear Cara curse at us from inside the bedroom, and I grin. "Maybe we should take this elsewhere?"

Darius doesn't argue. He pushes me back, fumbling with my belt as I guide us toward our room blindly, not letting his lips go. The moment the door's shut, I pull back to yank my shirt off, kicking my jeans off as I go. Darius wastes no time getting naked for me, his eyes hungrily running over my body as he stares at me. "Fuck."

"What?" I demand, looking down at my body. "Something wrong?" I've never been the type to give a shit about people's opinions of me, but Darius and Selene have knocked that wall down, and my insecurities are at an all-time high.

"Nothing's wrong, *amante*. You're fucking perfect," he groans, grabbing my hand and tugging me toward the bed. We should be keeping an eye on the cameras for the Diablos, but that's the last thing on our minds.

He pushes me back so I'm sitting on the edge of the bed, dropping to his knees instantly. I wish our girl were here to watch this, I know she'd enjoy the show.

The moment his lips wrap around my dick and his eyes peer up at me, I curse, fisting his hair. I hold his head still as I thrust down his throat, somehow getting harder as he chokes on it. Saliva runs down my shaft and soaks my balls, the wet choking sounds urging me on as I slam into him. I already need to fucking come, so I force myself to let his head go and push him back. "Get on your fucking knees. This won't be gentle."

"It never is," he grins, his lips swollen. The moment his ass is in the air for me, I grab some lube to make sure I don't split him in half, smearing it over his tight hole and pressing two fingers inside. He drops his forehead onto the bed, murmuring my name as I force in a third.

"San, fuck me," he begs. "Stop teasing me."

"It'll hurt," I warn, but he looks at me over his shoulder, his eyes dark.

"I'm counting on it." *Fuck.*

I remove my fingers and align the tip of my dick with the tight hole, grinning sadistically at him. "You asked for it." Then I forced my way inside, the sound of his discomfort sending tingles to my balls. I don't give him time to adjust, I just pull out and slam back in again and again, his desperate cries and praise bouncing off the walls around us loud enough for the entire neighborhood to hear.

I hope they all know who he belongs to.

Chapter Ten

Darius

Delicious pain. It's all I feel as Santos goes to town on me like he'll die if he doesn't, and I'm at his mercy in the best possible way. I'm biting the blanket so damn hard I'm sure my teeth will crack, but I don't stop him. I want him to hurt me because, this feeling? It's the best. Our relationship is built around pain and destruction, and every hard stroke he gives me feels like home.

"I already want to fucking come," Santos pants, his fingers digging into my waist as he holds tight. "So fucking good."

I've never cared about praise before, but something burns in my chest at hearing it from him. I want to please him and Selene all the fucking time, so knowing I drive them both so crazy is really good for my ego.

I reach underneath myself, finding his balls and giving them a firm squeeze, causing him to jolt. "Fuck, D."

I want him to fill me up, and I want him to come so hard he sees stars, so I slide my hand back further, just managing to reach his ass, and push a finger inside the tight ring.

I don't understand half the shit he's cursing, but that means I'm doing something right, so I push in further, stroking his tight walls as he continues to slam into me. He comes with a shout, his hands dropping to the mattress on either side of me as he presses himself as deep as he can, needing a minute to recover. His sweaty chest covers my back, and he lets out a chuckle. "Well, that escalated quickly."

My legs are shaking slightly from being in this position for so long, and the moment he pulls out of me, I flip him onto his back with a grin. "Hope you're not too sensitive."

"You going to top me, D?" he smirks, exhaustion filling his eyes.

"Yeah, I want to come so deep in you, you can taste it," I murmur, lying over him and grabbing the lube. "I'm slowing it down a little, though."

He seems confused but doesn't protest. It's rare we fuck at a slower pace, but sometimes it's what I crave. I prepare his ass before sliding inside, hooking his muscular legs over my shoulders. His eyes clench shut as I stoke deep, leaning over him more to press my lips to his. His mouth opens instantly, his tongue massaging mine. I'm surprised he's letting me go slow, to be honest, but he doesn't complain as I keep my thrusts slow and deep, our breaths mingling the closer I get to my release.

My balls are tight, but I hold on longer, savoring it as long as possible. I never know when he'll let me take it down a notch again.

"I love you," I practically whisper, his eyes flying open to look at me.

"I love you, too," he murmurs, running his fingers through my hair and giving me a content smile. I let go, grunting as my hot cum fills his ass, and by the time we pass out, he's curled up against my chest, snoring soundly without a care in the world.

Zander

I groan with relief when I see the front gates of Blaze's house—our house—up ahead. Being in this car with a woman who can't sit still, needs constant stimulation, and barely sleeps; and with a guy who's grumpy as all hell, has random screaming outbursts, and needs constant quiet has been exhausting. I want my bed so I can sleep for the next week straight, unfortunately, that won't happen. With lingering Diablos about, and Mack still on the loose, I know I'll have my work cut out for me. Why the fuck would the Diablos threaten to take our woman again? When it was her who slaughtered them all to free herself the first time? It makes no sense.

All I can determine is, they're trying to hit us in what they must think is our weakest point, and they'd be correct. We love her and we would do anything to make sure she stays safe. With that being said, she can also take care of herself, and it's a relief we don't have to coddle her. It's time we find Mack, kill him, and eradicate all Diablos. This finale has been decades in the making, and I'm ready to finally watch Mack meet his maker.

"If my house is a fucking mess, I'm kicking you all out." Blaze growls as we pull through the gates.

"What? What do Selene and I have to do with any of it?"

"Don't bring pets home if you can't house train them." He snaps, and Selene falls across the backseat laughing.

"I can't wait to get my beastiality on." She continues to snort, and I see the ghost of a smile on Blaze's mouth.

She's out of the car before we've come to a full stop, and she's running up the stairs, busting through the front door.

"Mommy's home!" She screams, her words travelling all down the street, "ready or not, come fuck me!"

"Why'd I think coming home would be easier?" I groan into my hands.

"Because you forgot this was your one and only vacation from the pets." Blaze snickers.

He gets out of the car, stretching his tall, muscular body, and shaking out those tree trunk legs. I don't even know how he got himself in here, he's so large. And he's large *everywhere*. I cringe when I remember him fucking Selene in the ass on the dancefloor at the MC building, which couldn't have felt as good as she was making it out to, I know now.

My cock begins to swell in my pants as I watch Blaze walk to the front door, thoughts of him fucking her in the ass still fresh in my mind. *No.* What am I hard for right now? The thought of my girlfriend getting rammed in the ass by a massive dick, or my best friend who owns said dick? Oh my God, am I becoming gay?

I stumble out of the car and slowly walk up to the door, giving my confused dick time to deflate. I get fucked in the ass one time by my girlfriend, and all of a sudden, my cock wants to harden to the thoughts of dicks in the ass.

As soon as I step over the threshold, I find Selene with her arms wrapped around Darius' neck, her eyes meeting mine over his shoulder.

"Maybe Zander will want to join us later," she gives me a wink as Santos grins. My cock pulses against my zipper, and I swallow down my apprehension. Join them how? Will one of them be doing to me what she did? My cock halts its pulsing as I imagine Santos plowing into me. Okay, so not a lot gay.

"I'm tired." I give her a half-assed smile, hoping she doesn't read too far into it.

"How about I come visit you after," she slips from Darius' arms and saunters over to me, pressing her body into mine, "I'll bring our little friend, too."

My cock springs to attention, throbbing and pressing painfully to my zipper. Okay, so maybe just a little bit gay. I can handle that.

"As fun as it is to listen to you four figuring out your train car formation, we need to get this Diablo thing under control once and for all." Blaze brings his laptop to the table and sits, "we'll figure out the *rail* complications later."

Asshole.

Selene cackles as she grabs Santos' ass, leading him to the couch, and when she sits, she looks around. "Where's Cara and our little Pepe?"

"Making wedding plans." Santos grins.

"What?" Selene's eyes bulge from her head. "They want to get married?"

"I wouldn't say that," Darius chuckles as I take a seat beside him on the couch, "but Santos and I caught them kissing in the hallway. Pepe is adamant it was innocent because he doesn't believe in sex before marriage."

"And since he wants to fuck my sister, they're getting married." Santos tosses his hands up, "I can't wait to walk the little fucker down the aisle."

"Your sister?" Selene looks at him shocked.

"No, my Pepe," he huffs, and I can't help but let loose a laugh.

"Can you guys shut the fuck up now?" Blaze snaps as his fingers fly over the keys of the laptop.

"I don't think Cara should be buying the cow without testing the quality of the milk first." Selene grumbles, and I laugh again.

"Listen up," Blaze turns the screen so we can all see it. "Mack has been MIA for a while now, and the Diablos were in hiding after the explosions, so what makes Pepe so fucking important to bring them out?"

We all fall quiet with thought. It is strange how much they're worried about a new member, and a seemingly useless one at that.

"Has he left since you've been back?" Blaze asks Santos.

"No, we won't let him because we're worried about the Diablos snatching him. But, he's been frantic about his abuela, and he calls her every day. I promised he could go see her with one of us."

Blaze points at the screen of the laptop, and we all lean in. It's an article dating back seven years ago, detailing a huge sex trafficking bust. The next article shows the key witness along with his mother and father killed a few days before the trial, resulting in the prosecution having to drop the case.

"What does this mean?" Selene asks.

"I remember this," I say quietly, "it involved my father and Mack. They celebrated when the case was dropped."

"They were implicated in this bust?" Selene gasps.

"No," Blaze answers, "but there was a good chance they would've been."

"I remember this, too." Santos leans forward, "we were so fucking pissed. It's when we decided to take down Walton and Delaney ourselves."

"Do you remember the survivors of the 'home invasion'?" Blaze asks, quoting the home invasion part because everyone knew it was a hit.

"The younger brother and the grandfather, wasn't it?" Darius scrubs at his chin.

"Grandmother," Blaze corrects, "an *abuela*."

The information all clicks for us at the same moment, and we all gasp. "That was Pepe?" Santos exclaims.

"Only one way to find out for sure. But I would say yes, and how much do you wanna bet the Diablos forced him to join?" Blaze nods. "Call him down here."

"No need." Pepe walks into the room, and we all snap our heads around to watch him, "that is in fact me. And that's why I have been desperate to get home to my abuela. I'm afraid they'll grab her."

"Why didn't you tell us this?" I ask him.

"Because I see the way you guys operate, and I really didn't want to put my abuela and myself in any more danger. You guys have a few things wrong though, I wasn't forced to join the Diablos, I did that on my own, with the help of my father." He sits on a chair and leans forward.

"The one who was murdered?" I ask him, slightly confused.

"No, he was the man who raised me. I'm talking about my biological father." His head drops into his hands as he exhales, "I guess it's story time."

"About time." Blaze snarls.

"My mother attended Columbia University; she was a little older than the other students because she had a baby—my brother—right out of high school. During her second year, they had a serial rapist on campus, and my mother fell victim to him. She knew exactly who it was and when she reported it, it was ignored."

"Who was the rapist?" Selene's eyes have narrowed, her jaw tightened, and I can see the bloodlust seeping through her body.

"Mack Delaney, he got off with the help of Henry Walton." We all stare at him with mixed expressions of pity and anger.

"I was conceived through that attack, but since my family is strict Catholic, my mother would not abort me. My father in everything but blood agreed, and that's how I came to be."

"Does Mack know who you are?" Blaze asks.

"Of course," he nods, "he's the one who found me, and when he offered to take me into his gang of sex traffickers, I agreed. I was going to compile as much information as I could on them to give to the police, and all the while make Mack believe I was truly interested in being his son. Then you came along and even though you weren't the police, I had a feeling justice would be better served through you. That's why I agreed to help."

"So, that's why you're so important." Selene scratches at her chin. "Looks like I need to start hunting some Diablos and try to smoke out Papa Mack."

"Don't call him that." Pepe shudders.

"Well, he can't be Daddy; we have one already." Selene points at Blaze.

Blaze

"We can't bring your grandmother here," I tell Pepe, "The Diablos could very well be watching her house, and I doubt they'll hurt her, considering who your father is. We need the Diablos to believe you're our hostage to keep her safe." I turn to Selene, "go hunting, and spread the word we have a Diablo captive."

"Yes!" she wiggles in her seat, excitement taking over. "Let's reap some motherfuckers."

"Zander will accompany you, looks like he needs the vacation time." I wink at his scowling face, "and I will train our newest pet in the art of defending himself." I grin at Pepe who looks on the brink of shitting himself.

"Oh, thank you, but I'm okay. I have God's protection on my side-"

"Let's go." I cut him off as I stand. "I don't have all day. Call your sister down, too." I tell Santos, "It wouldn't hurt for her to learn, as well."

I don't bother to listen to any other whining and bullshitting as I head off down to the basement and into our workout area. I'm tired from being cramped in that fucking car for two days, and even though sleep sounds like heaven, I need to make sure we're all prepared. This is it, the day me and the guys have been waiting for, taking down Mack Delaney and his empire of skin. He's been a slippery fucker over the years, and with Walton down, he's our last target.

I hear thundering on the stairs leading to the workout space and turn to see an excited looking Cara in yoga pants and a t-shirt.

"Let's kick some fucking ass!"

"It would've been good for you to have that mentality seven years ago when you were abducted." I point out.

"I was a kid."

"And?" I lift a brow.

"I always thought my brother and father would protect me, and now I know how wrong I was. I'm ready to learn, sensei." She folds her hands under her chin and bows.

Fuck, she really is like her brother.

"Where's your intended?" I smirk.

"We're not getting married," her fists land on her hips. "I just wanted to get laid."

I snort at her admission just as a skulking Pepe slowly comes down the stairs. His head is down, and his shoulders slumped at the prospect of having to learn how to fight. Then, I watch with shock as Cara leaps out in front of him, punching him square on the forehead, making his head snap up, and swiftly kicking him in the dick, making him tumble down the rest of the stairs with a garbled cry.

"Was that good?" She bounces on the balls of her feet, waiting for my praise.

"Actually, yeah." I nod, and she squeals as she rushes over to me.

We watch as Pepe struggles to stand, his fist gripping his cock, and his face green. "I really don't want to do this."

"Oh, knock it off, you pussy." Cara grins at him, "come play with me, and later I'll kiss all your boo-boos."

Pepe perks up at the prospect of getting his dick sucked, and hobbles over to us.

"What would Jesus think of you right now?" I tsk at him with a grin.

"Jesus would bless him." Cara nods, "all men love a good dick sucking."

"Blasphemy!" Pepe exclaims.

I'm in for a long ass day with Santos junior and the altar boy.

Selene

I missed walking these streets with my trench flowing around my calves, and my knife tucked into my belt. This has been my life since I was fourteen, and I'm glad to be back. I'm heading toward a strip club which the Diablos frequent called The Temple. The owner Carl knows Blaze well, and he let him know about a few Diablos who happen to be there now.

I get to The Temple and quickly look over my shoulder, seeing Zander not too far behind. He's not coming inside, but he'll meet up with me when I lure my prey from this place. I walk inside and look around. The ambiance is sultry with smoke obscuring features, and the dim lights giving off a romantic glow.

I find the bar to my left and head that way, sliding up onto a stool. A monster of a man comes forward and leans on the bar, giving me a slow once over. "You look like you should be up on stage, not down here with the rest of us scum."

"Thanks." I give him a wide grin, "I'll take a whiskey on the rocks, hold the roofie."

"That's it from our Queenie," the MC croons into the mic, "up next we have Tiny!"

I turn in time to watch a voluptuous woman saunter onto the stage, her long, light-brown hair swaying behind her, hitting just above her ass. She's wearing a metal chain dress and nothing underneath, save for a G-string. She grabs onto the pole and hoists herself up, twirling around it in a gleaming swirl of metal on metal.

I hear the glass settle on the bar behind me, but I can't take my eyes off the feminine display in front of me.

"Tiny can work that pole like no other." The bartender comments behind me. "We did have a stunner here before, her name was Tempest, you would've loved her, too."

"Is Carl around?" I finally drag my eyes from the beauty on the stage. "I'm here to see him."

"Are you sure you're not applying for a job?" He winks.

"No, I've come here to kill someone, and you're looking to get yourself added to the list."

He laughs heartily, and when I don't join in, he swallows thickly with a nod, disappearing into a door. *Idiot men.*

A well-groomed, middle-aged man comes out of the door with the bartender trailing behind him. He comes to stand in front of me, giving me a skeptical once over.

"You're here for the Diablos?"

I give him a nod and sip my drink. "Yes, point them out."

I get another look but finally he discreetly points to my left, I turn my head and see two thug looking guys sitting at a table, drooling over Tiny on the stage. I can't even fault them for it.

"Thanks," I nod. "Blaze said he would be by with payment."

I down the rest of my drink and slap a twenty on the bar. I keep my eyes on the two men I'll be dealing with, trying to keep my anticipation tempered, and make my way over to them. They're so engrossed in Tiny; they don't even notice I've slipped into a chair at their table until I've cleared my throat.

"Who are you?" One of them asks, completely taken off guard by my sudden appearance.

"My name is Candy, and the owner suggested I come over to keep you guys company." I undo my trench, showing the lace lingerie I'm wearing underneath.

"Carl?" The other looks toward the bar, raising his hand, "that guy is fucking bomb."

"What are your names?" I ask as I lean on the table.

"I'm Joe and this is Tommy." The first introduces us, and I run my finger along the rim of his glass.

"I hear you guys are real gangsters," I widen my eyes. "You don't understand how hot that makes me."

"Really?" Tommy leans forward. He's huskier than Joe, with black hair and dark eyes. He has a gorgeous smile and plush lips. He's a looker.

"Yes," I make my voice breathy, and let my fingers skim down over my chest, disappearing under the table, and between my legs.

"Sounds like she wants to have a party, Tommy." Joe leers across at me. He's not so pretty, actually, he looks a bit like a meth-head, skinny with greasy, brown hair, and dull, brown eyes.

"Can we?" I perk up. I look around while biting my lip. "It can't be in here; the things I want to do to you both are illegal." I give them a wink.

"Are you taking us back to your place?" Joe licks his thin lips.

"I don't think I can wait that long," I moan as I continue to play with myself. "I need your fat cocks in me now."

"Fuck," Joe stands abruptly, his chair tipping over. "Let's get out of here."

Tommy nods, standing quickly as well, "there's an alley to the side of this place. Real dark and private."

Like stealing candy from a baby.

"That's perfect," I nod as I stand, letting them have a full look at what I have on, including my fancy metal belt, then do up my trench.

"Fuck, you are so hot, I can't wait to destroy that pussy." Tommy mutters as he leads us out of the bar, Joe trailing behind us. All these men claiming they can destroy pussy is fucking pathetic. We can birth a whole ass human from that hole, there's no dick too big, bunch of fucking losers.

We get outside and quickly make a beeline for the alley, and they are right, it is dark and private. Only I know someone else is in here with us, and I want to give him a bit of a show before I have all my fun.

"Who's eating me first?" I throw open my trench and prop my foot against the wall behind me, spreading my legs wide. My lingerie is crotchless and regardless of how dark it is, I know they can see my pussy right there for the taking.

Tommy drops to his knees first, his face coming in close as he groans loudly, "fuck Joe, she smells so good."

"Hurry up, asshole." Joe sneers. "I want my turn." He undoes his pants and pulls out his dick, it's not bad for a skinny fuck lacking in nutrients. He begins to pump it in his hand, groaning as Tommy sinks his tongue into my folds.

He knows how to use his mouth, and I almost forget what I'm here to do as I drop my head to the brick behind me. I hear a soft throat clearing and know it's Zander, he's probably fuming. My head comes up, but it looks like both men are too absorbed with my pussy to have heard it.

I grab the handle of my knife and slip it from my belt, the metal scraping has Tommy pulling back from my pussy. He looks up just as I stab it into the side of his throat, the blood spraying onto me and Joe's dick, giving him some much-needed lube. Not that he appreciates it as he begins to scream, dropping his dick in the process. *What a waste.*

I pull my knife out and kick Tommy onto his back, his gurgling death noises masking Zander's footsteps as he comes up behind Joe, wrapping his arm around his neck.

"We need you to get a message back to your leader Mack." He says as I clean my knife off onto Tommy's shirt. "Tell him the Reaper Incarnate is looking for him, and she has something that belongs to him."

I begin to hum as I swipe up some of Tommy's blood and begin to paint the scythe on his forehead. Fuck, I really missed this.

"Put your dick away, Joe." I tsk as I look up into his frightened face. "Do you think your meth-damaged brain can remember the message or should we just kill you as well?"

"I got it." He stammers out as Zander shoves him forward.

"Hurry," I wave him off, "or else I may just chase you; I love to chase."

He runs off out of the alley just as I finish my finger painting, and I sit back on my hunches to admire the artwork.

"You were enjoying that a little too much." Zander growls.

"A lot actually," I agree, and look up at him. "I expect you to finish what he started." I stand and lean against the wall, using the same pose I did for Tommy.

"There's blood on the ground." He points to the growing puddle.

"And?" I pop a brow, and he rolls his eyes, falling to his knees. "Don't forget my ass, she's been wanting some love, too."

His eyes shine with a bit of anger mixed with a lot of lust as he grabs my waist and spins me around, my chest colliding with the rough brick. I grab the bottom of my trench, hanging it over my arm as my pussy clenches in anticipation. Then he surprises me by grabbing the crotchless portion of my lingerie and ripping a bigger hole up the back. He spreads my ass cheeks, and his tongue begins to work my asshole, sinking deep inside.

"Fuck," I moan, my forehead hits the brick. His fingers begin to work my clit, and then three sinks into my pussy as he stands.

"That's a good idea." He says into my ear, "I'm going to fuck this tight ass."

I look over my shoulder and watch him spit into his palm, dragging it along his length. He spreads me back open and begins to sink into my ass, chuckling when I begin to cry out. It burns and it's almost painful, but when he begins to finger-fuck my pussy at the same time, I feel the beginnings of an orgasm.

"You love your ass being fucked, huh?" He snickers into my ear.

"Yes," I nod and turn to look at him over my shoulder, "and that makes the both of us, baby Walton."

Santos

My sister is a fast fucking learner. She took on anything Blaze threw at her, but Pepe? Not so much. He spent more time praying and picking himself up from the floor than inflicting damage. Pretty sure he was looking forward to Cara kissing his boo-boos better like she promised, because every time she laid him out like she was training for the UFC, he got this stupid smile on his face.

"You didn't even try to defend yourself!" Cara whines, kissing the bruise that's forming on his cheek.

"I wasn't going to hurt you," he scoffs. "I'm not like that."

"You're a little bitch."

"Confirmed," he nods, eyeing me warily as she keeps fussing over him. It's kind of cute, I can't lie.

"You know I'm going to hang a massive photo of your wedding day on my wall, right? You're so cute," I smirk, ignoring the filthy glance Cara gives me. I don't care if she doesn't want to get married. They need each other. Well, Pepe needs her to keep him safe, I can't be there all the time to watch him, but that's beside the point.

Pepe clears his throat, his eyes remaining on Cara. "I bet she'd look beautiful, too."

Cara grins, her expression softening as she looks at him. "You think?"

"I know you would. You're gorgeous," he shrugs like it's no big deal, a yelp coming from him as she knocks him back and kisses the hell out of him. Darius grins from the doorway, watching the scene unfold, but Blaze rolls his eyes like the grumpy fucker he is.

"Is it weird this is making my dick hard?" I ask, earning a scowl from Blaze.

"Yes, it's fucking weird. She's your sister."

"They're just so cute! Ugh, when will my baby girl be back? I need to sink myself in her so bad right now," I groan, rubbing my dick through my pants, stumbling when Blaze shoves me.

"You're disgusting. Go dick your boyfriend if you're horny."

"Right here?" I tease, moving to unzip my jeans, but Blaze grabs the front of my shirt and hauls me closer, his angry eyes burning into me.

"No. Keep your dick away. You'll poke someone's eye out with it otherwise," he growls, making me cackle.

"Says the man with the python in his pants! You're restraining the hulk behind that zipper!"

"You're lucky I'm not into guys, San. Because nothing would make me happier than shoving it down your throat and choking you until the light left your crazy fucking eyes," he sneers, letting me go with a scowl when I moan.

"Oh, please, Daddy. Choke me."

"You're one sick, little fucker."

"I know you are, you said you are, so what am I?" I sing-song, his eyes flashing with irritation.

"Real mature."

"You love me."

"Someone fucking has to," he grunts as he leaves the room, giving Darius the side-eye. "Tag, you're it."

"We're playing tag?!" I beam, but Blaze keeps walking, throwing his answer over his broad shoulder.

"No. Darius is on Santos duty, that's all. I've had enough for one day." *Asshole.*

Pepe's blushing like mad when I finally look at him again, Cara still kissing his face and arms as if he'll die without the affection. Like I said, they're so cute. I can't wait to be an uncle.

"Santos! I'm not having kids any time soon!" Cara snaps, confusing me.

"I said that out loud?"

"Yes!"

"Oops! That conversation wasn't for you. Pretend you didn't hear it!" I reply, glancing up at Darius who's chuckling at us. "I say we knock Selene up. I bet being a dad's cooler than being an uncle."

"I think that suggestion would get you killed," he grins. "But totally. I say we bet on who manages it first."

"I might put my money on Blaze. Her womb would be too scared to say no to him," I laugh, ordering Cara and Pepe to shower before Darius and I head out of the kitchen. Blaze looks relaxed, which doesn't happen often, and I can't help but taunt him some more.

I throw myself across his lap on the couch, wiggling my ass in the air. "I've been a bad boy, Daddy Blaze. Spank me."

"I'm close to shoving a gun up your ass and firing, San. Don't push me," he grunts, trying to shove me off, but I hold tight.

"Kinky! Which gun would you use? The big one? Oh! Where's my machine gun?!"

"You mean *my* machine gun?" he snorts. "You're not touching it again. Darius, get him the fuck off me, before you lose him."

I smirk over my shoulder at Darius. "Don't worry, babe! I won't leave you for him, despite his good looks and obvious charm!"

Darius sniggers, but my eyes flash to the front door as Selene and Zander walk in, blood splattered on both of them. Zander's knees are covered in blood, and by the way Selene's smiling right now, I know just what happened. Lucky bastard.

"Baby!" I shout as I scramble off Blaze's lap and dive at Selene, kissing her hard as I hold her body to mine. She smells like death and vengeance. Well, like blood, which is the same thing. My sexy, little Reaper.

She grins, running her hands through my hair. "Hey, San. Have you been good for Daddy Blaze?"

"Stop fucking calling me that!" Blaze barks, but he kisses her cheek on his way past to grab a beer, apparently not too angry.

"I was *super* good!" I wink. "But now I'm fucking horny. I mean, look at you! You're a walking wet dream, baby girl."

She swoons, leaning into me, and giving me a light kiss. "You're always horny, but thanks."

"So, what now?" Darius asks, hauling Selene from my arms and dragging her to the couch. She looks so pretty on his lap.

"Now, we wait," Zander shrugs, sitting down and taking a beer from Blaze as he returns.

"I say you give us a play-by-play of what you two have been up to. I'm jealous, whatever it is. Did you fuck on their corpse? Oh! Did you fuck their asses, Zan? Next time can I watch? If that's a kink, I want it. Dead-body-ass-fucking show!"

"I didn't fuck anyone's ass," he rolls his eyes then stops to grin at Selene. "Well, I didn't fuck the Diablos' asses, anyway."

I fucking love story time.

Where's my popcorn?

Chapter Eleven

Zander

It takes a few days, but we do receive a message from the Diablos, and it's one that comes from Mack himself. I know how he operates, and he knows that I do. Him and my father were close, and I know every single one of his signature moves. So, when a car explodes just outside our gates, I know it's his message, and I know just what he's conveying.

"We have to hand Pepe over or be prepared." I tell them as we sit around the kitchen table. We just finished dealing with the cops and after a few hours of hard questions, they reluctantly left, not at all buying that we know nothing.

"For what?" Cara asks.

"War." I shrug.

"How would he get to us?" She asks.

"Every time we need to leave, they'll be waiting." Blaze intercepts, "I remember the time he used a drone to fly a bomb into someone's house."

"Yeah." I nod. "He's not as dumb as he looks."

"He won't be making the same mistakes twice. He won't capture hostages anymore," Darius joins in, "Selene got away and left a house of body parts for him to find."

"It'll be a kill on sight order." I nod.

"Do we have enough time to do this last kill?" Selene grins, her eyes looking unhinged.

I shrug, it's going to happen anyway.

Pepe told us about the guy who lives near the harbor, he brings in girls from Manhattan and hides them in cargo containers until Mack picks them up. These girls aren't junkies off the street or prostitutes. They're taken from elite prep schools or locked inside Ubers on their way to upscale parties. Selene wants to take him out to send another message to Mack. No more high-end virgin girls to auction off.

"This time I'm coming with you." Santos grins, and my stomach flips.

"Is that a good idea?" I ask, "no offense but you both need to be supervised."

"We've killed together before." Selene winks at Santos.

"In the back of that limo," he nods, "I want a repeat."

I know what they're referring to, so I leave them to eye-fuck each other and grab Blaze's laptop. I hack into the city's traffic cams and bring up the one nearest to the harbor drop-off. We all know it well; we've watched these runs plenty of times when Henry thought we were there to help. It's the end of the month and around the time a drop off is done. Pepe also confirmed Mack was waiting for that container before making another trip to Nevada. The Highway Knights buy them to auction off to the MC members to do as they wish with them. Selene told us Jan spent a month at the Knight's compound, being abused constantly, and that's how Papi found her.

"Let's call Loqi and see if he's heard anything about a shipment for the Knights." I look at Santos.

"My brother probably has a mole in the Knight's compound, I know over the years my father has caught many of theirs in Dientes compound. It's how they operate. You can never be too sure if a prospect is a genuine person or a spy." Cara chimes in.

"Fine, I'll call the asshole." Santos pulls his phone from his pocket. Once he's dialed the number, he turns on the speaker, and places it in the center of the table.

"Is Cara okay?" Loqi asks as soon as he picks up, causing his sister to roll her eyes.

"Of course I am," she sneers. "I'm being looked after properly."

"Okay," Loqi sounds a bit defeated, "that's good. I will try to get up there to see you soon, we've been a bit tied up here."

She shrugs, completely unaffected by her brother trying to make an effort and leans back in her chair, the silence hanging heavy around us.

"Hello?" Loqi calls into the phone, and Santos clears his throat.

"Hey."

"Santos, what's up *hermano*?" Loqi asks.

I can see the slight change in Santos' demeanor with Loqi calling him brother, "we're closing in on Mack up here, but I was wondering, have you heard about any monthly shipments headed for the Knights?"

"Yeah, we have a guy in there who feeds us info. The shipment is already on its way. It'll be here in a few days. Why?"

"Fuck," I growl, "we need to intercept that transport."

"Those shipments are moved like armored trucks, there's no intercepting it. Why? Is there someone on it who you know?"

"No, we're trying to flush Mack out, and we figured the best way would be to fuck up his shipment before he got his hands on it."

"I see," Loqi hums, "we don't usually get involved in those until the girls have been discarded, it's too risky. But, let me see what I can find out, and if we go forward on intercepting, be prepared for a bloodbath."

"Is there any other way to bathe?" Santos snickers, and his brother chuckles.

"Not in this life, *hermano*."

The phone call ends, and Selene huffs from her seat, “does this mean I don’t get to kill the guy at the harbor?”

“You can kill whoever you want.” Santos grins at her.

“You’re with me tonight.” She snaps her fingers.

“Hopefully it catches Mack’s attention.” I tap my fingers to my chin.

“I have his phone number.” Pepe straightens, “maybe you could send him a detailed video?”

I fucking knew this kid would come in handy. “Good idea.”

I’ve pulled up everything I could find on Christos Alexopoulos. His parents immigrated here from Greece, bringing their small, overseas shipping company with them. Over the years it’s expanded into a large corporation, with Christos at its head.

He’s a model citizen—as most of them are—with his foundations and charities. Tonight, he’s holding a charity gala at the Ritz Carlton to raise money for children with terminal cancer, and I’ve purchased two plates at twenty thousand a pop. It’s all worth it to see the excitement on Selene’s face, and not to mention how her body looks in a red, silk cocktail gown. Her hair is swept up into an intricate updo, with pieces curling down around her face, and her makeup is subtle, but those lips shine a bright red.

“You’re gorgeous,” I breathe as I haul her into my body.

“I can’t wear my belt.” She pouts.

“That’s why you have me with you.” Santos comes to stand beside her, looking dapper in an all-black three-piece-suit. His black, curly hair is brushed back over his head and gleaming with gel.

Selene is soaking him in like he’s a tall glass of water on the hottest day, her mouth hanging open. I have to agree with her, he’s never looked this put-together.

"Doesn't he look handsome?" Darius comes up behind him and kisses his neck. He reaches beyond Santos and grabs Selene's arm, pulling her from me and into Santos.

"Yes." Selene smiles, finally finding her voice. "It's nice every now and then, but I still love my boy rough around the edges." She kisses Santos softly, then kisses Darius over his shoulder.

"Let's run over the details before you three leave." I motion for us to sit on the couch.

Darius is their chauffeur tonight, and we've packed the rental with a few necessary things for tonight to go smoothly.

"We go in for dinner," Selene looks at Santos who's rubbing his hands together.

"I can't wait for some filet mignon." He grins, "extra bloody."

"I can't wait to kill this guy." Selene wiggles in her seat.

"At least his blood will be disguised by that dress." I grin. "Run through what will happen after dinner."

"I will find Christos and ask him to have a drink with me." Selene grins, "maybe flirt a little, and then act drunk, letting it slip how badly I want to fuck him in my limo."

"I'll leave right after dinner, and wait for them in the limo," Santos adds.

"We'll knock him out and bring him back to his port at the harbor." Darius tags on.

"And then the real fun begins." Selene nods, her teeth gleaming a bright white against the red of her lips.

Selene

Dinner is finished, and I'm still fucking starving. There were about a hundred different courses, and each plate had portions that wouldn't fill a toddler. These rich people are fucking ridiculous.

I watch as Santos leaves the banquet room, his tight ass bulging with each step. I have to find a way to get him into suit pants more often. Once he's out of sight, I get up out of my seat, and head over to the small group of men enjoying crystal tumblers of amber liquid. They look important and they must be if Christos is in the center of them. Maybe he's trying to entice them to join his lucrative skin export business.

I saunter up and lean against the bar, waiting to be noticed. It doesn't take long because most men love tits and the color red.

"Johnny," a man calls out from the group beside me, I don't look to find out which one, "get this beautiful lady a drink. We mustn't keep her waiting."

"Yes, sir." The bartender hurries over.

I look over my shoulder and find all four of the men looking at me with predatory smiles. I want to give them one of my own, but I swallow down the urge. Instead, I give them what I'm hoping looks like a timid uptick of my lips, "thank you." I say softly.

"What can I get you, miss?" The bartender asks. I'd kill for a fucking whiskey, but I'm supposed to be a gentile lady.

"A glass of champagne, please." I answer softly, my voice barely above a whisper.

I feel the heat of a body moving in closely behind me, and I once again have to tamper down the urge to turn around and deck a bitch.

"Which company are you from?" I turn slowly at the sound of his voice and come face to face with Christos himself. He's handsome in an older gentlemanly way. He sort of reminds me of Henry Walton, only more refined.

"I'm here for a friend who couldn't make it this year." I bleed sadness into my tone, just as Zander told me to do.

Christos' blue eyes crinkle around the edges and curiosity shines from his dark olive complexion. He tips his head, and his dark hair slips a bit out of place. "Who might I ask is your friend?"

"Was," I drop my gaze from him, making sure to put a slight tremble in my bottom lip, "Henry Walton."

"Henry was your friend?" He sounds skeptical and he should, that old fucker didn't have friends, only whores and business associates.

"We were… um…" I look around for effect, "intimate friends."

"Oh, I see." He nods and gives me a once over, "it's sad what happened to him."

"I was told it was a break in," I sniff and let my eyes water, "but I can't believe, it just doesn't add up."

I turn back to the bar and find my champagne glass, tipping it back and drinking it all down in one gulp. I sniff again and lift my hand to the bartender; I'm using my so-called grief to pretend to get myself drunk.

I look at Christos over my shoulder and find him studying my ass, "sorry. I just get so worked up whenever I think about it."

"I understand," his eyes are darker now as he begins to see me in a different light. "How long did you *know* Henry?"

"Two years." I suck back the next glass and set it on the bar. "I shouldn't have done that," I stumble a bit and right myself with a hand to his chest, "I've never been able to hold my alcohol." I hold a hand to my stomach.

"Do you need me to call you a car?" He places his hand on my shoulder, the fingers gliding over my skin.

"My car is outside. But thank you, mister?"

"My name is Christos Alexopoulos." He smiles, and I let my eyes widen with false shock.

"Oh my!" I hold my hand to my mouth, "I'm so sorry, I had no idea. I must look so foolish."

"On the contrary, Henry was a good friend of mine, as well. How about I walk you to your car, miss?"

"Oh, I couldn't ask you to leave your own gala." I give him my best seductive eyes, "I may not let you return. My name is Selene."

"Is that right?" He grins, his hand slowly making its way down my arm. "I think I could disappear for an hour and make it back in time for my speech."

Nope, the only speech you'll be making will be to my knife as I cut you open.

I bite into my bottom lip and look him over slowly, letting my desire saturate the air around us. "Okay." I whisper.

He leads me out of the gala, leaving behind his snickering friends, and places his hand on my lower back.

"I see a tattoo peeking out above your dress," his fingers skate along the top of my shoulder blades. "What is it?"

"Let's get to my limo and I'll show you." I grin at him over my shoulder.

I can't wait to show him just what that tattoo means.

"What about your date? Did you come alone?" He asks as I take out my phone to text Darius.

"He came for the food; I haven't been able to replace Henry." I give him a sad, wide-eyed look.

He hums his reply, and the hand that's resting on my lower back slips down further over my ass. We step out from the hotel entrance, and I see my limo idling there. I step down the first stair when Christos grips the nape of my neck in a tight hold.

"Did you think I was fucking stupid, whore?" The pure venom in his words tells me he didn't buy my act.

"You're hurting me," I whine. "What are you doing?"

"Henry never entertained anyone for longer than a few nights," he halts our descent down the stairs, his fingers biting into the column of my throat. "He was a very close friend of mine."

"Couldn't have been too close," I try to continue to play my part, "he was with me for two years." I hate that I didn't wear an outfit that matched my belt.

"Wave your driver off and come with me." He demands. I wave Darius off, throwing a grin to his window, knowing he's watching me. He won't let me out of his sights.

"Where are you taking me?" My voice shakes, and I congratulate myself, acting scared is not easy.

He leads me to a white limo parked in the lot, and taps on the roof, his hand still firmly around my neck. It's really starting to ache, and I'm about five seconds from jabbing him in the eyes. The driver gets out and comes around to open the door for us.

"You couldn't open your own door?" I sneer, unable to control myself.

He shoves me inside, and I fall across the seat, cursing when my six-inch heel twists my ankle in an awkward position. I reach down to undo the buckle as he gets in the seat beside me. The door shuts, and I settle back in my seat, not in the least bit worried.

"Where are you taking me?" I ask him. "Or are we doing this right here?"

He gives me a strange look, "I'm going to dispose of you."

"Why would you want to do that?" I huff, "I'm nothing but a simple whore."

He yanks me around, so my back is to him, and unzips my dress in the back. So, he wants to fuck then dispose.

"Ah," he chuckles, "there it is. The Reaper Incarnate." My heart stills. "Did you think our circle doesn't know about you? We know you were the one who killed Henry, I saw the top of your scythe tattoo while you were at the bar."

Fuck.

"And?" I sneer over my shoulder, "you're not even the slightest bit afraid?"

"No." He hollers out a laugh as the car pulls out into traffic, "I'll have you disposed of and back in time to make my speech. You're really that cocky to show up to this thing without backup?"

"I'm the Reaper Incarnate." I give him a large grin, "why would I need backup? You heard about what happened to Henry, so, why aren't you scared?"

His fist collides with my cheek, and I immediately see stars. "That wasn't nice," I tsk. "Where are we going?"

He ignores me as he types something on his phone, and I turn to look out the window. I hope Darius is following us since he has the weapon stash. We head to the harbor, and I bite into my cheek to hold my scowl in place. He's falling into our trap even though this isn't going as planned.

"Are you going to drown me?" I snicker.

"No, I'm going to slit your throat and leave you in a shipping container. Your body won't be discovered for months while you're out to sea."

"That's cool, I've always wanted to take a cruise." I smile sweetly.

"Oh yeah?" He laughs, "while you're dead?"

"It's all an adventure, am I right? Life, death." I wave my hand over my head. "And I'll meet back up with my lover Henry. I'll give him one final pegging while we wait at the gates of Hell."

He screws up his face in disgust.

"His son tends to like a good pegging, too." I say as we pull into the pier, "must be something in the genes."

"You're working with Zander Walton?"

"Working? Oh no, he's my boyfriend." I wiggle my foot in my unbuckled shoe, "he helped me take down Henry, and you're just a stepping-stone on our way to Mack Delaney."

"Then why the fuck did he let you come here alone?" He asks as I cross my leg over my knee.

"Who says I'm alone?" At my words, he turns his head to look out of the window, and I grab my dangling shoe, striking the thin stiletto into his cheek. It sinks through the delicate flesh, and the car slams to a halt at the sound of Christos' screams.

I hear tires squealing behind us over Christos' squawking, and then gunfire. I grab the stiletto out of his cheek, and the blood begins to gush down over his suit.

"Oh no, how will you make a speech looking like the Bride of Chucky?" I put my bloody shoe back on and open the door, finding the driver's dead body lying on the asphalt. "Oh, look." I point to the body, "maybe we'll send him on a cruise instead?"

I get out of the limo and step over the body, turning to see two of my men striding toward me. This is like the part of an action movie where the good guys are walking in slow motion, guns in their hands, and sadistic grins on their faces. I practically moan at how gorgeous they are.

"Is my baby okay?" Santos gets to me first, hauling me into his chest.

"Yep." I look over my shoulder as Darius yanks Christos out of the limo, "that man promised me a cruise and I don't think he'll be able to keep up his end of the bargain." I pout up into Santos' face.

"We'll go on a fucking world cruise once we take out these motherfuckers." He grins down at me, and I swoon.

"Selene," Darius calls out as he holds onto a struggling Christos, "what did you jab through his face?"

"My heel." I lift up my foot to show him the evidence, "whose face has my shoe been stuck in?" I begin to sing along to the tune of a Shania Twain song as I walk toward Darius and Christos.

Santos chuckles behind me and hums along. I stand in front of the sack of shit and slap him hard on the cheek, my hand sticking to the blood there. Christos grunts through the pain, and Darius groans.

"Fuck, I just want to sink my cock so deep into you right now."

"Why don't you guys head out?" Santos stabs his finger through the hole in Christos' cheek, laughing when the man screams. "You two have yet to pound each other alone." He gives me a wink, "don't break him, I want my turn when I get back."

Darius groans again and pushes Christos into Santos' arms. "Make sure you put the scythe on him baby," I kiss his cheek, "we're all the Reaper Incarnate now."

Santos

My dick's so fucking hard right now, it hurts. Between being left to torture this piece of shit, and knowing Selene and Darius are off fucking each other's brains out, it's no wonder. They need some alone time, and let's face it, I don't need help torturing someone. I'm in my fucking element.

I drag Christos toward an empty shipping container, ignoring his grunts of protest. I always find it hilarious how these big, tough assholes show no mercy when abusing and trading women and children, but the moment they meet someone who can fight back? They cower and cry. Pussies.

"Let me go!" the pussy demands, his voice sharp but with a hint of fear. I take a deep breath in, reveling in the scent. "This all comes back to Mack, go after him instead, you heathen!"

"Wait, you think I'm pissed at you over that? Pfft, I'm going to rip you apart for that awful excuse of a dinner. I'm feeling insulted, and I'm fucking starving. Sorry if it makes me a little moody," I grin, shoving him into the container and causing him to stumble, his body sprawling across the ground with a thud.

He scrambles to his feet and tries to lunge at me, but I shoot one of his kneecaps, dropping him back to the ground with a cry of pain. It's a shame Selene's not here. I would have bent her over his corpse when I finished and coated our skin in his blood to celebrate. Another time, I guess.

Christos is wailing like a baby, clasping his bloodied knee in his hands while tears track down his cheeks. Pathetic, really.

"You want me to stop?" I ask with fake confusion. "I bet all those women you kidnapped probably asked the same thing of you. Such a shame you didn't listen. An eye for an eye, and all that jazz."

I fire a shot into his other knee, stopping him from going too far if he tries to seize the opportunity. Two bad knees are better than one, in my eyes. His agonizing scream sends a shiver of pleasure down my spine, I smirk at him as I step closer, and he attempts to crawl away. “Uh, Uh. Where do you think you’re going? Don’t run off, I have to set up a little something for Mack, then we can get started!”

He’s sniveling in the corner now, giving me time to turn and set my phone up against the opposite wall of the container. The lighting is awful, so I turn the phone light on then turning my attention back to the little bitch I left on the floor. “So, in the words of my baby girl, do you want to play a game?”

“No! I’ll cut Mack off! I’ll never touch a woman again! Let me leave and I’ll…”

I pull one of my blades from my belt, flicking it at him so it sinks into his shoulder with ease, his screams music to my ears. “Too little, too late. You should count yourself lucky it’s not my girl in here with you. You’ve heard what she did to Henry, right? Or would you have preferred her methods over mine? I can call them to bring me a big dildo if you wish, no lube, of course,” I murmur, stepping closer to yank my blade out of his flesh.

“No! Look, let’s talk. Man to man. That little blonde cunt of yours just…”

I grab his throat and drag him to his feet, forcing him to stand on his damaged legs. “My little what? I didn’t quite hear you. Now, I know you didn’t just insult my baby girl. Would you like to repeat that?” I ask in a low voice, grinning when he cries out. I make him take his own weight, seconds before letting him go, and watch him crumble to the floor. Kneecaps are important when you want to stand, you know?

“Your crazy girlfriend must have gotten her facts wrong! I’m not even that involved in Mack’s skin business!” he spits, anger filling his eyes.

I tut, my lips curving into a sadistic smirk. “But you admit you’re involved? Besides, my girlfriend’s not crazy, she’s enthusiastic. You should see the way her pretty eyes light up when she kills someone. She…”

“But I…”

I sink another knife into him, not meeting his eyes. "Excuse me, Daddy's talking! Anyways, as I was saying before I was so *rudely* interrupted, my girl's really enthusiastic about our cause. You see, this is personal to her. She's seriously fuckable when she gets wind of creeps like you. You don't even have to touch the women involved, but you're still involved. An accessory to the crime, if you may." Then I throw another knife at him, nailing him in the crotch. *Oops*?

He screams, his voice already rough. "What was that for!"

"I don't really like you, Christos. I also have a twitchy hand, so I have a tendency to throw things by accident. You know what? I have a fun game we can play. Take off your shoes."

"I can't, you psychopath! You blew out my knees!" he snaps. I shrug, reaching down to grasp his ankle firmly, bending his knee painfully to take his shoe off. His cries bounce off the confined walls, making me smile. I whistle, wanting to feel like my baby girl is beside me while I play. Her energy usually gets me going, and by the time I have both of his shoes off, I'm fired up and ready to go. Now the party's started.

I sit on the floor, tilting my head slightly as I pull pliers from my pocket. I'm more into stabbing people and calling it a day, but I want to change things up. I like being spontaneous.

I hold his ankle firmly in my hand, squeezing his big toenail between the tips of my pliers. "This little piggy went to market."

"No!" he screams, just as I yank and twist, ripping the toenail from the skin, blood flowing like art down his foot. I can't help but stare at it, the bright crimson drawing me in like a moth to a flame.

He tries to sit up and shove me away, but I pull one of the blades from him and plunge it into his unharmed shoulder. That should slow him down a little. I soak in his sounds of pain, going for the next toenail with a smile. "This little piggy stayed home. Silly piggy, that sounds boring."

He continues to scream through my nursery rhyme while I work. Starting over on his other foot. He's skin is covered in sweat, his feet bloodied, and his voice horse. This is only the warmup; I have no idea what he's crying about. I haven't even fucking started yet.

"Give me your hand," I ask nicely, scowling when he shakes his head. "Fine. But for the record, I tried to be nice."

I get to my feet and walk around him grabbing his hand, flattening it on the cold ground. His fingers curl, trying to hide the nails, but I'm not going for those. I lift my foot and stomp down hard, hearing the magical sound of bones crunching from under the sole of my boot. He screams, blubbering and getting snot all over his face. It's disgusting.

I do it again, making sure to grind my foot in the process, drawing as much pain out as possible. I suddenly remember my sister, and anger takes over at knowing these pricks are the reason she was taken. I make quick work of his other hand, then I grab a knife and cut down the center of his shirt, exposing his chest and stomach.

"Please, stop! I'll tell you anything you want! Don't kill me!" Christos begs, halting my movements. I stare at him thoughtfully for a second, before grinning darkly.

"Don't you see? We already know everything. You're here as a message for Mack. He's next on our list, but you're just a little steppingstone in our path to get to him. You know, my sister was taken years ago. I didn't even know she existed, but I've found her and can't help but hold a grudge. She's family, and no one fucks with my family, *comprende*?" I move toward my phone, turning on the camera before squatting down beside the piece of shit. "Say hi to Mack."

When he stays quiet, I punch him swiftly in the ribs, pulling a groan from him. "I said, 'say hi to Mack'. I don't have all night, believe it or not."

"Mack! Help me!" he sobs, making me cackle.

"What, you think this is live? You'll be dead before he gets it. Right, Mack? You know the drill. Where should I start cutting? Maybe here?" I question myself out loud as I start dragging my knife through his flesh, ignoring his agony as I carve patterns. I start whistling again, getting lost in the sounds of pain and the smell of blood. I'm covered in it. I wish my baby girl were here so I could mark her body with my bloodied handprints, my knife leaving scars across her perfectly imperfect skin.

I snap out of it when Christos makes a wheezing noise, my eyes going wide. "Oops! I got a little carried away. Hold tight, I'm not done yet."

He doesn't answer me, his body weak from the blood loss, and I can't help myself as I stand and start kicking his ribs until blood flies from his lips. I've punctured something with his broken ribs, most likely his lung. The more he wheezes, the harder my dick gets. I can't wait to watch the light leave his eyes so I can get out of here and sink myself into my lovers.

I set to work, drawing Selene's famous scythe on his forehead, chuckling as I add, *The Reaper was here*, down his one arm that's not as bloody as the other. Now he looks good and ready to meet his maker.

"Hey, Mack?" I grin into the camera, holding it close to my face as Christos makes one final, wet choking sound behind me. "We're coming for you. Enjoy this little gift, courtesy of the Reaper Incarnate. If you keep hiding like a little bitch, I'll have to play with Pepe. You know, your son? I've taken quite a shine to him. I might even fuck the Jesus right out of him before letting him bleed out. We'll be seeing you soon," then I wink for the fun of it and show him the mess I made of Christos again before ending the video, grinning as I send it.

Of course, I'd never hurt my Pepe, but Mack doesn't know that.

I grab all my toys, wiping them off on Christos' shirt, then I leave him in the container for Mack to find. I head toward his car, whistling to myself as I go, looking forward to getting home to my family.

Darius

I don't even get in the front door before Selene attacks my mouth with hers, almost making me trip. Her teeth nip at my lip sharply, while her hands yank at my shirt, demanding I take it off. Someone chuckles, drawing our attention as we stumble through the door, my shirt on the floor and my pants undone.

"Good night?" Zander smirks, eyeing Selene as she shamelessly pulls her dress off, not caring that we have an audience. Pepe sputters from the couch, and Cara scowls at him, muttering under her breath about getting a spoon and carving his eyes out.

"Yep, Santos will be back soon," I reply, Selene's lips crashing into mine again as she starts pushing me backwards toward the hallway.

"Wait, you left him alone?" Blaze barks, and Selene pulls back from me with a huff, her hands going to her hips.

"He's fine. He needs to let out some demons, and I needed to fuck Darius. What's the issue?"

"What if someone followed you? Or someone catches him? Stop thinking with your pussy!"

She stalks over to him and jabs a finger in his chest, glaring up at him with defiance. "Santos told us to head back, and we scoped out the place properly, double checking on our way out. Let him play."

"How about I fucking spank you?" he grits out, her eyes gleaming with heat.

"Later, Daddy. I have a date with Darius. You get in line."

He goes to argue with her, but I grab her hand and haul her toward the hallway, shutting us in my room and shoving her toward the bed. She looks perfect, laid out across my blankets, her hair fanning around her and making her look like the goddess she is.

I kick my pants off, my boxers flying with them, and then I'm on her. She moans into my mouth as I grind against her, my hands grabbing hers to yank them above her head, pushing her delicious tits up more. She mewls, the soft sound sending electricity down my spine. I pull back and leave her in nothing but her fuck-me heels, an idea popping into my head suddenly.

"Trust me?"

"With my life," she says at once, licking her lips in anticipation.

"I have a surprise for you," I smirk, climbing from the bed and rummaging in the closet until I find what I've been looking for. The metal chains clank as I pull them out, her eyes widening.

"I was looking for those!"

"Well, I wanted to hide them in case Blaze got any ideas of throwing them away. You look so pretty when you're tied up at my mercy," I growl, heading toward her and closing one of the metal cuffs around her wrist.

"I'm supposed to be in charge!" she whines, but she doesn't attempt to pull her hands away, telling me she likes being dominated by me. It's strange not having Santos beside me, murmuring curses about her stunning body, and I know he'll barge in the moment he's home, so I have to work fast.

Once she's secure, I don't hesitate to push her thighs apart with my shoulders and go to town on her pussy with my mouth. I don't want to restrain her legs, loving how they clench around my head. If she suffocates me with her pussy, I'll die a happy man.

The chains rattle as she tries to touch me, an annoyed huff coming from her. Surprisingly, she doesn't voice it, letting me take full control from her, knowing I'll have her screaming for the heavens in no time.

I run a finger through her dampness as I suck at her clit, moving my finger down until it reaches her tight ass, her breath hitching a fraction as I toy with her. It doesn't take long for her to get impatient.

"Hurry up and fuck me!"

I chuckle, not changing pace until I'm suddenly pushing my finger into her ass, her back arching off the bed. "Oh, fuck!"

I push it in and out of her faster, my tongue worshipping her clit until her thighs tighten around my head, almost crushing my skull. She comes loudly, and I have to press my free arm across her stomach to keep her on the bed. I don't let up, my name sounding too good coming from her lips as she screams.

I finally ease off, letting her recover for a moment before I climb up her body and kiss her. The chains rattle again, making me grin as I stare into her eyes. "We're only just getting started, baby."

"I'd like my hands back now," she pants. "I want to touch you."

"Nope," I reply, popping the *P* and kissing down her neck, biting her hard. She groans loudly, her legs wrapping tight around my waist.

"Even if I say please instead of '*get fucked*'?"

"I'm not letting you go. Ever," I murmur, her eyes narrowing. It's fun winding her up, and it gets my dick hard. Obviously, I'll untie her when I am finished ravishing her, but not yet.

I lift one of her legs over my shoulder, aligning my painfully hard dick against her soaked pussy, not giving her any warning before slamming home. Her eyes squeeze shut as she screams, her fists bunching since she can't do anything else with them, and I growl.

"Eyes on me, baby."

They fly open, holding mine as I lean further over her and piston hard into her, her tits bouncing against my chest, her hard nipples dragging across my skin. She feels like home, just like Santos, and I know I won't last long if I don't slow down.

"You look so perfect chained up," I groan, slowing enough to lean down and take one of her pert nipples in my mouth. She gasps, trying to pull her hands out of the metal cuffs by force, and I wonder if she'll break her hands trying to get to me. Knowing she'll hurt herself in order to touch me causes a primal growl to burn in my chest, and I slam into her as hard and deep as I can.

It sends her into a sudden climax, and she almost deafens me with her screams, urging me on as I fuck her through it. Her body's quivering under mine, completely spent, but I know she can still walk. We can't have that.

I pull out and flip her over, her wrists twisting awkwardly, and I lift her to her knees. My eyes roam over the reaper tattoo down her back, and I run my fingers over the dark ink, mesmerized by her beauty. She's turned all four of us into sappy pricks, and I have zero problems with that. Being alone with her makes me realize how serious this is. I mean, I've always been serious about her, but Santos isn't here to banter with, we aren't playing games. It's just Selene and I, getting lost in each other, and it feels so fucking right.

I fist her long, blonde hair, yanking her head back sharply as I sink myself into her pussy from behind, her arms straining from the chains. "Fuck, I love you."

She's quiet for a moment, but she answers when I start thrusting in and out.

"I love you too, D. So fucking much."

"Brace yourself," I warn. "This will be hard and fast."

She grunts a response, but I don't pay much attention. I keep her hair tight in my fist and fuck her hard, the headboard slamming against the wall, letting everyone know what we're doing. I'd be concerned about their hearing if they weren't already aware, but that isn't the point.

She's screaming my name within minutes, her body convulsing around me as I yank her back sharply by the hair, fucking into her and drawing her body back to mine, my sweaty chest plastered to her back. I reach around and tease her clit, wanting to pull one more orgasm from her before I bust myself.

"I can't!" she moans. "It's too much!"

"Fucking come for me!" I snap, hardly recognizing my own voice. When the fuck did I channel Blaze? Oh well, it works for me.

A low groan leaves her at my command, and when she finally clamps down on my dick again, I come, burying myself inside her, as deep as possible, my legs shaking from the intensity of it. We collapse in a heap, catching our breaths, and she rolls over to face me, her eyes soft.

"Hey, D?"

"Yeah, baby?"

Her eyes narrow and she gives the chains a tug, reminding me she's still tied up. "Unlock the shackles before I kill you."

"Since you asked so nicely," I grin, managing to unchain her and drop the metal in a heap on the floor. I pull her against my chest and press a kiss to her forehead. "Better?"

"I can't feel my hands," she snorts, nuzzling into me affectionately. "But yeah. Better."

I sit up and shuffle back against the headboard, hauling her in front of me. Her back sticks to my chest from the sweat, but I don't give a shit. I'll get messy with her any day.

I reach around and take her arm in my hands, massaging her soft skin to help the blood flow, a content sigh leaving her. I do the same for the other arm, leaving kisses across her shoulder as I dote on her.

"I like spending time with just you," I admit, her head tilting to the side to look at me.

"Me, too. We should try and do it more often. Just because you and Santos are together too, doesn't mean we have to always share. Next time, I'm tying you up," she grins, and my dick jerks in agreement. "You like the sound of that?"

"Chained to the bed with you riding me? Sounds like Heaven," I grin, my hands moving to her thighs to continue the massage. The little sighs coming from her warm my chest, and without thinking too much, I slide out from under her and roll her onto her stomach.

"What are you doing?" she mumbles, tired from our fun.

"Giving you a massage," I reply, thinking she'll argue. Instead, she melts into the mattress as my fingers work over her tight muscles, eventually putting her to sleep.

I curl up beside her, giving in to my tired body and sleeping too, only waking up when a hard body presses against my back, and cool liquid is rubbed over my asshole. I shift onto my stomach more, parting my legs, and hearing Santos' groan, the scent of shampoo and soap filling my nose.

"I missed you guys tonight."

"We missed you, too," I murmur, glancing at Selene's sleeping form. Santos chuckles softly, his lips trailing along my neck.

"Seems like you wore her out. You're not too tired for me, are you?"

"Never. Fuck me."

He sinks into me, not seeming hurried, his lips brushing my ear as he speaks, "I love you, D."

"I love you too, *amante*."

Blaze

I watch as Zander books seven first class tickets to Vegas and tut. He gives me a look with his brow raised.

"What?"

"Do we really need first class?" I raise my brow right back.

"You tell me, brother," he leans back in his seat. "All seven of us crammed into coach, how many times will we have to pull Santos off Selene? How many times will we have to keep watch over Cara and Pepe? Then, who's going to stop you from dragging Selene to the bathroom?"

"No one is fucking stopping me if that's what I want to do." I snap at him.

"Exactly," he shakes his head, looking weary, "at least we'll have a bit more privacy."

I don't have any other argument because he's right. All seven of us crammed in coach would be catastrophic.

"Did we get anything else back about the shipment?"

"Yeah, Loqi's guy inside the Knights compound said they're meeting up with Mack himself the day after tomorrow. That's why I booked the tickets for the first flight out tomorrow. We need to plan this perfectly, like Loqi said, this one is going to be tricky." His brows crease as worry takes over his features. "I don't want anything to happen to us."

"Nothing will happen." I scoff. "It's a miracle we've survived this long."

"I know," he exhales, "something feels off," his hand lands on his chest. "I don't like it."

Maybe this feeling he's getting is the same one that's been keeping me on edge. I feel like everything is about to explode and we're not getting out of this unscathed like all the other times.

Or, maybe I'm becoming as big of a bitch as Zander, and I need to remember my balls are bigger than his.

We touch down in Nevada—surprisingly after a quiet flight—around mid-day, and the heat is already stifling. I hate this weather; I could never live in Nevada all-year-round. Selene, Santos, and Darius are stretching and yawning, waking up from their naps on the plane. It was a quiet flight because they slept the whole time, and I'm thankful they burned themselves out last night.

After we grab our bags, we find Loqi leaning against a blacked-out SUV with another one parked behind it. He looks tired, but when he sees his sister, he perks up. I chance a glance at Cara and watch as her features soften. As much as she went through, she can't completely blame Loqi. He was young as well, and really, a lot of kids disappear from their guardian's sight.

"Cara!" He steps forward, unsure of how she'll react to him.

"Hi Luis." She goes forward and wraps her arms around his waist.

"Who's Luis?" Zander asks, and Cara laughs as she pulls out of her brother's embrace.

"You really didn't think his name was Loqi, did you?"

"I never really cared," Zander shrugs. "What's Papi Loco's real name?"

"Santiago." Santos answers, and we all fall quiet. "Similar to mine."

"We don't have much time," Loqi says, "we need to plan this out, and be prepared for every scenario."

We get into the SUVs and head to the compound. I'm not at all happy to see it again so soon, and I can't wait to be done with all this. We head inside and a few of the guys we've come accustomed to holler out our names. As fucked up as this place is, they really are like a large family. Not that I have room to talk, the five of us—now seven—are the same, just on a smaller scale.

We leave Cara and Pepe to sit at the bar with Licker and follow Loqi down the narrow corridor toward Papi's office. It's quiet, not one snicker from any of us, and I can't help the ominous feeling that washes over me. My feet are following behind Loqi, one step in front of the other without hesitation, but my instincts are screaming for me to stop and turn around. I look over my shoulder to find Selene gripping Santos' arm, her teeth worrying into her bottom lip. Zander is on her other side, that crease between his brows a constant feature, and Darius shuffling beside me, watching the back of Loqi's head like he wants to take a bite out of it.

Loqi doesn't bother to make us wait this time as he opens his father's office door. Inside are a few guys and sitting on Papi's lap is Henny.

"Selly!" She jumps up and rushes to Selene. They embrace and Selene's eyes close as she takes in a deep breath.

"Hey, Jan." She says quietly.

"I don't like this," Henny looks around the room. "I think we should find another way to take down Mack."

"He has a shipping container filled with girls, Jan" Selene cuts in. "Surely, you know what they're feeling."

Henny's shoulders deflate and she grabs her sister's hand. "This is going to be very dangerous, and I wish I could command you to stay here with me."

We all make our way around the large table, taking seats as Henny and Selene continue their hushed conversation.

"Son." Papi nods to Santos, who grumbles as he sits down. He's a long road away from forgiving his father.

"The Highway Knights are a ruthless group of animals." Loqi spits out. "The shipment we intercepted before was small, and they sent mostly prospects for the pick-up. That's why we took them down so easily."

"Our bomb specialist, Boomer, is in their compound now, and he's been with them for the past two years." Papi Loco cuts in, "he's our eyes and ears to the internal going-on in that compound. Their monthly shipment of young girls is their most lucrative business."

The room falls quiet as everyone silently seethes. We've been fighting this stain on our home soil for years, but to know it's rampant all over the US is daunting. There's no way we can bring it all down on our own.

"We can make an impact," Darius says, cutting through the silence, "we know Mack is a big player in the distribution of these girls and we've taken out three of his well-known associates. We can do this, and we have to do this." He looks from Santos to Zander, then his eyes land on me. "We've been fighting this war for years, he's the last piece of the puzzle. We can't back down now."

"We're not backing down." Santos' fist hits the tabletop, "not after what they did to the girls we love. Even if we all die tomorrow while killing him, it'll be worth it. We'll continue to kill him for eternity in Hell."

"I'm with you, brother." Loqi reaches his fist across the table, and Santos smashes his to it. "Let's go out in a blaze of glory."

I want to be on the same page as them, I want to feel what they're feeling, but I just can't settle this bubbling anxiety inside of me.

"I think Selene should stay here." Santos says, as he turns to look at our fuming woman. "I need you alive."

"Fuck you," she snaps at him, "you need me out there to keep your unpredictable ass alive. Without me, you'd have been dead the first night I met you."

I can see the tears building in her eyes, and Darius' chuckle draws our attention, "I think that was the moment he fell in love with you, when your blade cracked open that Diablo's skull."

"Without a doubt." Santos nods, his face still solemn.

"The drop off point is never the same place twice, but Boomer has found a way to be there, and he'll text us the location as soon as he has it. This gives us a disadvantage because we don't know the terrain, and we'll lose our spy inside their walls." Papi states.

"It'll be nice to have our boy back home, though." Hook chimes in, his one eye shining with anticipation.

"Agreed." Papi nods. "So, this is how it's going to go down, and listen closely because Boomer left us a few surprises."

Chapter Twelve

Zander

Three hours locked in that room planning what could be our very last hit. Our final fight, and instead of being afraid, I feel elated. Something inside of me is so proud of what me and my brothers have become, and we wouldn't have gotten this far without Selene.

I was seventeen when I saw my father strangle my mother to death, then throw her body into the pool. I was petrified. Back then, I knew he was shady; I knew his company did some illegal shit, and the thought of confronting him scared me. So, when the cops showed up and proved they were on my father's payroll, helping him cover up his murder, I knew something had to be done. My mother's death certificate says drowning due to intoxication, and I can never change that, but I've worked hard to avenge her murder.

In a heated argument a few years later, he admitted to killing her, and all because she threatened to go to the cops about his business in our basement. He fed me the same threat time after time, thinking he was molding me into his protege the whole time my brothers and I were planning his demise.

With Selene's help we succeeded, but then uncovered a whole can of worms. This became our life's mission, but I can't wait to see it come to an end. I want to watch Mack bleed out at the hands of one of us, not caring who, just wanting to be able to see it with my own eyes.

We're lying in a room with two king-sized beds pushed together, care of Sunshine who I'm sure is warming up to us, even though she called us a warren of rabbits. We're quiet and that's saying a lot since both Selene and Santos are here.

"Is this going to work?" Selene says, breaking the silence.

"It has to." Santos replies, his response sounding doomed.

"All for five and five for all." Selene whispers, and I don't know why that makes my throat clog with emotion.

"Always." Darius whispers back, "whether from here or beyond."

My vision blurs as I contemplate any of us *beyond*.

"Pepe has to come with us tomorrow," Santos cuts in, "Mack needs to see him, I need him to see how his son has chosen us over his father. But Cara needs to stay here."

"She won't be separated from him." Selene groans. "But yes, I agree."

"We'll have to tie her up somewhere." Blaze growls, "she has a mean left hook, and loves to go for the fucking balls."

Again, we fall into silence, something we've been doing for the last few days, and it's tinged with worry. I feel like our time is slowly drawing to a close, like sands in an hourglass, slowly tumbling until not a single grain is left.

"I love you guys." I blurt out, because I need them to know it, "each one of you is as important as the next, and I can't imagine anyone else when I think of family."

"Family forever," Darius joins in.

"No matter where we are, we'll always be together." Selene sniffs, her hand slipping into mine.

"Fuck this." Blaze gets up with a snarl, "I'm not sitting here and listening to our fucking eulogies. I need a drink."

He storms out of the room, slamming the door behind him, and making the walls vibrate with the force. It's silent again, not even the sound of our breathing penetrates the heavy fog, and I close my eyes to try and block out the worries of the unknown. My heart races as I try to imagine how tomorrow will go, and I'm worried the others will hear its pounding beat.

"I think Blaze has the right idea," Darius grunts as he rolls off our massive bed. "Let's go have a drink together tonight." He walks for the door; Santos follows close behind him.

Selene and I get up as well, and I grab her hand. I won't say it out loud, but it was almost as though Darius meant this would be the last time.

Selene

The sun is starting to set on the desert around us, casting reds and oranges, making the sand a vision of fire. Like the land is gradually transforming into Hell around us, a fiery premonition to what could come in the next hour or so. We're all tense, worry radiating from our pores in thick waves, nearly suffocating us. None of us wants to die when we feel like we've just begun to live.

Kevlar covers our chests and back—more mine than the guys whose bulky chests span wider—and our bodies are looking much like weapon arsenals. Both Darius and Santos have tied red bandanas around their heads to stave off the sweat, but I giggle at how closely they resemble Rambo.

Zander has been pacing a trench into the sand as he's stuck in his head, trying to control every aspect, and Blaze is a ball of burning fury on the cusp of exploding. I'm sitting next to a quiet Pepe as we play Tic-Tac-Toe in the sand. He's pretty calm considering we're thrusting him into battle with his father, while he believes the father in the clouds is protecting him.

"How many times do you think Cara has bitten Henny?" Darius snickers.

"None," Pepe answers solemnly, "she'll just feel abandoned all over again."

"She has never been abandoned." Loqi snaps back.

"That's how you see it, not her, though." Pepe meets Loqi's eyes, "if you make it out of this, I need you to make it right with her, no matter how hard she fights it. She deserves a family."

I prepare for Loqi's retort, expecting it to be filled with venom, and instead he gives Pepe a nod, his eyes softening for the man who cares for his sister. The other Dientes are huddled in a group not too far away, waiting for signs of company. Boomer told us they're coming in with twenty of their best enforcers, men trained to kill with their bare hands if need be, and he said they won't hesitate to take us out. No questions asked.

Not that we didn't already know that. Getting Mack and eliminating him is now our priority, no matter the cost.

I feel the vibration first, a soft tremor dancing along my fingertips as I draw my X in the sand. The sensation skates up my arm and slices through my heart. My head pops up at the same moment as Pepe, only he jumps to his feet quicker.

"They're coming." He pants.

Everyone is still, listening for the distant sound of engines, looking for the dust to kick up, and releasing our bated breaths. No matter what we're feeling on the inside, it's fucking showtime. As soon as the rumbles grow louder, we all scramble to our designated spots, and I end up beside Blaze.

He grabs my chin, looking me deep in the eyes, then crashing his lips to mine in a bruising kiss. "I love you," his teeth nip at my lip, "don't you dare get yourself killed, do you understand me?"

"Yes, Daddy." I whisper as I try to swallow down the lump in my throat.

"Good girl." He kisses me again.

We hear a soft whistle, the signal for the large eighteen-wheeler hauling a shipping container of young girls. Then the loud rumble of bikes reverberates off the Sierra Nevada mountains surrounding us, ramping up my heart. I stiffen, worrying about my guys. Are they in their spots? Should I have insisted the five of us stay together?

"I can taste your anxiety, Little Reaper." Blaze whispers harshly, "get yourself together, warrior."

"I'm scared." I whisper back as the sounds of the engines form one loud rumbling anthem.

"So am I." He whispers back, and I swallow down a sob.

"You're not allowed to die on me either." I grab the back of his shirt in my fist.

He gives me a nod and hauls me further down behind the boulder we were assigned to. Papi Loco has strategically placed us around the area giving us maximum coverage and opening up more targets, but it also leaves us in pairs with not a lot of back up if we ourselves are targeted.

The dust is thick around us in obscuring plumes, and I can barely see my hand in front of my face. This is bad, how can I aim if I can't fucking see? Blaze curses, probably feeling the same way. This isn't our everyday climate; we're not used to shooting in this environment. We'll be forced to follow the Dientes lead.

The engines finally stop, and the dust still hangs dense in the air, filling my lungs. My throat becomes dry, and I feel the overwhelming urge to clear it. My eyes begin to water just as we hear the first few voices. They're talking about the females inside the container, guessing at what they might look like, and how their tight, virgin cunts will feel later. The bile works its way up from my stomach, threatening to spill with my disgust.

"Hey!" Someone calls out, and my heart lurches up into my throat, "Mack himself came with this one, it must be a special haul."

"We gotta make this quick, boys." I hear the walking dental nightmare himself, "I have people who need killing back home."

The asshole, I grit my teeth, loving how the sound of the fat cunt's voice is bringing in an all-consuming rage, tearing through my fear. My hand finds one of the guns strapped to my waist and I grip the smooth handle in my palm.

"They have a bus with them." Blaze whispers, "the Knights. I bet that's where the girls will go."

"Yeah, when we bring them back to the Dientes compound." I snarl.

I hear the scrape of metal doors opening, and then the sudden onslaught of tears and screaming. My stomach twists as the men begin to hoot and holler, calling out to the young girls with obscenities.

"How much longer?"

"Papi said he wants the girls safely in the transport vehicle before we attack." Blaze reminds me.

"It's taking too long."

"Get yourself under control." He snaps.

I huff out my breath and roll my eyes, sticking my tongue out at the back of the bastard's head.

"You'll be punished for that later." He grumbles, and my mouth drops open.

"How did you see that?" I whisper.

"I know you." He shrugs. "They're moving them. Fuck, the girls are young. Maybe twelve to fifteen."

"Fuck." I growl.

I hear doors shut, and then Papi Loco's voice ringing through the air, "I heard this belongs to someone here?"

This is where he walks out with a gun to Pepe's head. This whole plan makes me nervous because I don't know how much Mack actually cares about his son, and I'll never forgive myself if something happens to Pepe.

"How the fuck did you get here, Joey?" Mack calls out.

"I was traded." Pepe calls, his rehearsed words sounding scared.

"I don't like this." I moan.

"Papi Loco, let my son go." Mack calls out, his words slurred from his lack of teeth. His tongue must feel like an unrestrained slippery eel.

"Can't do that, Mack." Papi calls back. "Not until you hand over that bus full of girls."

"Not in your fucking dreams!" Another voice yells. "You fucking Dientes need to get the fuck out of here before someone dies."

A shot rings out, and I nearly jump to my feet, Blaze's hand on my shoulder is the only thing that's stopping me. Gunfire echoes around us, sounding like thunder as it claps off the mountains and flings back around our heads.

Blaze turns and gives me a wink, his grin tugging at his scar and making him look irresistible. Then he's gone, running into the fray. I jump to my feet and see the chaos in front of me. When I see a man running toward me, his leather cut showing a knight riding a motorcycle, I lift my gun and shoot him in the throat. He drops like a fat log of shit hitting toilet water.

I rush out, trying to dodge bullets, and looking for my guys. Red dust clouds the space around me as people run for cover, and bullets hit the ground at our feet. I find Pepe cowering in a fetal position where Papi Loco must've dropped him, and I grab the back of his shirt, dragging him with me behind a boulder. We find Santos there changing the mag on his gun, his face red from the dust.

"You found him!" He grins wide when he sees Pepe. "Little fucker must've been burrowing to Hell when I went out to look for him."

"No," Pepe shakes his head, "I was praying for one of you crazy assholes to find me."

"Well, Jesus must really love you today!" Santos exclaims as a bullet hits the rock we're behind.

"Hey!" Santos stands up and lets loose a string of bullets. "Who the fuck you shooting at, assholes?"

"Get the fuck down here." I yank on his shirt.

He crouches back down and gives me a wink, "I got one."

"Where are the others?"

"I lost Darius," he points to his right, "he ran that way. Zander was over there, too."

"I lost Blaze."

"They'll be fine," he nods, "this is what we live for."

A biker runs behind Santos and stops, raising his gun. I see the Knight's emblem and don't hesitate to knock a bullet between his eyes.

"That's twice now." I smirk at him.

"I wouldn't have needed it if you weren't distracting me." He winks. *Asshole.*

"Let's find the others." Santos darts out from the rock, and I go to follow when I remember Pepe.

"Are you coming?" I ask him.

"No. I think I'll stay here." He looks shaken, his skin ashen. I get it, this isn't fun for him.

"Here's a gun." I hand him one of my spares, "shoot anyone who tries to shoot you, understand?"

"I don't want to-"

"You were willing to kill me at one point." I remind him, "you can do it and Jesus will understand. We'll celebrate by taking you to a priest to be molested after."

He snorts and looks up at me with watery eyes, "I can't imagine not having you around, Selene. May God be with you and protect you today."

"God bless you and your nuts." I nod and scramble out from behind the boulder.

The gunfire is tapering off, and I see bodies littered along the sand. My heart slams into my ribcage as I try to squint through the dust, hoping not to recognize any of them.

I get to a large rock, finding Santos and Loqi. Loqi has a bad gunshot wound on his thigh and blood is shooting out like a fountain.

"They hit his artery." Santos grunts as he ties his bandana around Loqi's leg, trying to stop the worst of the blood loss. "Can you stay here with him while I try to find Darius?"

"Yeah," I cringe at the sight of Loqi's grey skin.

Santos runs out, and I hear a few more shots ring out as I crunch down lower.

"I've always wanted a brother." Loqi moans, his words slurred and slow.

"Well, you lucked out. You ended up with the best brother ever." My throat is tightening, and my eyes are burning as I watch him slowly die in front of me.

"Don't worry," he gives me a wink—so much like his brother— "I'm not afraid to die."

"Don't you dare fucking die." I growl and grab the front of his shirt, "you have a brother and sister who need you."

"Loqi!" I turn and find Papi Loco running toward us, his face and hands covered in blood. "Don't you even fucking think of it, boy."

"Hey, Dad," Loqi grins, "I got him, I shot Daniel in the head."

"Fuck, that's war for sure. Boomer!" He yells over his shoulder, and an older man rushes forward. "Take him to the bus, we need to get out of here."

"Who's Daniel?" I ask as Boomer throws Loqi over his shoulder and runs off.

"The Knight's president's only son and VP." He heaves out a tired breath, "they were best friends as kids."

"That's going to be messy." I nod.

"Hey, Walton Jr!" I hear Mack call out to Zander, "bring me my boy and maybe I'll let this one live."

I stand quickly and find Mack standing in the middle of the settling red dust with Blaze on his knees in front of him, holding a gun to his head. I lift my own gun aiming for Mack's head when a couple Knights step out, holding up guns.

"You shoot me, and they've been ordered to kill him." Mack snickers.

"Little Reaper," Blaze calls out just as Santos makes it back to my side, "don't hand Pepe over."

Mack slams the butt-end of his gun into Blaze's temple, making him grunt out in pain, and fall to the sand.

I dart forward with a scream, "you toothless son-of-a-bitch!"

Santos grabs my arm, yanking me back, when a warning shot is fired near my feet. That does it. Santos lifts his gun and shoots one of the Knight's, causing a second round of mayhem. I see Darius run forward to Mack and Blaze, his gun firing, and I shrug out of Santos' hold, needing to get to Blaze.

The next few moments are in slow motion. I watch as a Knight steps up in front of Blaze, aiming his gun at me, then Santos runs in front of me, shielding me from the bullet that's fired. I slam into his back, trying to shove him, when Darius jumps in front of the both of us, his body jolting in mid-air.

"Darius!" Santos screams, dropping to the ground beside his lover. I hear another shot ring out and watch as the Knight drops to the ground, then Zander runs over to us.

Blood is blooming on the back of Darius' shirt, and I know it's bad. He took a hit to the chest outside of the Kevlar vest. The scream that rips from my throat is fierce and animalistic, not at all sounding natural. I jump over the guys on the ground in front of me, and my feet hit the red sand in loud thumps which resonate through my chest. Mack lifts his gun, pointing it at me, a sadistic smile on his face as Blaze begins to get up.

"You have one shot, motherfucker!" I scream, "you better pray you kill me!"

My hand wraps around the hilt of my knife as I yank it out of the sheath, and Mack takes his shot. I skid to the side, and the bullet which was destined for my chest, slams into my shoulder, jarring me back a few steps. My shoulder screams with fire as I laugh maniacally.

"You missed!" I continue to cackle as I jump on him, stabbing my knife through his eye. He falls back with a shout, his back hitting the sand, taking me with him. His gun skates across the ground as I yank my knife back out, glancing up when I hear a click.

Blaze is standing over us, the gun pointed down at Mack's head, "this has been a long time coming." Then he fires the shot into Mack's forehead.

I hear the cries behind me, knowing it's bad, too scared to turn around. Instead, I continue to stab my knife into Mack's head repeatedly, the blood spraying up all over my face.

"Selene," Blaze calls me, but I'm too lost in grief; in bloodlust; in complete rage.

Mack's face begins to resemble minced meat when Blaze drags me off of him. I turn quickly, finding Papi Loco and Hook rushing Darius to the bus. His vacated spot on the sand is completely saturated with blood. Santos turns, his eyes on me, their darkened depths filled with pain. I shake my head, the movement making me stumble as the world tips around me.

I'll never forgive myself if Darius is dead.

My vision begins to blacken around the edges, and when I turn to see where Darius is, everything tips on its axis. The ground rushes up to meet me, and I feel arms wrap around my waist.

"Reaper, what the fuck happened?" Blaze growls, but it's hard to form words around the pain of my breaking heart.

"She's been hit!" Santos yells, running forward. "No! Blaze, she's been hit!"

Oh, yeah. I try to reach for my shoulder, but my arm doesn't comply, and my head falls forward. I no longer have strength nor the will to try. I want to be where Darius is.

"No, no, no." I hear Blaze chant just as the world turns dark around me.

Darius

I don't even think about it before jumping in front of the bullet Santos is trying to save Selene from. I'd do it for any of them, needing them to finish what we started. I know this may be the end for me, but I'll die knowing the people I love are still alive.

The bullet hits my flesh, sending hot searing pain through my body, the desperate scream of my name filling my ears from Santos as I hit the ground hard. It's hard to breathe, telling me this is bad. I can't form words as my vision starts to dim. Selene's screaming somewhere, her pain burning into me. She'll be okay, my brothers will look after her.

I'm getting cold, but I feel hands on me as I choke on my blood.

"Don't you fucking die on me!" Santos cries, trying to apply pressure to the wound that's quickly sucking the life from me. I want to tell him I love him, that I'd do it all again to save him, but my mouth won't work, and the darkness starts seeping in.

"Stay with me, please. I fucking need you!"

I think it's Santos, but I'm not sure anymore. Everything's going fuzzy.

"I love you, don't leave me!" Definitely Santos.

I hear a gunshot just as I fight for air, someone's hand squeezing mine as everything goes black. As my life is taken from me, all I can think about is how my family has to be okay without me.

They have no other choice.

Santos

I zone out the sound of young girls crying as we drive to get medical help. The bus is packed, but the only thing I see is the devastation to my family. Darius' skin is pale from the blood loss, his hand cold in mine as I will him to be okay. He's been my anchor for so long now, I can't face the world without him.

Selene's just as still, both of them covered in blood as it seeps into their clothes. Panic swirls inside me, knowing the odds of saving everyone is so low.

I glance over to watch Papi with Loqi, my brother's body looking more like a corpse. He can't die either, I've just fucking found him. I curse myself for spending so much time hating him, knowing I might not get the chance to get to know him.

I hate myself for fighting with Selene before coming into this, wishing she was awake so I could spill my heart to her. If she'd stayed back, she'd be okay, but that isn't her style. I can't be angry at her for that, because if someone told me to stay behind, I would have bitten their heads off.

"Come back to me," I whisper, giving both their hands a squeeze, hoping for a response. I don't get one, and my throat goes tight with emotion at knowing this is it. We aren't all going home together to celebrate our victory, some of us are going home in a box.

I don't give a shit that I'm crying like a baby as I cling to them, taking a page out of Pepe's book and praying they'll come back to us. I choke on a sob, my grip tightening on their hands as someone wraps their arms around me. If they try to make me let go of them, I'll flip out.

Instead, they just hold me, Zander's voice reaching my ears. "I've got you." That just makes my tears fucking worse. I'm glad Zander and Blaze are alright but losing Darius or Selene will kill me. They are the calm to my storm, my tether when I lose control, and they are my home.

"I can't lose them," I force out, leaning into him for comfort. He doesn't answer, telling me everything I need to know. He doesn't think we'll all make it either and he's not going to sugar-coat it with lies for my sake.

Blaze sits close by his face tight with pain as he stares at Selene, wearing his heart on his sleeve for once. He meets my gaze, his voice rough.

"If the Grim Reaper even tries to take them, I'll fight that fucker myself. He's not taking them anywhere, San. I won't fucking let him."

"You'll fight death?" I choke on a small laugh at the image of him standing off with the Devil, not letting our family be taken to the darkest depths of Hell.

"You bet your ass I will. I'll do anything for them," he grunts, his eyes going back to Selene, ending the conversation.

Once we arrive, Digs carts them away, and Zander has to hold me back from following. "Let him help them. We'll only get in the way."

"I need to stay with them!" I snap, but there's no anger in my words, only pain. He takes my hand, tugging me toward some chairs, pushing me gently into one and dropping an arm around my shoulders, Blaze dropping into the chair on my other side. He doesn't hug me, but his shoulder brushes against mine, showing me he's there for me. I know deep down, he's chasing comfort too, not used to being so out of control in a situation.

I never thought the grumpy bastard would soften for anyone, but as we sit here, I feel his fear and misery. His love for Selene is so strong it almost chokes me, and I wipe my cheeks as more tears spill.

"Santos."

I glance up, finding Papi in front of me, and I have no idea how long he's been standing there. I'm drowning in grief, the worry eating me alive at what comes next. Will they all die?

"Yeah?" I manage to croak out, surprised when he squats in front of me and takes my face in his hands.

"I'm sorry. For everything. I can see what they mean to you. I know I never understood your relationship with Darius, but I see it. I respect him so much for what he did for you. He's your family, which makes him mine."

I want to lash out, scream at him for saying shit like that when he has no right, but he leans forward and hugs me, the anger vanishing as he tries to hold me together while I break.

"I'm sorry about Loqi, he's a pretty cool brother," I mumble, pretending I don't hear him sniff back tears of his own.

"When we all get home, we'll celebrate. No one's dying today," he states firmly, leaning back to look at me with a stubborn look in his eyes.

"Promise?" I rasp, needing him to make it all okay. He doesn't say anything, his jaw tight, but the sound of a heart monitor flatlining draws each of our attention to the closed door, my heart leaping in my chest.

"No!" I scream, launching out of my chair, but Zander and Blaze hold me back, their hands tightening as I struggle. "Let me go!"

Papi stares at the door silently, as if his eyes can laser through the wood and will things to be alright. Nothing's alright, though. Not when one of them just died. I hear them trying to bring them back, charging up the shock paddles, and I need to see who it is. I keep fighting against my brothers, but it's no use. My body goes weak, and I slump against Zander, my tears soaking his shirt as he clings to me.

Am I saying goodbye to my brother? Or the two people I love more than anyone in the world?

Epilogue

Selene

I stare at my reflection in the mirror.

My hair is shining a light blonde, shimmering with whatever oil is in it. My makeup is subtle, my eyelids shimmering in the light beside the vanity. My hand glides down over the long, black dress made of the softest material that hugs every one of my curves like a dream. It's strapless, the front dipping down to create the deepest sweetheart neckline.

The door opens, and I turn my head to see Pepe step into the room, looking handsome in his suit. My shoulder aches from the sudden movement, and my hand comes up to press at the still healing wound. The feeling of the raised, puckered flesh threatens to pull me back under, but it's Pepe's words that draws my attention instead.

"I don't think that dress is appropriate for a wedding." He gives me a confused look.

"Do I look appropriate to you?" I retort.

"You look beautiful, regardless of what you're wearing." His face softens.

Pepe has blended into our family of misfits perfectly, and it helps that he's dating a groom's sister. He still drones on about Jesus, prays for us every day, and truly believes all of our souls are salvageable, making it his mission to ensure we all end up in Heaven together. As long as I end up with *all* of my guys, I don't care where I am.

"Thank you," I whisper as a bout of nerves wash over me.

"I printed off the certificate," he holds up a piece of paper, "in case any of these guys want to question the validity of today's ceremony."

Pepe took an online course to become an ordained minister so he could officiate this wedding. There's no one else who could do the job justice.

"We'll frame it later and hang it on the walls when we get home." I smile at him.

We're still here in the Dientes compound. Digs wouldn't let me leave until I was back on my feet, and to be honest, I wouldn't want anyone else looking after me. He's a compassionate man who only lives his life to save others.

He saved *me*.

It's beautiful here, with the mountains as a backdrop, and the sky always a bright blue. Perfect for a wedding. Shockingly, Papi Loco was so excited about the prospect of a wedding, he planned every detail, and decorated the large open field. Flowers, fancy chairs, and the food, he did it all. He's been doing everything in his power to win over his oldest son, hoping for forgiveness. I think he may have succeeded after today.

Loqi steps into the room, his cane clicking against the hardwood flooring. "Damn sis, you are fine!"

He's taken to calling me sis since he's had a second chance at life. I accept it because it makes Santos happy to see us getting along, especially when he's working on solidifying his relationship with his brother.

"That sounds like maybe you want to fuck your sister, *Luis*." I tut, "incest is a crime here, no?"

"I'm willing to do at least ten years for it." He gives me a slow perusal.

"I'm going to head out." Pepe says as he shakes his head, clutching the crucifix around his neck. He may be one of us, but we still tend to shock him regularly.

"How can I convince you to marry me next?" Loqi asks, a twinkle in his eye.

"I'll consider it when you don't limp like a gimp anymore."

"Ouch." His hand lands over his chest, "I may always be gimpy though, doc says I need a lot of *physical* therapy."

I saunter over to him, and pat his cheek, "your hand has been such a good companion up to this point, let's not ruin it now."

His head tips back on a laugh, so similar to his brother's, I can't help but laugh with him.

"Come on, gorgeous." He holds out his arm, "people are waiting on you."

The sun is setting, shooting reds of all shades across the sky, and the outline of the moon is already high above our heads. It's picturesque and perfect, just like today. I'm walking between two of my guys, our arms interlocked, and our hearts beating as one. The love between us has only grown the two months we've been here, and we are the strongest we've ever been.

We reach the end of the aisle and I take Santos' face in my hands, leaning forward to give him a sweet kiss. He quickly deepens it, making it nearly inappropriate, causing snickers to sound around us. He lets me go with a mischievous grin on his face, as I slap his chest.

"Naughty boy," I whisper. "I'll be punishing you later."

"As long as I get the same punishment Zander did." He gives me a wink over Zander's audible groan.

I turn to my left, taking in my next man, his eyes looking down at me, filled to the brim with love and appreciation. Their blue shining bright, filtering through to my very soul.

"Darius," I croak, my voice losing its strength. "Thank you for fighting for us… for me." I can feel the tears coursing down my cheeks, the accumulation of stress and worry for the life of my lover, dissipating as I look into his smiling face.

It has been a rough two months. There were a few times we thought we were losing him, but he pulled through, later telling us he only saw our faces while he fought. He had lost a lot of blood but thankfully, Papi Loco's blood type is universal, and he helped save my man's life.

"There's nowhere else I'd rather be, angel." He leans down, capturing my trembling lips in his, and I vow—as I have been vowing every day—to love them all with my whole being because tomorrow is never guaranteed.

"Who gives these men to be wed?" Pepe's voice rings through our kiss.

I grab Santos' hand and then Darius' as I step back, linking them together. "I do."

Darius looks so handsome and *alive* as he stands there looking into Santos' eyes. The sight of them looking so in love, and ready to take this next step chokes me up. Just as a sob pounds against my chest, Blaze's heat is at my back, his arm slipping around my waist.

"Come sit with me and Zander and let our boys get married, Little Reaper."

I begin to cry softly as Blaze leads me back to our seats, and Zander wraps an arm around me, dragging me into his body. "You big softy." He kisses my cheek with a snicker.

"Do not start," I point at him, while wiping my tears.

"You'll get that ass beat again." Blaze mutters.

"Really?" Zander's eyes light up, "did you bring it with you?"

I slap a hand to his chest as we watch Santos and Darius get married. There's not one dry eye in the place as they recite their vows. Even, as Santos reads out his, filled with threats of death if Darius ever decides to try and leave us again.

I've never been so proud of anything in my life.

Zander

My arms are around my girl, and her blonde hair is illuminated by the twinkling lights around us. We're swaying to a slow song, and she's smiling as Darius and Santos dance in the moonlight. It's been a rough two months, and life really comes into perspective when you fear you're losing someone you love. All of us have been to Hell and back, and now, we're thankful for every day we have together.

When Santos came to us, professing his need to marry Darius, we were all shocked. I was surprised because Santos has never spoken about marriage. Then there was the worry they were breaking apart from Selene, from all of us. But they're not, they just want to solidify their individual relationship, and we all support them for it.

"Where will they go for their honeymoon?" I ask my beautiful girl, and she looks up at me with a scowl.

"In my pussy, that's where."

I choke on a laugh at the seriousness on her face, knowing none of us will be let out of her sight for a long while. We all feel the same about her. When she was shot, it scared the living shit out of me, and I saw everything I was living for slowly drain away. There's no me without her, and I promised her when she woke up the next day, she would have to deal with me for the rest of her life.

"I'm so thankful my father paid you to fuck him." I tell her, a smile dancing across my mouth.

"Me, too, baby Walton." She coos, "the dick on that man." She lets out a long sigh, her eyes taking on a dreamy look. I pinch her waist, and she breaks out into giggles. "I'm really glad, too, Zan. It was always meant to be." She finally looks up at me with love in her eyes.

"I love you," I tell her as I press a soft kiss to her lips.

"I love you, too." She grins, and I prepare myself for whatever it is she's thinking, "how soon is too soon to leave? I really want to sink a big dildo into your ass."

And there it is.

Blaze

Nothing in this world will ever compare to what I feel for the annoying woman dancing in the arms of my best friend. I fought the pull I felt the first moment I laid eyes on her, and I did everything in my power to push her away, only to have her cling on tighter.

I never thought love was possible for us four, but especially not for me, having never felt it for myself. Then this Little Reaper comes along and rips my heart out of my chest, holding its bloody warmth in her hands. She owns it through and through.

Zander tips his head back and groans while Selene grins like a sadistic bitch, making me chuckle. I wonder what she said to him this time. Darius and Santos have been inseparable all night—for two months really—and I'm happy to witness their pure love as they sway together on the dance floor.

"Thank you for taking care of my little sister," Henny sits down next to me.

"It's a group effort." I shrug.

"She's lucky to have you all."

"Are you needing more than just Papi Loco?" I ask her with a knowing grin.

"What?" She looks around wide-eyed. "Don't say that. He'll gun us all down."

I chuckle as she keeps looking around for her crazy old man.

"Pepe!" We hear Cara squeal from the dance floor.

Pepe is down on one knee, holding a little black box, his arms shaking with nerves. We knew he was going to be doing this today because Santos basically threatened him if he didn't. Not that he needed much pushing, it's not hard to see how much they mean to each other.

"Cara, I believe God brought you into my life, and I want to make this official." He opens the box and Cara gasps. "Will you marry me?"

"Say yes, Cara!" Santos bellows, and everyone begins to laugh.

"Of course!" Cara squeals as Pepe slips the ring on her finger.

Papi Loco and Loqi rush them both on the dance floor, forming a large group hug. It's been a rough go with them, but they're on the road to healing.

"Damn," Henny wipes the moisture from her eyes, "that's beautiful."

My Little Reaper comes running toward me, and drops herself in my lap, her arms circling my neck. "Did you see that, Daddy?" Her words sound husky and winded from excitement, causing my cock to swell against her ass.

"Yeah, baby." I smile at her.

"We're going to be planning another wedding." She squeals with excitement.

"We?" I snicker, and Henny joins in.

"More like Papi will," Henny corrects while Selene scoffs.

"Fine, we get another open bar!"

My face burrows into her neck and I drag my tongue across her skin, tasting her. She shivers in my arms, and I chuckle into her skin.

"How soon is too soon to leave?" I ask her, and she gasps.

"I want to know that, too!" She exclaims just as someone wheels out a large wedding cake, making us both groan.

"Still too soon, apparently," I growl, and she giggles.

"Come on, Daddy." She stands and yanks on my hand, "I'll spread some cake icing on my pussy and let you clean it out."

Henny groans in disgust behind us but I don't give a fuck. Now, I want a piece of that cake.

Santos

I don't think I've let go of Darius all fucking day. I let Selene dance with him, but I lingered on the side, not wanting to be too far away from him. Hell, I don't want to be away from any of them. Honeymoon? Family fucking vacation. No exceptions.

"If you hold me any tighter, I'm going to bust my stitches," Darius chuckles lightly as we slow dance, an edge of pain in his voice. I quickly ease my hold on him, giving him a sheepish smile.

"Sorry. I zoned out," I admit, glancing around the room to check in that the others are okay. He gives me an understanding look, leaning forward to kiss me.

"We're alright, *amante*. Not even the Devil can have me, I'm yours."

"That fucker nearly did get you," I growl quietly. "He won't be getting a second chance. If anyone even knocks on our door, I'm shooting first. I don't care if they're Girl Scouts selling cookies."

"You can't start shooting Girl Scouts, I doubt they're a threat," he teases, pressing closer to me as he urges me to keep dancing.

"That's what they want you to think. Then once you buy the cookies and put them in the kitchen, *BAM*, explosion. Do you know how many cookies Zander usually orders? That's a lot of explosives in our house," I snort, making him roll his eyes.

"I think you'll find that *you* are the one who orders a million cookies."

"Not anymore! I'm onto those little, pig-tail braided assassins!" I declare, spotting Selene motioning to me with a handful of cake. I didn't even let Darius' hand go when we had to cut the cake. I was too worried the fucking thing was wired and ready to blow.

"C'mon, our baby girl's summoning us," I grin, tugging him after me to make sure he stays with me. As we approach, I notice the cheeky glint in her eyes, making me smirk. "What are you plotting, my little blood queen?"

She runs her finger through the icing, popping it into her mouth and sucking it off, pulling it out slowly. "As much as this wedding has been perfect, how about we sneak off for a while? I have some fun places to put this icing where you can eat it out from."

My dick stirs at the thought of her body covered in it, my tongue licking her clean while she screams.

"Done deal. I'll just let Papi know we're going. He can keep an eye on Cara."

"She'll be fine, she has Pepe," she whines, making me snort.

"I think he needs more training before he can do much. I'll be two seconds. Meet us in the bedroom," I chuckle.

"I'll grab Grumpy and Zan," she exclaims before turning and skipping off to find them, leaving us to track down Papi.

It doesn't take long, he's boasting about Cara's up and coming wedding to a bunch of his guys, Loqi standing beside them with the biggest grin on his face.

He meets my gaze and winks, amusement all over his face. "Your girl getting antsy?"

"What makes you say that?" Darius frowns, and Loqi laughs.

"Because she's practically piling up all the cake that's left onto a plate and I doubt cake makes her horny, but she looks ready to burst."

We glance back to find Selene with a massive plate of cake, her ass rubbing back on Zander who's whispering in her ear with a devilish grin. She says something to Blaze who ends up with his hand around her throat, his lips crashing into hers so hard she almost drops her mountain of cake.

I look back at Loqi with a shrug. "What? She loves orgasms and we love cake. It's a win-win situation. The best flavored cake is pussy flavored."

He cracks up, grabbing my shoulder and tugging me close for a hug. "You guys are hilarious. Enjoy your night. And San?"

"Yeah?"

"Congrats on your wedding. Thanks for the invite," he grins, turning to Darius and gently pulling him in for a hug, too. "Welcome to the family, brother."

Before I can reply, Papi pulls me in for a hug. "My boy! You sure you don't want to relocate to Nevada?" He's spent a lot of time over the past few days, trying hard to convince us to move closer to them.

"Sorry, Papi. We can't handle the weather. Blaze is still grumbling about it. We'll visit, promise," I smile, patting him on the back as we pull apart.

"Make sure you bring the rest of the family with you. It will be a party every time you stop by," he beams, turning to Darius and shooing Loqi away from him. "I know I've said it already but thank you for saving my boy. You always have a home in Nevada if you ever need one. If you have any issues, you call me. We've got your back."

Darius is grinning so hard I'm surprised his jaw doesn't snap.

"Thanks. It means a lot."

"And call me Papi! You're my son now, after all," he scolds, my heart warming at his words. We still have a little ways to go on building trust since he'd abandoned me, but we're off to a really good start. He treats Darius like family, the same as Selene, Blaze, and Zander.

"Excuse me, I need to steal the grooms. There's been an... uh, incident in the cake department and they need to see to it right away," Selene says quickly as she grabs my hand, her breath fast. Papi grins, glancing over at Zander who has icing all over his fucking suit.

"You'd better see to that right away. It sounds important," he states dryly.

"It is. I'll bring them back in the morning after it's dealt with," she nods innocently, dragging us across the room, Blaze and Zander following with the plate of cake.

Zander already has his shirt off, his pants undone as we enter the bedroom, but I hesitate when I eye Selene stripping Darius beside me. "Uh, is this a good idea? Darius…"

"Darius can lie back on the bed like a good boy and let nurse Selene look after him," she coos, peppering kisses across his bandage. "I'll be gentle, won't I, baby?"

Darius snorts, giving her a dirty look. "You better fucking not be gentle, or I'll flip you over and ram your ass until you bleed."

She moans, shoving his pants down and fisting his dick. "Don't threaten me with a good time." She steers him toward the bed, encouraging him to sit. "Seriously, though. You really need to take it easy. Just a little. Lie back."

He looks ready to argue with her, but I glare at him, making him do as he's told. Blaze makes quick work of stripping the beautiful black dress from Selene's body, his lips trailing across her back as she sighs and leans into him.

"I need to be inside you, right fucking now," Zander groans, completely naked as he pumps his dick in his hand. His eyes are heated as he watches Selene turn and kiss Blaze almost savagely.

"I have an idea, but Darius isn't allowed to do the work," I smirk, stripping off and moving toward the bed. Darius scowls.

"I don't like the sound of that."

"You will in a minute," I promise, grabbing some lube before lying back on the bed, slicking my dick up before reaching for him. "Come here."

He raises an eyebrow but moves closer, seeming confused. "How do you want me?"

"Sit on my dick and lay your back against my chest," I instruct, helping him get into position. I align myself with his tight hole, slowly pulling him down onto me until I'm fully seated inside him. He groans, dropping his head back as he gets used to it.

"Now what?"

"Now we lean back so Selene can ride you."

"We'll squash you, idiot."

"Doubt it. Blaze and Zander can fight over her ass," I chuckle, both of them turning to each other with a grin. Selene's eyes go wide as she takes a step back, shaking her head.

"Nope. Daddy is not putting his big dick in my ass right now."

"I hope you're ready to choke on it then, Little Reaper," Blaze smiles sadistically.

"This won't work. It's…"

"Shut up and ride me, baby," Darius cuts her off, motioning to his solid dick. "It won't fuck itself."

She huffs, glancing at the plate of cake that's now on the bedside table. "But the cake…" Before she can finish her sentence, Blaze grabs her and throws her down on the bed, grabbing a fistful of cake and rubbing it all over her pussy, not hesitating to dive into it face first, making a meal out of it.

She moans, grinding on his face, and smearing cake and icing all over him, but he doesn't give a fuck. I sit up more, keeping Darius against my chest as we watch Blaze eat her like a man starved. It's hot seeing my wedding cake on her naked body.

Zander chuckles, grabbing the plate and plonking down on the bed beside them. He silently smears icing on her breasts, leaning down to lick it off with a groan. "So fucking good."

There's cake everywhere by the time she screams her release, and I fucking love it.

Without warning, Blaze drops onto his back and hauls Selene against his chest, her sticky tits pressing against his pecs.

"But, oh, fuck!" she gasps as he forces himself into her pussy, not giving her time to adjust. He holds her hips firmly as he fucks up into her, determination on his face. Making her come has been the best game we've ever played.

I take the hint, nudging Darius to climb off. Now Blaze is in her pussy, no one will be able to drag him back out. He holds her tight to his chest, slowing his thrusts as Darius shuffles toward them. She looks ready to snap at him to lie back down, but he lubes up and eases inside her ass, her protest dying on a strangled moan.

Darius is obviously hurting a little, but he ignores it as he starts moving in and out, fisting her hair and pulling her head back. Blaze instantly claims her lips, muffling the noises coming from her, and as Darius leans forwards a fraction and parts his thighs, I know what he wants.

I waste no time as I scramble behind him, making my way inside his tight hole again, trying to be gentle so I don't end up making him tense too much. I don't mind him hurting, but I don't want to risk his stitches. If they tear, we can end up with another emergency trip. I never want to be sitting in a waiting room for him ever again.

"Dammit, Santos. Fuck me!" he snaps over his shoulder, groaning as I pull back and slam in a little harder.

"Better?"

"Keep going, fucker," he grits out, not seeming satisfied until I'm fucking him as hard as I can. Selene's cursing as Blaze picks up the pace, him and Darius almost competing to get her off, and Zander chuckles as he steps closer, swatting Darius' hand away from her hair so he can fist it.

"Open wide. You're being a little loud."

She does as she's told, almost making me laugh. It's a rare sight, one that makes my dick harden even more. Darius grunts as she comes apart, her body shaking between him and Blaze as if she's been electrocuted, and Zander keeps her quiet as he fucks her mouth, his eyes flicking up to me.

I can't help myself as I smirk, cocking my head slightly as I slow my pace. "You want a ride next? I promise I'll blow your mind faster than that plastic you copped last time."

I expect him to get angry, but he just smirks back, pushing deeper into Selene's throat and making her gag. "The only one of you fuckers allowed near my ass is our girl. My ass is too good, you'll fall in love with me, and Darius would have to share."

"Like fuck," Darius snarls, slamming into Selene and coming hard, only giving it a second before pulling out and shoving me back. Zander laughs as Darius straddles me, sinking onto my dick as his mouth finds mine, but we know he's not really jealous. He doesn't have to compete with anyone for me, and he knows it.

I vaguely watch Zander slide into Selene's vacated ass, but my attention is quickly drawn back to the man on my lap, his lips on my neck as he grinds his hips, trying to get me deeper.

"You're going to hurt yourself," I warn, biting his shoulder sharply when he ignores me. "Darius."

"Let me," he begs, but my eyes dart to his bandage as he leans back, a small drop of blood seeping through. It's not bad, but it will get worse if he keeps going.

I flip us so he's below me, lifting one of his legs over my waist. "Just lie back and take it. I'm close."

He sighs, forgetting all about it as I start fucking him harder again, the sound of skin slapping together filling the room. Without Zander's dick in Selene's mouth, she's moaning and begging loudly, close to her next orgasm. The moment she screams their names, I'm a goner, coming hard inside Darius as I drop my forehead to his, our breaths becoming one.

"I love you so fucking much," I murmur, his eyes peering into mine as he smiles softly.

"I love you too. I've always got you."

"Promise?" I ask, needing him to say it. He's mine forever, despite the piece of paper that proves it, and if death ever tries to take him again, that bastard had better be taking the rest of us, too.

Blaze comes with a roar, Selene not far behind. Seconds later, Zander does too, and the three of them collapse beside us in one sweaty, cum covered pile. Darius' hand runs through my hair, and he gives it a playful tug, leaning up to kiss me.

"I promise, husband."

Darius

We spend the entire night fucking. Sometimes just Santos and I, other times Selene would join in with the others. I'm between Santos and Selene, her hand on my chest near my bandage. She's been worried about me, but sleep is finally starting to take its hold over her.

"I love you guys," she mumbles, yawning as she snuggles closer to me. Santos mumbles that he loves us all too as he drifts off, clinging to me as if someone will snatch me. They'd bring me back if they succeed, no one could manage me, let alone my family coming for them. Santos has nothing to worry about.

"Love you too, Little Reaper," Blaze mumbles from her other side, a soft snore coming from Zander who's curled up at the bottom of the bed, passing out after fucking her one last time. I can't imagine a better wedding day, my heart full at knowing our family was all witness to my love for Santos. Maybe one day Selene will be ready to take that step with the rest of us, but we aren't in a hurry. We're happy, and that's all we care about. I've been worried Selene would feel hurt about us getting married without her, but she has been thrilled, making me realize nothing will ever get between any of us.

Selene starts snoring softly, and I place a kiss on her head. I can't even remember a time when she wasn't with us. She came in like a tornado and swept us off our feet.

She softens Blaze.

She matches mine and Santos' crazy.

She balances Zander.

And she makes our house into a home, soothing our demons a little at a time. Sure, she also encourages those demons to come out and play, but they have leashes now and we're in control of them, not the other way around.

I stare at her in the dark, not being able to help the smile on my lips. It's pretty funny how she was just someone we heard about once upon a time, hiding in the shadows, her name whispered on people's lips in passing as she left a bloodied trail behind her.

But it's not just her they need to fear anymore, and even though we have brought down Mack and the others on our list, we know more will pop up eventually. We will be ready to bring those fuckers down the moment they surface.

Without mercy, we will avenge those who have been silenced or can't save themselves. Those we slaughter will die knowing our name.

We are the Reaper Incarnate.

Acknowledgments

C. A. Rene

Thank you to Rach for taking this journey with me and seeing it to the end. I love these characters and I love that we created them together.

To my family for putting up with my constant disappearing act and half paying attention moments, I love you.

To our betas: Jocelyn, Kristen, Lo, Jaime. You are all so awesome, thank you for all your help.

To our editor Lori, you are the bee's knees. Love you.

To all the readers who took a chance on psycho Selene and her unhinged boys, thank you!!

R.E. Bond

Thank you so much to everyone who gave this series a chance! We never expected our novella to turn into a series, so thank you for wanting more of Selene and her guys! Chrissy and I had so much fun writing it! I'm sad it's over, not just because I fell in love with these characters, but because writing with Chrissy has been fucking awesome.

I hardly knew Chrissy when she asked me to co-write in the Violent Tendencies anthology with her, and I possibly shit my pants a little, but I'm so glad I took the chance because I have definitely found my soulmate. Whether it's a co-write or my own writing, she is always there to support me and cheer me on. Love you Papi Peanut!!!! Xx

To everyone who shared, recommended, or promoted this series, thank you so much! We couldn't have done this without your support! Xx

Until the next time you pick up a book of mine, love you all bunches.

Rachael Xx

About the Authors

C. A. Rene

Words that drip blood and tears... Lover of all things dark. I love to read it, write it, own it, eat it, whatever it. My addictions include Coffee, books, and WINE, in that order.

R.E. Bond

R.E. Bond is a dark romance author from Tasmania, Australia. She is obsessed with reverse harem books, especially if they have m/m! She collects paperbacks as a hobby, has read or written every day since she started high school, and constantly needs music in her daily life. She loves camping and rodeos in the summer, and not getting out of bed in the winter. Coffee and books are life, and curse words are just sentence enhancers.

Also by R.E. Bond

Watch Me Burn

Pretty Lies
Twisted Fate
Beautiful Deceit
Ignite Me
Perfectly Jaded
Don't Fear the Reaper
Wrath of Rage

Reaped

The Reaper Incarnate
Hunting The Reaper
Claiming The Reaper

Also By C.A. Rene

Whitsborough Chronicles

Through the Pain
Into Darkness
Finding the Light
To Redemption

Whitsborough Progenies

Ivy's Venom
Carmelo's Malice
Saxon's Distortion

Desecrated Duet

Desecrated Flesh
Desecrated Essence

Hail Mary Duet

Blue 42
Red Zone

Reaped

The Reaper Incarnate
Hunting The Reaper
Claiming The Reaper

Sacrificial Lambs

Sing Me A Song
Song of Tenebrae
A Verse for Caelum

CPSIA information can be obtained
at www.ICGtesting.com
Printed in the USA
LVHW030714080622
720770LV00017B/1844